PRAISE FOR

Praise for Compulsion

"Darkly romantic and steeped in Southern Gothic charm, you'll be compelled to get lost in the Heirs of Watson Island series."

—#1 NEW YORK TIMES BESTSELLING AUTHOR
JENNIFER L. ARMENTROUT

"The perfect Southern family saga: charming and steamy on the surface, with cold-blooded secrets buried down deep."

—KENDARE BLAKE, NYT BESTSELLING AUTHOR OF
THREE DARK CROWNS AND ANNA DRESSED IN BLOOD

"A fresh twist on the Southern Gothic—haunting, atmospheric, and absorbing."

—CLAUDIA GRAY, NYT BESTSELLING AUTHOR OF
A THOUSAND PIECES OF YOU AND
THE EVERNIGHT AND SPELLCASTER SERIES

"Beautifully written, with vivid characters, a generations-old feud, and romance that leaps off the page, this Southern ghost story left me lingering over every word, and yet wanting to race to the compelling finish. Martina Boone's Compulsion is not to be missed."

—MEGAN SHEPHERD, NYT BESTSELLING AUTHOR OF
THE CAGE SERIES AND THE MADMAN'S DAUGHTER

BELL OF ETERNITY

ALSO BY MARTINA BOONE

LAKE OF DESTINY: A CELTIC LEGENDS NOVEL

COMPULSION

PERSUASION

ILLUSION

BELL OF ETERNITY

—A CELTIC LEGENDS NOVEL—

MARTINA BOONE

MAYFAIR
PUBLISHING

Bell of Eternity is a work of fiction, and the characters, events, and places depicted in it are products of the author's imagination. Where actual events, places, organizations, or persons, living or dead, are included, they are used fictitiously and not intended to be taken otherwise.

MAYFAIR
PUBLISHING
712 H Street NE, Suite 1014,
Washington, DC 20002
First Mayfair Publishing edition April 2017
Copyright © 2017 by Martina Boone

Jacket design by Kalen O'Donnell
Interior Design by Rachel & Joel Greene

Published in the United States of America
ISBN 978-1-946773-08-1 (trade paperback)
Library of Congress Control Number: 2017905183

For Susan Sipal with thanks for her magic wand.

BELL OF ETERNITY

BURNT OFFERINGS

"There were no tears in her.
The wound went too deep, or she was
not so constituted to give way to it."

WINSTON GRAHAM
ROSS POLDARK

E MMA LARSEN HAD BEEN known to cry over animal shelter commercials and ads about starving children, so it came as a shock to find she had no tears to shed when her mother died. The ambulance came and went, leaving behind the empty wheelchair and pink, vacant rooms that suddenly felt even larger without Evangeline's oversized presence. Emma drifted numbly through the aftermath, the clearing up, and the funeral arrangements. She answered condolence cards every night until she could no longer keep her eyes open and, more from force of habit than anything else, rose each morning in the silvery dawn hours to pull weeds in her kitchen garden.

The reading of the will changed all that.

Whatever emotions Emma felt or wanted to feel burned themselves away as she watched the video in the lawyer's office. And she was left with an anger so incandescent it made her hair crackle and sent a sizzle of electricity through the air.

She wasn't an angry person. She didn't want to be.

Only how was it that in the nearly twenty-five years of Emma's life, Evangeline Larsen hadn't managed to realize that her daughter was not a character in one of her best-selling romance novels? Someone to be shaped and manipulated to suit the plot that Evangeline was writing?

Regardless of what Evangeline had seen fit to put into her will, Emma had no intention at all of marrying Treave Nancarrow. Treave was Emma's best friend—just about her only friend after four years of having no life to speak of— but she didn't love him. When it came to that, she wasn't even certain that love existed. A lifetime of watching Evangeline jump from one relationship to the next before the accident hadn't exactly given her much faith in happily-ever-afters.

She was barely able to look at Treave as they left the lawyer's office together, and he cast her wary, worried glances with increasing frequency as he drove her home. Easing the Ferrari to a stop at a red light on M Street, he finally shifted around to look at her.

"Right," he said in the upper-crust British accent he'd never lost in all the years since he'd left his family's castle on the coast of Cornwall. "Out with it. How upset are you, really? On a scale of one to ten?"

"Eighty-seven and a half. Possibly an eighty-eight," Emma said, sitting stiff as a hardcover spine in the passenger seat.

Treave grinned, that grin that had always been infectious and endearing and was now suddenly just embarrassing. But his gray eyes were still worried in his slightly hawkish, handsome face, and his hands gripped the steering wheel too tightly. "I don't suppose it's a good time to wonder what you think of the idea, then?" he asked. "Would you mind very much?"

"Would I *mind*?" Emma should have been beyond humiliation, especially with Treave. His friendship had been her lifeline since the moment she'd met him at the hospital where he'd been comforting Evangeline in spite of having just lost his father in the same accident. The very fact that he'd been Evangeline's lifeline, too—had been Evangeline's lifeline *first*—made him too much like family to ever be anything else.

Treave had seen Evangeline at her worst, helped Emma get Evangeline through the worst. He'd heard the most awful and heartbreaking of Evangeline's rants and caught glimpses of the computer screen over Emma's shoulder before she'd managed to erase the hours of *I hate you, Emma*'s and *You're useless, Emma*'s and *Why won't you just let me die, Emma?*'s that Evangeline had scattered between the pages of the novels she dictated into her microphone when the pain had gotten to be too much.

Maybe it was because of that, because Emma had

counted on Treave to be the one person she didn't need to pretend with, that the ache of embarrassment now cut all the way to the marrow of her bones.

"You don't have to offer to marry me," she said, her voice muffled as though she was speaking through a mouthful of pebbles. "I don't want you to."

Treave shifted gears and the engine revved. "But we could give it a try, you know. We'd be good together."

"Absolutely not." Emma stared straight ahead, unwilling to look at him. Unwilling to see him pitying her.

"What about the money?" He glanced at her sharply, turned in his seat to study her. "What are you going to live on?"

"I'll figure something out." Emma hesitated, not wanting to hurt him, but at the same time, she'd had as much as she could take. "Look, I'm sorry, but would you just drop me off, and I'll meet you later at the funeral home?"

"You don't want me to stay? Or come back to get you?" Treave stole a look at her from beneath hooded eyes, and for an instant—there and gone again—something oddly like panic made the bones stand out beneath his skin.

"I'll be fine driving by myself." Emma squeezed his hand where it rested on the steering wheel. It was easier to convey gratitude and regret that way than it was to say the words aloud. "I'm tired, that's all," she said, "and I don't want to talk about this anymore."

Honestly, she didn't even want to think about it. Much less about the dozens of details she still had to attend to before the funeral and reception so that Evangeline could have the send-off she'd requested. Spending the afternoon smiling and listening to people telling her how wonderful Evangeline had been now seemed an impossibility.

It didn't help that Evangeline's face was everywhere inside the house: on awards and in photos with various celebrities, and on the back covers of ornately framed book jackets that hung upon the walls. Emma kicked off her shoes and threw them at the stairs, then padded down the long corridor to what had, these past years, become her sanctuary. Decorated when Evangeline had first bought the house, the kitchen was the only room Evangeline hadn't since redone in shades of lavender or pink. After leaving college to come back and take care of Evangeline, Emma had made it into her own, softening the sealed brick floor with rugs in warm, neutral colors and relieving the austerity of the stainless steel countertops with a collection of herbs and edible flowers in simple, hand-painted pots. The air still held the lingering aroma of spices and fresh-baked bread.

She felt calmer the moment she walked through the door, and she breathed in deeply as she brewed herself a cup of chamomile tea, reminding herself that staying angry with Evangeline wasn't helpful. In any case, the funeral and the reception were less for Evangeline's benefit than for the Angels, the most loyal of Evangeline's readers. For them, Evangeline had been a hero, someone they truly loved and believed they knew. Many of them had already planned to brave the heat and dizzying DC traffic to say their goodbyes. Emma didn't want to let them down.

Swallowing the last of her tea, she simultaneously squashed the remnants of her pain and fury into a neat, tight ball and hid them out of reach. She phoned the caterer to make sure the food for the reception was still on track and checked over the three pages of single-spaced notes that Evangeline had dictated about the arrangements. That done, she went upstairs to tame her untamable blond waves into an acceptable bun, wiggle her hips into what Evangeline would have considered a stylish black crepe dress, and wedge her feet into three-inch heels. Early enough that she ran no risk of being late, she drove to the funeral home to read the eulogy that Evangeline had written for herself, and after the burial, she drove home again.

All of that without letting herself give in to anger.

She even managed to stay calm through most of the funeral reception despite a constant stream of Angels and local writers and Treave hovering at her elbow, worried and trying to pretend he wasn't.

But by six o'clock, with two hours still to get through, she was ready to stand on a chair and scream if anyone else mentioned how *kind* Evangeline had been. It was very nearly a relief to turn and find the caterer rushing toward her.

"Julia, is something wrong? Do you need me in the kitchen?" Emma asked with a shameful twinge of hope.

Julia Hurley, a sweet-faced young woman from the local battered women's shelter whom Emma had met at Costco, looked like she was about to cry, and there was a streak of something that looked suspiciously like soot across her cheek. "I think the oven's broke," she said in a hissing whisper. "Everything's cooking too fast and the last batches of Gruyère puffs are charcoal. I'm so sorry. What do you want me to do?"

"The oven?" Emma repeated, and as the realization sank in, a bubble of near-hysterical laughter tried to push its way up her throat.

Julia blinked at her as though she'd gone mad. Which was, frankly, entirely possible.

"Want to come and look?" Julia asked, still gaping at her.

Her heels clicking on hardwood, Emma worried at the pearls strung like moons against her black sheath dress while she and Julia hurried toward the kitchen. And as they drew closer, the stench of burning appetizers seeping from beneath the swinging door struck her suddenly as all too appropriate. The broken thermostat was just one final blow on top of the others, fire and brimstone and sulfur, and by this point, Emma wouldn't have been surprised to learn that it was Evangeline's ghost behind that, too. She could just picture Evangeline perched somewhere on a cloud of motherly disapproval, surrounded by bare-chested romance cover models and still—still—unable to resist getting in one final parting jab at Emma.

Shoving the door open harder than strictly necessary, Emma marched into the kitchen. Instead of the habitual order in which she had left it, the room now had every surface littered with trays and baking sheets, most of them half-empty and the rest either not yet baked or blackened around the edges. A thin, acrid haze of smoke hovered beneath the ceiling despite the hastily opened windows.

"You see? Ruined! Every one of them." Julia picked up

what was meant to be a Gruyère and caramelized onion pastry from one of the baking sheets and waved it at Emma. Dropping that, she picked up a rubbery meringue cookie from another tray. "These, too. I opened the windows and the humidity turned them limper than my drunk ex-husband's you-know-what, so that's no dessert and no more appetizers. The guests will all stand 'round the next hour and a half with their stomachs growling, and I may as well go start flipping burgers. No one's going to want to hire me," she said, bursting into tears.

Trying to stay calm herself, Emma pulled Julia into a hug. "Oh, honey, don't worry. We can figure this out."

She spoke with as much certainty as she could muster, but she couldn't help acknowledging that Julia wasn't wrong.

Most of the Angels and guests would neither care nor notice if they ran out of food; many had driven long distances or stopped briefly before hurrying back to work or going home to chauffeur kids to dance practice or lacrosse. Others, though, those who lived in the neighborhood, would stay until the last possible minute, talking and reminiscing. Eating. Emma had taught herself how to cook feeding them at Evangeline's monthly book nights, and because they all did a lot of entertaining themselves, she'd hoped they would be willing to help Julia get her business off the ground. Unfortunately, a handful of them—Regina Humphries in particular—wouldn't overlook a single flaw. And Regina would share her opinion with anyone and everyone who'd listen.

Emma had been trying to *help* Julia, not ruin her

reputation. And all right, maybe when Evangeline had instructed her to "hire a real caterer" instead of "playing at doing the cooking" herself, giving the job to Julia had seemed a bit like poetic justice. Julia *was* an excellent cook, though.

Really, it came down to the oven. That was clearly Emma's fault. If she'd only scraped up the courage to stand up for herself, she'd have had the oven replaced years ago. Instead, she'd coaxed it along with mail order parts and instructions she'd downloaded from the Internet because, if she'd so much as hinted at replacing it, Evangeline would have swept in, hired a decorator, and made the whole kitchen as modern and perfect and *pink* as the rest of the house.

In four years, hiring Julia and choosing not to replace the oven were the two things Emma had done that came closest to defiance. The broken thermostat was clearly a message from behind the grave. Punishment for both transgressions delivered in a single, Machiavellian master stroke that left Julia paying for Emma's lack of courage.

No, Emma wasn't about to let that happen.

Hoisting her chin, she marched over to the equally ancient refrigerator, flung the door open, and scanned the nearly naked shelves. The past weeks had left her little time for shopping, so the choices were slim: a few staples, some yogurts approaching their sell-by dates, the usual jars of her homemade jams and pickles, and the remnants of three casseroles brought by well-meaning neighbors. But the refrigerated air cooled her cheeks, and by the time she took out butter, milk, and a half-empty carton of chicken stock, she had begun to devise a plan of salvage.

"Okay, so here is what we're going to do." She rummaged in a nearby drawer for a lemon-zester and dropped it into Julia's palm. "You scrape away the blackened bits, and I'll make up a cream sauce to add back a little moisture and sweetness. Genevieve can circulate fast so that no one gets too much of anything, and by the time we're done, no one will know there was anything wrong."

"*Honey.*" Julia raised both eyebrows high enough to make her forehead wrinkle. "Unless you're planning on putting medical marijuana into that sauce, I could scrape these cheese puffs until they disappear, and people would still know they were eating charcoal. Come to think of it, making them disappear would be the best thing we could do."

Emma laughed—she always felt better with a plan. "This will work, believe me. Burning things is the one cooking skill I mastered right away, so I've learned a few tricks here and there."

She disappeared into the butler's pantry and emerged again with an armload of ingredients that she dropped beside the stove. Then she let herself out into the garden, where brick walls draped in a tangle of moonflowers and climbing roses enclosed her carefully tended beds of vegetables and herbs, of yellow sunchokes and red nasturtiums, of bright orange marigolds and purple-blooming chives. She snipped a few sprigs each of roseroot and lemon balm to give the sauce a mood-boosting lift and took them back with her into the kitchen.

She was standing at the stove tying on a checkered

apron when the kitchen door burst open. Half-expecting Treave, she turned with a sinking feeling, but it was only Julia's niece with an empty serving platter and a hurricane of bouncing corkscrew curls.

"Man, have you seen the way those skinny women can eat? It's crazy." Genevieve dropped the empty serving tray on the counter with a clatter. "Tell me you've got a way to get more food ready. That oven was so hot I was about to call the fire department. No way we're going to use that again."

"Your aunt and I are working on a solution now. Do you think you can help us stall? Walk through quickly with the next batch and don't let anyone catch your eye," Emma said.

"Tease them don't feed them. Cool. I'm on it." Genevieve's grin was wicked. She set down her platter and started filling it with the last of the polenta and prosciutto chips, prawn and chorizo skewers, and stilton and chutney rarebit minis from the half-empty baking trays.

Julia scraped at the Gruyère puffs, sending furious clouds of soot in a fine layer across the countertop. "I still don't see how this is gonna work. But that's the problem right there—I don't *know* enough." Her face crumpled, making the worry lines even deeper. "What am I doing, thinking I can start a catering business? I'm hopeless."

"You're the opposite of hopeless," Emma said. "You're taking a risk, being brave. Taking care of your family. The rest of the food was perfect, and that oven was on its last leg, so put this down to Murphy's Law."

Or Evangeline's retribution.

Julia didn't deserve to fail. Not only would the catering let her reduce the money she had to pay for child care, but she could cook, truly cook. The rest would come. Thinking back to that first panicked book night when the regular caterer had stormed out after a shouting match with Evangeline, the tight tangled knot of Emma's anger threatened to surface again. Over the course of fifty-odd book nights, she'd moved slowly from hastily doctored frozen appetizers to gourmet food, and it hadn't even struck her until the reading of the will that she would never get to hear Evangeline pass along the Angels' compliments or give Emma any little bit of acknowledgment for the work. Now that Evangeline was dead, all the things Emma wished she could have heard her say had been buried with her, along with all the things she should have said in return.

Emma didn't even know what those would have been exactly. "I love you" and "I hate you" didn't begin to cover it. When she'd gone away to Stanford, she had never meant to come back. If not for the accident, she never would have. But how could she have left her mother's care to strangers?

She'd never regretted that choice until the moment the lawyer had pressed the button on the DVR and Evangeline's face had appeared on the screen. Even then, for the first few moments, Emma had simply been happy to see her mother's face again, the remnants of her smile still beautiful as her head lolled back on the high black support pillow of the wheelchair, her long hair pulled up into the coronet she'd had Emma braid for her each morning.

"Emma," Evangeline had said in her breathy, wavering

voice. "If you're seeing this, I'm dead. And about time, too. If you'd understood me at all, you'd have helped me die on my own terms years ago, but you've never had either courage or imagination. The truth is, you're far too earnest, which is why I'm not leaving you my money. You'd only let it lie around in a bank vault or let yourself be taken in by some useless charity.

"You need someone to take you in hand, get you to stop being such a stick-in-the-mud. I want you to get married. Now, before you get fat and lose your looks. Hopefully, Treave will marry you. He's always seemed to like you well enough. If not Treave, then it'll need to be someone the lawyer approves of, and it needs to happen within a year. None of this waiting around, not being able to make a decision. I've no patience with that. Also, the house will be turned into a museum—the lawyer has all the instructions—so you won't be able to hide away in there. Get married within a year, and you can have the rest of my money. Otherwise, it'll fund an annual writing conference and memorial writing scholarships in my name. So that's it. Your choice. And Treave's. Treave, I promised you'd have something in my will, so I'm leaving you my Daphne du Maurier pen and $50,000. If you want more, you'll have to take Emma with it."

Emma had sat frozen after the video was over, her nails dug into the arms of her chair. All she'd wanted to do was escape and go somewhere to scream and scream, but Treave had come over and crouched in front of her, drawn her into his arms and held her, trying to sweep away the awkwardness.

Realizing she was beating the whisk too hard in the pan, Emma slowed the motion before she broke the sauce beyond repair. She made herself concentrate, stirring chicken stock and balsamic vinegar into the roux, letting the lemon balm and roseroot steep in the cream and remaining ingredients and simmering them together until the sauce was unctuous and sweet.

By the time it was ready, Julia had half the Gruyère puffs scraped off and back to a reasonable semblance of golden brown. Emma sauced one lightly and handed it over. "Better?"

Julia took a bite. "Okay." Then her eyes opened wide. "No, wow. That's *edible*."

"See?" Laughing, Emma used a fork to drizzle the remaining puffs.

The door swung open again on a wave of distant conversation, and because she was expecting Genevieve, Emma turned, still smiling.

Only it wasn't Genevieve.

"There you are," Treave said. "I might have known you'd be hiding out in here. But people are asking for you." He stepped the rest of the way into the kitchen and straightened to his full, considerable height. In his well-cut suit, he looked solid and comfortingly familiar, the same dark hair, the same gray eyes that saw too much, the same handsome face. But he was also different. No longer just Treave, her friend, but someone she was seeing through the filter of her mother's instructions.

Marriage.

The humiliation of it made Emma furious all over

again. That and the fact that Evangeline had put Treave, too, into this position so that he'd felt honor-bound to offer Emma his help.

PLOT TWIST

*"Here is one with a gift for loving and a gift for hating,
and when he hates,
God help the man who earns his hatred."*

ROSEMARY SUTCLIFF
TRISTAN AND ISOLDE

T REAVE TOOK ANOTHER STEP into the kitchen, his expression growing worried as Emma didn't answer. "Earth to Emma? Are you all right, sweetheart? Did you hear what I said?"

Emma looked away, unable to meet his eyes. "Sorry. I was thinking about something else. I left you to the Angels with no protection, didn't I?"

"That's no hardship, but they're asking questions about the plans for the museum and Evangeline's last book, and I don't want to presume to answer for you. Not to mention that there are more people arriving all the time who'd like a chance to see you." He turned his smile on Julia with an apologetic shrug. "Sorry to have to steal her away."

That smile made Julia suck in her stomach and stand up a little straighter. "It's all good," she said to Emma. "I can finish myself."

Emma shook her head. "A few more minutes won't change anything. Treave can hide out in here with us if it's awkward for him. Or he could go on home," she added, forcing herself to look at him. "You could, you know. You've more than done your duty."

"You think I'd abandon you? *Loyal unto death*, that's the Nancarrow family motto, isn't it? Now step away from the food and leave the catering to the caterer."

That was close enough to something Evangeline would have said to sting a little, but Emma laughed as he'd intended, and Julia waved her toward the door. "The man's right, honey," Julia said. "You're supposed to be out there. Just tell me what to do about dessert. Want me to skip it?"

"What about making some chocolate cups to replace the meringues?" Emma peeled the apron from around her waist. "You could fill those with the fruit and cream you've already made up, and everything you need for that is in the pantry. Or you just dip dried apricots in melted chocolate. That would be easier." She paused with the apron in her hand. "No, it's still too much to do. I should stay and help."

"Stop it." Julia leaned in close. "Even I can manage to paint melted chocolate on some cupcake liners." Glancing at Treave again, she added in a whisper, "And I'll tell you, if that gorgeous man was looking at me the way he's looking at you, I wouldn't keep him waiting. *Go.*"

Emma bit her lip and glanced at Treave, then quickly looked away again. She smoothed her dress down over her hips and checked for food spills, but there wasn't a thing she could do about her hair. Given the humidity, short of a flat iron or a razor, there was no smoothing that.

"You still look beautiful," Treave whispered, holding the door open for her. Beyond the door, the fuchsia wainscoting of the corridor gleamed in the evening light cast by the recessed lamps overhead. The door swung shut, and he turned her toward him, his expression both drawn and serious. "So tell me—honestly. Did everything get too overwhelming, or is it only me you've been hiding from in there? How worried should I be?"

"That was burnt canapés, not hiding," Emma said.

He ducked down so that she couldn't avoid his eyes. "I know you. You're hurt and confused, and I realize I muddled everything this morning about the will, only please don't shut me out."

"Not now, all right? And definitely not here."

He straightened with a sigh. "You're forcing me into drastic measures, aren't you? Ice cream and a film as soon as this lot leaves."

"Fine, as long as it's not another soppy Nicholas Sparks movie."

"If you're going to insist on explosions and car chases, I'll insist on pistachio ice cream."

"Deal," Emma said, and because pistachio ice cream

was her favorite, not his, that was no concession. For a moment as the two of them walked down the hall of the old house and slipped in side by side among the guests, she could almost forget that the will had changed things between them all.

The house was one of the old grande dames on the east side, where the roots of ancient oak trees pushed up the sidewalks and the branches dappled spotless streets removed from most of the city rush. A granddaughter of Martha Washington had built the home with her husband, and the front still had the twin parlors that had doubled as a ballroom in a pinch—or as a perfect place to hold a big reception.

The crowd had thinned now, but a few dozen Angels remained, some newly arrived, others lingering, talking, fanning themselves with paper napkins or memorial leaflets in the heat that drifted in each time the front door closed and opened. Regina and another of the locals had designated themselves as unofficial greeters, chatting with everyone who came and went, pointing out the drink station, the guest book, and the photo album that Emma had put together before the will was read.

Treave was still the only male. Not a single one of Evangeline's husbands or lovers had bothered to come. Not even Emma's father, though Emma had tracked him down and left a message on his voicemail. That didn't surprise her much. After the divorce, he'd sent birthday presents for a few years, but those had stopped by the time that she'd turned eight.

It struck her, as she looked around now, that the people who had remained in Evangeline's life the longest were the ones who knew her least. Those who, like the Angels, loved an image of her that wasn't real.

The Angels had become the closest thing Evangeline had to family. They'd become Emma's family, too. She knew the names of their dogs and children, knew which of Evangeline's stories were their favorites and which characters they loved to hate. For the first time, she realized that she was saying goodbye to them tonight, too, and she couldn't help wondering what was going to be left of her once all these farewells were over. She was like a supporting actor in a play where the star and all the other characters had disappeared, suddenly left on stage not knowing what to do or where to go.

"Emma, Treave! There you are!" Regina Humphries, wearing a perma-frown and a steel gray Chanel suit that matched the force of her personality, waved from across the room.

Regina was the one Angel whom Emma wouldn't miss.

Groaning, Emma ducked behind a group of people who stood beside the grand piano. "Head her off, would you?" she said to Treave. "You're good at charming her."

"No one's good at charming Regina. Except possibly with a flute and a turban and a large basket with a snake-proof lid," Treave said, heading for the exit.

"Chicken. Think of your family motto."

"That's about loyalty, not courage. We Nancarrows have been proudly embracing cowardice since the English

Civil War." Grabbing Emma's arm, Treave steered her with him into the other parlor. "As a survival mechanism, I highly recommend it."

He guided them through the crowd toward the drinks cart and started to pour himself a Scotch with an exaggerated look of relief that Emma realized was meant to make her laugh. But then Regina caught them.

"Well, there you both are! No one knew where you had gone. And Treave, you've been so busy that I haven't managed to catch you all day. I've been calling your office all week. Haven't you gotten any of my messages?"

"Oh, Regina. Hello." Treave turned and stooped to kiss the crepe-paper cheek Regina offered. "No, I haven't gotten any messages. I'm only just back from St. Petersburg and Moscow, and I've been with Emma all day. As you can imagine, under the circumstances."

"Well. Yes." Regina colored lightly, her helmet of steel-colored hair not moving as she nodded. "Evangeline's death has been a shock, hasn't it?" She sniffed and turned to Emma. "For all of us, though I must say, Emma, you're holding up very well. You didn't cry once at the service. I suppose that's better than making a scene, though, isn't it?"

Emma counted to five very slowly. "Evangeline wouldn't have appreciated a scene," she said. "She wanted a dignified service."

"It was quite nice, actually." Regina shifted forward, the lapels of her suit flapping as she peered at Emma through the shadows cast by the grand piano in the corner of the room. "She was worried about you being able to manage it all, you know, but I thought it went off rather well. The reception is more disappointing. Still, I don't imagine you were able to get her regular caterer on such short notice. I suppose one can't complain."

Treave's lips tightened. "One *shouldn't*. Especially given that it was Emma who usually catered the food for book nights."

"Emma?" Regina's eyebrows rose. "But Evangeline never said . . . "

"She didn't like to call attention to it," Emma responded hurriedly. "And I thought the food tonight was excellent. The caterer is just starting out, and her rates are a bargain. I expect she might still have time in her fall schedule if you'd like to try her. Maybe for the Historical Society picnic?"

Regina raised her head slowly, nose first like a smug sort of puppet with the string positioned very badly. "I've had that planned for months. One does, you know, if one wants an event to go off smoothly. Things always go wrong if one hires someone willy nilly at the last possible moment."

"Not always," Emma said, smarting from the jab in spite of herself. Then it hit her that she didn't actually have to stay and listen to Regina anymore—that Regina was one person she *wouldn't* miss having in her life. She bared her teeth in something she hoped would pass muster as a smile and edged around the end of the drinks cart ready to bolt for freedom. "Oh, gee. Look, there's someone I desperately need to talk to. Excuse me."

Treave caught her elbow and moved to follow. "I'd better go with her. Lovely to see you, Regina."

"Wait." Regina caught his other arm. "I really do need to speak with you about my investments, Treave. I've been worried, and my husband—"

Feeling only mildly guilty, Emma didn't try to save Treave. She peeled his fingers off her arm and smiled at him as she rushed away. The doorbell ringing a few moments later gave her a legitimate excuse, and she went to answer it.

Evangeline's longtime editor from Ransom House stood on the threshold in an outfit that screamed New York: a short black dress, burgundy lace tights, and spike-heeled shoes that made Emma wince just looking at them. Marie Jackson swept inside as the taxi that had deposited her in the driveway backed away. After giving Emma a perfunctory hug, she glanced around the room, and a frown marred the smooth brown skin beneath the tightly crimped curls that the she wore cropped close to her head.

"God, it's sweltering out here," she said. "And isn't this thing nearly over? I assumed nearly everyone would be gone by now. You've got to be exhausted. In your shoes, I'd be half-drunk in self-defense by now."

Emma laughed and eyed Marie's stiletto heels. "In your shoes, I'd fall down and break a leg without the need for alcohol. Anyway, if I start drinking now, I'll never stop. How are you? I didn't think you were going to make it."

"I caught the train after that lunch meeting I couldn't cancel, and here I am."

"I'm glad you made it. Thank you for the flowers, by the way," Emma said. "They were beautiful. Enormous and beautiful. Please thank everyone for me."

"They all send their condolences. I know it's been expected, but it still seems unbelievable. She was so brave about it all." Lightly, Marie touched Emma's arm with an unusually timid movement. "This is a little embarrassing to admit," she said, "but honestly, I'm here for your sake as much as Evangeline's."

Emma paused beneath an oil painting of her mother. "What do you mean?"

"The company—by which I mean Patricia—sent me down with instructions to camp out on your doorstep until I could get you to sit down for a conversation. It's awful to do this now, I know, but do you have any time tomorrow? Breakfast? I have a million and one things I have to get done this week, so you'd be doing me a huge favor if you'd give me an hour or two so I can get back."

"An hour or two for what? I don't think I can handle many more surprises these days."

"Oh, Em, I'm sorry." Marie caught both of Emma's hands. "Of course you can't. Listen, I know it's early days yet, but you haven't made any decisions about what you're going to do next, have you? Apart from the museum? You'd mentioned wanting to go back to finish school at one point, and—"

"I haven't had time to think much yet."

"Good, because that's why I wanted to talk to you. I've loved working with you since your mother's accident. I don't know what we would have done without you running interference with her, and the truth is, her manuscripts have ended up stronger since you started helping. Warmer. More compassionate—I think that's the word I'm looking for. Not that I could ever have said so to Evangeline, but it was obvious how much time and work you must have put in beyond just transcribing her dictation and keeping her on deadline. To make a long story short, we'd love to have you continue publishing with us."

"Publishing?" Emma asked, not quite processing what Marie was saying. "Books?"

"Of course books," Marie said, smiling faintly.

Emma blinked. "What kind?"

"Romances would obviously be ideal. What we're hoping is that you'll be willing to finish this last book Evangeline was working on, which is the reason we're rushing this a bit. I'd give you whatever help you needed, of course, and we could publish it under both Evangeline's name and yours. Then the next one would be under your name alone. You'd bring a lot of Evangeline's fans along with you that way and get a nice fat sales bump."

A visceral shudder ran through Emma at the image of herself trying to step into Evangeline's shoes—into Evangeline's life—like a little girl playing dress-up in her mother's clothing. She opened her mouth to say that she was thinking of going back to college and maybe medical school—something sensible and grounded—if she could find a way to pay for it, but what came out instead was an idea she hadn't even realized was forming in her brain.

"I'm going to open a catering business," she said as Treave stepped up beside her. She smiled both at him and Marie, and now that she had said the words they filled her with bone-deep certainty. Excitement tingled across her palms, and she turned to Treave wanting him to be as excited about the idea as she was. "What do you think? It's perfect, isn't it?"

"A catering business?" Treave repeated, his expression growing remote. "I know it sounds good, but it would be risky. And time consuming."

Emma couldn't help bouncing a little on her toes. "Not so very risky. With so many events in this town, there's always a need for new caterers."

"Because the old ones go out of business having lost their shirts in the process. Most food service ventures fail within the first five years. They make terrible investments."

"I have the contacts to get referrals, and I can cook well enough—or get some professional help," she said, thinking of Julia.

Treave's brows snapped together, leaving deep furrows above his eyes. "Em, there's much more to catering than cooking."

"I *know* that." She tried to swallow down her disappointment and her surprise—Treave was usually the first one to support her.

"I, for one, think it's a fantastic idea," Marie said, giving Emma a warm, wide smile. "That raspberry mousse cake you made the last time I was down here was seriously one of the best things I've ever eaten. Oh, wait. I have an idea—what about writing a cookbook? We could include some of the food Evangeline mentioned in her books along with the recipes you've made for the Angels' book nights. Evangeline's fans would eat that up, and it would be wonderful publicity if you wanted to start a business."

"Em," Treave said with a slow shake of his head. "Don't rush into anything before you've had a chance to think things through. There's too much happening for you all at once."

"I'm sure Marie isn't expecting an answer right this minute," Emma said.

"Of course I'm not." A flush darkened Marie's cheeks. "You take whatever time you need. The offer will be open when you're ready. Call me directly, or talk it over with your mother's agent. I'm sure she'd be happy to walk you through this. Only tell me you'll think it over?"

"I will. Of course I will." Emma glanced at Treave, whose eyes were suspiciously bright with something that looked like anger.

Nursing a confusing mixture of excitement over the idea of making a profession out of her cooking and disappointment in Treave's reaction, Emma managed a convincing smile. But the idea of opening a catering business was too perfect, too luminous and shining, to let him spoil it with talk of numbers and common sense.

Hadn't she envied Julia for being brave? Here was her opportunity.

Maybe, at least in part, because Evangeline's video still buzzed in her head like a swarm of bees, this seemed to be one decision that she didn't think needed much mulling over.

It was past time she started taking some risks of her own. After all, where had caution ever gotten her?

PROPOSAL

T REAVE HELD THE TRAY for Emma after the guests had gone, wandering around behind her while she picked up gold-rimmed coffee cups and lead crystal glasses from behind the potted orchids and picture frames on top of the piano. What Emma wanted rather desperately was to be left alone.

"You're leading with your heart, Em," Treave said. "You realize that? Ordinarily, I'd stand and cheer for you, but you haven't had time to think through the financial aspects and the amount of work involved."

Emma set a glass onto the tray, the ruby red dregs of

wine gleaming like blood against the silver surface. "I don't need much to live on; I proved that in college. I can get a second job or a third if I have to until the business takes off, but I want to do this for myself. To try something that makes me happy."

"You'd hate it if you tried and failed."

"Which is why I need a brilliant business plan—your specialty." Emma swung back to face him. "Please, Treave, help me figure out how to make this work instead of telling me why it won't."

"Of course I'll help, that's a given. But haven't you given any thought to the will at all? I know that I made a proper muddle of it this morning, and this isn't at all how I envisioned asking you, but I was hoping . . . I've always hoped that you and I would someday marry."

Emma stiffened. "You don't have to say that. It's fine. I'm fine."

"I'm not just saying it." Treave moved up next to the piano. "What I'm trying to tell you—admittedly very badly—is that I've been falling in love with you for years, so gradually I didn't even realize it had happened. Now I try to think of my life without you, and I can't imagine it."

"We'll always be friends—it's not as if I won't be in your life. You don't have to be nice."

"Nice isn't something I'm often accused of being." Treave shook his head. "Certainly not nice enough to marry someone I don't wish to marry. Look, Evangeline did catch us both by surprise, I realize that. If I'd had any inkling what she'd planned, I'd have done my level best to talk her out of it, and the last thing I want is for you to feel like you have to marry me—or to marry me for any reason other than that you want to, come to that. I'd hoped we would have the time to let our relationship evolve naturally now that there are only the two of us in the picture."

"You've never said anything."

Treave set the tray on the piano. "How could I? It would only have introduced more stress between you and your mother, and Evangeline would have hated being the extra wheel to our pair. Or I thought so anyway until I saw the video. In any case, I assumed you suspected how I felt—I hoped you felt the same way. You still could, couldn't you? Given time? Friendship is a good foundation."

"Not always."

"Are you saying you won't even try?" Treave searched her face then looked away abruptly, over her head, as if he didn't want to watch her when she answered.

The idea that she could hurt Treave romantically, genuinely hurt him, hadn't occurred to Emma until that moment. But the stiffness of his shoulders and the wounded look in his eyes said that her words mattered to him very much.

"It isn't you," she said. "You're wonderful. I just don't think I'm cut out to marry anyone. And I'd hate to spoil our friendship, throw away what we already have."

"That wouldn't happen to us. We're good together. At least don't close your mind on the subject before you've had a chance to recover from the surprise of it all. Will you promise me that much?"

Emma stared back at him, not wanting to agree, but not wanting to make him even more upset. The whole idea of marriage made her skin itch. She'd seen too often what it had done to Evangeline, how often the delusion of happily-ever-after had left her mother sliced bare and bleeding.

Then, too, it was time to stand on her own two feet, follow her own passions, and do what *she* was good at doing. Cooking was the one thing she knew beyond a shadow of a doubt that she loved to do.

Treave stepped closer, smiling ruefully again. "All right, that's fine. I'd rather have silence than a refusal, so I don't intend to push you. You're still furious with Evangeline, and I understand that, too. But don't let her ultimatum influence your decision. That wouldn't be fair to either of us." He scrubbed a hand through his hair with an uneven hiss of breath. "I bloody hate all this, you know. I especially hate leaving you alone for three weeks in the midst of it, but I can't cancel my trip to St. Petersburg tomorrow. Then there's my brother's wedding straight after I get back."

"Three weeks isn't long."

"Then come to the wedding with me." Treave put his hands on her shoulders, his eyes suddenly alight. "It's the perfect solution. If you don't come, I'll be stuck on my own as the odd man out for two weeks while everyone else pairs up. You more than deserve a holiday, and you've always said you wanted to visit Cornwall anyway. We'd have time together away from here without any pressure, a chance for you to see me differently. We could even take a crack at putting together a business plan for you at the same time, if you like. What do you say?"

What could Emma say? She had no real reason to turn him down, not when she'd wished for years she could see where he'd grown up. An island castle in Cornwall, a business plan, a chance to get away, a chance to clear her head. Why would she want to turn him down?

"When you put it like that," she said, "Of course I'd love to come."

THE CASTLE ON THE HILL

*"And the ashes blew towards us
with the salt wind from the sea."*

DAPHNE DU MAURIER
REBECCA

T HE STORM THE NEWS had warned about since Emma
and Treave had first landed in London was little more
than a gathering cloak of shadow, dark and distant on the
horizon as Treave drove the rented black Range Rover
southward. Already exhausted by the long flight to the
United Kingdom, Emma was content to watch the
landscape unfurl beyond the window, unspeakably lovely
landscape of apple orchards, green fields of barley, and
acres of yellow rapeseed so bright they burned the eyes.
Salt tanged the air as the road veered toward the sea. Treave
slowed now and again to drift around—or crawl through—

picturesque seaside towns swollen with crowds of sunburned tourists, colorful beach umbrellas, and recently constructed holiday homes.

At first, he kept up a running commentary, a rundown on the history and geography of the west country and the fiercely independent Cornish coast. He was more comfortable with facts and finances and numbers than with literature, but Emma was her mother's daughter, and novels and legends were what kindled her imagination. The drive stirred up thoughts of *Poldark* and Daphne du Maurier and *Tristan and Isolde*, made her long to have Treave stop the car so she could run out onto the edge of a cliff and see the wild coastline and the water churning down below her while the wind made tangles of her hair. But bit by bit, as the road crossed toward the other side of the peninsula, the storm swept toward them. By the time they reached the ocean again, the water had lashed itself into ropes of froth, trees whipping ominously above it, and trash swirling in the increasingly deserted village streets.

Hunching deeper in his seat, Treave stopped talking to concentrate, driving at a ground-swallowing speed that, since the oncoming cars were on the opposite side of the road than Emma was used to seeing them, made her feel as though an accident was more certainty than possibility. Not wanting to seem too obviously a coward, she folded her hands tightly in her lap and watched out the window as though she could make the storm and the traffic behave if she just concentrated hard enough.

"Don't worry," Treave said, picking up on her nerves.

"We know a thing or two about storms in Cornwall, and this one won't be bad as storms go. I'm only hurrying because if we don't get to Mowzel ahead of it, we'll be hard pressed to find a boatman to take us over to the island. The causeway will be underwater already."

Emma wrapped her hand around the seat belt. "We have to go by boat in this? Wouldn't it be better to wait it out somewhere until the storm is over?"

"I can't imagine we'd find rooms anywhere decent at this time of year, and I'd hate to come this far without being able to get home. But trust me, we'll be safe as houses crossing over. Any self-respecting Cornish boatman knows these waters better than he knows his wife." Treave steadied the wheel as the wind tried to wrench it from him.

He didn't seem bothered by the weather much at all. He drove the car like he did everything else, with a self-assured competence that made it impossible to doubt him. His jaw was stubborn, his nose just slightly beaked—an aristocratic nose, a conqueror's nose worthy of a man whose family had won an island fortress in the English Civil War and held it ever since. He'd have been a soldier in another lifetime. Or a pirate, Emma thought, smiling to herself at the way the landscape was already making her fanciful.

"What are you thinking that's made you look at me like that?" Treave asked, taking his attention off the road for a moment to raise an eyebrow at her.

"I was wondering how owning an entire island affects you as you're growing up. Knowing that your family has literally helped turn the tide of history."

Treave's laugh transformed his face back to something more familiar. "Our history is nowhere near that romantic, I'm afraid. The Royalists lost the war and abandoned St. Levan's Mount to the Parliamentarians, at which point we got it in exchange for sinking masses of cash into repairing the castle and the fortifications. Then Parliament went and restored the monarchy anyway and made the whole war moot. All those lives lost, homes and abbeys destroyed, but that was Cromwell for you. In any case, the family hasn't technically owned St. Levan's Mount or the island since my father left it to the National Trust four years ago. The Trust does the repairs, and the family has a 999-year lease, so my brothers still operate the tours along with a new B&B and winery. Personally, I think they're both starkers, sinking more money into keeping the place afloat, but they're determined to give the people who still live on the island a way to support themselves."

"That's kind. Responsible."

"Kind and responsible, even wonderful—but not terribly wise, unfortunately. Bankrupting themselves to keep the village limping along won't do anyone any favors in the long run. The jobs will still vanish eventually, and if the Trust had taken over the tours, they would still have found work for as many people as they could. We'd have been better off letting them do that and giving the rest of the workers a reasonable severance to help them carry over while they found additional work."

"Is there other work?" Emma asked. "How many

people live on the island?"

"Only about thirty, but we employ more from Mowzel, and of course most of Mowzel's tourism comes from its proximity to the Mount. Here, you'll catch your first sight of the place in a moment." Treave pointed ahead through the windscreen.

The car rounded a bend on the smaller road they'd taken, and Mount's Bay stretched out in front of them, grey and frothed with whitecaps, sweeping from Lizard Point to Gwenapp Head as if some enormous sea creature had taken a bite out of the southernmost stretch of Cornwall, leaving the shape of a giant claw clutching at the English Channel. Nestled amid greenery and fields that undulated nearly to the water, the towns of Marazion, Penzance, and Mowzel dotted the shoreline, spaced roughly equidistant, with Penzance, by far the largest, in the center.

Mowzel, on the farthest end, was little more than a fishing village, and offshore, about a quarter mile out into the bay itself, an island rose steep and green from the water, its jutting height made even greater by the walls of a castle that seemed almost to have grown organically out of the cliffs at the summit. Terraced gardens climbed the hillside above a row of small buildings at the base of a tiny harbor protected by a sturdy pair of sea walls. Even with the waves crashing against the stone, the place looked battered but enduring, and it was easy to see how it had stood there steadfastly since the twelfth century, commanding a view of the shipping lanes and giving its owners control not only of the harbor but also of the wealth passing through the

English Channel.

Pirates wasn't, perhaps, a term too far out of reach. If not Treave's family, then others must have profited from that wealth.

The thought stirred up the sediment of all the gothic stories Emma had read while growing up. She'd cut her reading teeth on *Jamaica Inn*, *Rebecca*, and *Frenchman's Creek*, on tales of smugglers and wreckers and women so memorable that they had become immortal. But now the thought of *Rebecca* somehow conjured images of Evangeline. Another woman larger than life. Another woman for whom pride was everything.

Flinching at the thought, Emma turned her attention back to the bay, to the gusting wind and the waves that thundered against the rocks and sent geysers of water high into the air.

A city girl through and through, and a landlubber to boot, she couldn't help dreading the idea of crossing the water in this kind of weather. Her only experience on a boat hadn't been a good one.

The summer that she'd turned fourteen, her mother had rented a yacht on the premise that they could combine a Caribbean vacation with research for her newest series. Emma had spent two miserable months trawling from island to island, sick as a dog on her bed every night while the boat rocked and she waited for the sputter of the dinghy's outboard motor pulling up in the early hours when Evangeline and the crew returned. Now as an adult, she could recognize that the nausea had probably derived from worry as much as anything else. Still, as the car shuddered in the wind and the water churned in the bay beneath an increasingly ominous sky, she wasn't optimistic about her ability to keep from embarrassing herself by getting violently seasick. Showing up to meet Treave's family with vomit splattered over her clothes wouldn't be the most auspicious introduction.

"Maybe I'd better call around to some of the hotels and see if we can find some options—just in case," she said.

"Trust me, it looks far worse from here than it is, and the backside of the causeway is sheltered by the island, so it's always calmer."

"You're sure there will be someone willing to take us over?"

"The boats'll go out as long as it's safe and not a minute less. We don't often get summer hurricanes up here, but the boatmen are used to coping with winter gales." Treave sent her a sharp look before wrenching his attention back to the road. "If it truly makes you uncomfortable, though, of course we can wait it out."

"No, as long as you think it's safe, I'll trust you." Emma smiled at Treave and told herself not to be an idiot.

She'd wanted to be braver, more exciting and adventurous. This was her chance.

Her mother would have been thrilled by the prospect of a little danger. Before the accident, Evangeline would have been the first to sit beside Treave in the bow, laughing as the boat bounced on top of the waves. Maybe that was part of Emma's own problem with Treave, the reason she still couldn't see him as more than a friend. She'd seen the way he was with Evangeline, the way the two of them were together. He routinely flew all around the world, to Paris, Moscow, St. Petersburg, Hong Kong, Malaysia, Thailand. Places her mother had known well, too. In his own way, Treave had Evangeline's talent for living a large life, an exciting life. Emma couldn't help feeling she was too small for him.

But the undeniable fact that she hadn't inherited the adventure gene from Evangeline wasn't a valid reason for rejecting Treave. Not really. Not when that rejection stemmed from fear, Emma's lifelong companion. Fear of being left behind, fear of change, fear of doing the wrong thing, fear of being the wrong person, fear of failing. And if she failed at a relationship with Treave, she'd end up losing more than her heart—she'd lose her best friend. She'd already lost touch with nearly everyone else in her life these past few years.

Clearly the first step in trying out a relationship was to change her way of thinking. She couldn't make Treave smaller, she wouldn't want to, but she could try to be a little *bigger*. Live life harder instead of standing on the sidelines quite so much.

Live, full stop.

Forcing her hands to unclench, she pressed the button that opened the sunroof of the Range Rover and let the wind fill the car with the scent of the oncoming storm.

"What are you doing?" Treave reached over to close

the roof again.

Emma caught his wrist. "Leave it. Please? For once, I want to feel the storm instead of looking out at it through the glass. Is that crazy?"

He watched her a moment, then slid his hand down until his fingers wrapped around hers a moment and gave a squeeze. "You of all people deserve a bit of crazy. Here, I'll open the windows as well, if you like."

He pressed the driver's side button, and the wind swept in, whipping Emma's hair against her cheeks. She let it, welcoming the sting and the tangles and the messiness of it all. Because what was life if it wasn't a little messy?

HOT AND COLD

"There are things that I canna tell you,
at least not yet."

DIANA GABALDON
OUTLANDER

B RANDO MACLAREN PAUSED ON the threshold of his
sister's upstairs office. With the storm pelting fat drops
of rain nearly sideways against the leaded windows, Janet
hadn't yet noticed his approach. She stood at the window
huddled into a summer sweater, though if she felt a chill
that was probably more from worry than from the draft
that persisted within the thick stone walls of St. Levan's
Mount. After a decade of living in the castle, she had to be
accustomed to the fact that tapestries, rugs, and even
central heating couldn't make a medieval fortress entirely
comfortable. This being Brando's first visit to Cornwall

since Janet had married the oldest of the three Nancarrow brothers, though, Brando had to admit that if this was how the other half lived, they could bloody keep it.

Aye, but he wasn't here for luxury, was he? Or warmth, come to that. Not even for the upcoming wedding that had given him the excuse to come. He'd traveled down to make his peace with Janet, and seeing her standing at the window with the sunlight revealing the first gray in her hair and hints of change in her face made him realize how much time he'd already allowed to slip away.

Janet was the last of his family, as he was hers, and he was older and wiser and generally less resentful than he'd been when she'd turned her back on him, her home, and her roots in the Scottish Highlands. He was more tempered, he liked to think, by the weight of his responsibilities. Janet, on the other hand, looked a bit worn-out and worried, but he'd seen already that she was no less a spitfire than she'd ever been.

Clearing his throat, he let her know that he was there.

She spun away from the window already spoiling for a fight. "It's you, is it? I forgot how you can creep up on a person."

"You were wandering away in your thoughts," he said, moving to stand beside her. "Give you a penny for them?"

"They're no secret. Only that Treave Nancarrow is still as daft and selfish as he ever was. Imagine dragging poor Jack the Boatman out in this weather. And what will the poor girl he's dragging along with him think of us, I ask you? Her with her mother just dead and the weight of grief still weighing on her. We'll be lucky if we don't end with having to turn out the lifeboat to fish all three of them out of the sea."

"If the girl's come all the way from America with Treave, I expect she knows exactly what he is already. Or it could be he's changed some since he threw your wedding dress into the mud and I broke his nose for him." Stopping beside her at the window, Brando smiled at Janet hopefully, but she kept peering out into the driving rain. "We all change," he said. "We all grow up a bit."

She glanced up at him. "Is that an apology at last for ruining my wedding day, Brando MacLaren? Bit late for that."

The old anger came swift and thick, bubbling up, but Brando tamped it down. He had to tamp it down. "I wasn't the one who ruined it for you."

"You and Treave, the pair of you. And you were never happy for me."

No. He hadn't been. Brando couldn't argue that.

Down the hill at the castle harbor, alongside the handful of long red-roofed homes and shops that nestled along the base of the cliff, waves battered the rocks and sent plumes of spray into the air. The five boats anchored in the harbor bobbed and swayed, a wild dance of dipping masts and brightly-colored flapping tarps. Beyond the relative safety of the sea wall, the cobblestoned causeway to the mainland emerged like a serpent's tail now and then through the churning wave, and close beside it, a boat chugged determinedly against the wind.

Brando didn't pretend to be a seaman. The closest he ever came to water in his day-to-day were the two small lakes that attracted tourists to the restaurant and small hotel he'd started in what had once been the family farmhouse. But he'd swum in those lochs of Balwhither Glen often enough, and even protected as they were by the heather-covered Highland braes, he'd seen them produce waves strong enough to drown a man or tip a boat. Then, too, he had a Highlander's healthy respect for weather, enough that he wouldn't disagree with Janet about the sanity of a man who insisted on trying to cross a quarter mile of open water in the tail end of an Atlantic hurricane. Nor, deep down, could he dispute Janet's opinion of Treave Nancarrow when it came to that. He'd only met the man once at Janet's wedding, but that had been enough acquaintance.

He might not have been the one to spoil Janet's wedding—at least not intentionally—but it was true enough that he'd been angry. At nineteen, he'd hated the world, and it had taken him the better part of the decade since to work himself into a sounder frame of mind. On the other hand, Treave had deserved everything Brando'd given him and more.

"Och, well." Janet released a pent up breath. "If you're going to stand there like a great lump not saying anything at all, I'd better be heading down with the car to get the two of them. If I'm late in this weather, none of us will hear the end of it. You could do me a favor, if you like. Fetch Kenver and Perran up from the cellars? Treave will sulk all evening if they're not turned out at the door to greet him. Although . . . "

"Although what?" he asked.

Janet glanced at his kilt and dark gray T-shirt with the faint air of disapproval she'd worn too often since the moment she'd taken on the mothering of him when he was a hellion of ten and she was just seventeen. "You might give a thought to changing."

"And what's wrong with a kilt, woman?"

"Nothing if you're at a Highlands Games. But this is Cornwall."

"Aye," Brando retorted, "and I'm still a Scot, last I looked. I'll wear the same as I wear every day—what I'm comfortable wearing. Treave can go hang if he doesn't like it. Since when do you care tuppence what he thinks anyway?"

"I don't." Beneath her riot of hair that was the same deep chestnut as his own, Janet's cheeks flushed pink. "Only I don't want trouble for Christina's wedding. Be on your best behavior. Hold your temper, that's all I'm asking."

"Me?" Brando pulled up short. He opened his mouth to retort that Janet of all people should talk about tempers.

But what would be the point?

"I came for the wedding because you invited me," he said quietly instead. "Though if it makes you fret, there's no need for me to stay. I had a hard enough time finding a chef to take over at the restaurant for me, and we've a full schedule of events booked for the hotel. Only don't expect I'll drop everything to come make peace with you the next time."

"Peace, is it?" Janet's hands flew to her hips, a posture with which he was all too familiar, and she narrowed her eyes. "We may have lost touch a bit, and an apology wouldn't come amiss, Brando MacLaren, but I'd hardly call that needing peace. Could be we'd squabble considerably less if you weren't liable to take offense over every little thing."

"Or if you were less mule-headed and contrary. Not to mention that you still can't see as far as the nose in front of your face. Otherwise, you'd not be pretending you don't know why I dropped everything to come when you invited me."

They glared at each other, him a good foot taller than she was, and the way she stood with her temper flaring and her chest heaving, Brando couldn't help a sudden grin. On some level, he'd missed arguing with her. Good thing he was a sight too old and solid these days for her to grab him by the ear and drag him back from wherever she had found him. But just as he was thinking he ought to apologize before she threw whatever was to hand at him for laughing—a paperweight or a sheaf of the file folders that littered her desk, for example—the sound of a throat clearing in the doorway shifted his attention to where Christina Healey, the bride-to-be, stood on the threshold watching them both wide-eyed.

Head tipped sideways and her dark pixie tumble of short curls glistening with rain as if she'd just dashed across the courtyard, she was even smaller than Janet and possibly the only woman Brando'd ever met who could best his sister in a brawl. Although her official title was Director of Marketing for the bed and breakfast and the winery, like the rest of the family she pitched in wherever she was needed. And like the rest of the family, she had the same worried shadows beneath her eyes.

"Are you two planning to stand here arguing much longer?" she asked. "Because the boat's nearly here. I'll go myself if you're not going down to meet it. Kenver and Perr are still in the cellars and no telling when they'll be back up."

"Sooner rather than later, if they know what's good for them." Janet set down the reading glasses she'd been holding on the corner of her desk. "I was sending Brando down to get them now, and I'm off to the harbor. You can come with me, if you like."

"I've only just come back from the boathouse, so if you don't need me, I'll go glam up before they get here. The girl he's bringing is bound to be posh and a bit superior with it."

"Aye, though we shouldn't judge before we've even met her," Janet said.

"Seeing as she's coming with Treave and who her mother was, she's likely to be a bit high-maintenance. That's all I'm saying and nothing against her. It takes all sorts to make the world." Exiting the office alongside Janet and Brando, Christina walked with them down the corridor past the six guest rooms that were operated as a B&B then veered off at the staircase, let herself through the chain that said, "Private. No Admittance," and climbed to the third floor where the family had their rooms.

Janet and Brando went the opposite direction, descending the wide, blue-carpeted steps. The castle, having begun as a tenth century abbey near the site of the original priory on the headland, had been added to continuously through the years, until the residence and battlemented twelfth century towers and curtain walls had formed a full square around the courtyard and swallowed up the tenth century stone chapel and tower that still stood at the center along the front. The carriage house and security rooms to the left, and the armory and lobby to the right occupied the rest of the side along the entrance and two front towers, and the residence and remaining public spaces occupied the remaining buildings.

Adding to the challenge of navigation, the guest drawing rooms and dining area had been segregated from the banquet rooms, library, and other spaces that were only open on the public castle tour as well as from those that belonged to the family section of the residence. The result was a labyrinth of passageways that made getting anywhere in a hurry nearly impossible. That was another reason Brando was happy to leave the ownership of a place like this to the other half. Having paying guests in his own home was hard enough—he'd learned that the hard way himself running a boutique hotel. He didn't envy Janet having to add in hundreds of tourists traipsing through the castle on any given day.

At least, given the storm, that was one less worry. The

public tours had been cancelled, and Janet had phoned the guests who'd been expecting to check in that night and warned them not to come. Still, with no safe way off the island, the guests who were already there were stuck indoors, which only added to Janet's worries. But Tamsyn, the castle housekeeper, while clearly not quite right in the head, had at least had tea and scones and a fire laid in the drawing room where three elderly couples were already playing bridge.

In that respect, staying at the castle amounted to a busman's holiday for Brando. Walking past the drawing room, he couldn't help noticing that one of the men was tapping his foot impatiently, wanting some more exciting occupation, wanting to escape. That was a bad review in the making right there.

Not that Janet would listen if Brando made suggestions.

She stopped as they reached the lobby at the base of one of the square towers nearest the portcullised castle entrance. "Right," she said. "That's me off from here, then, and you can tell Kenver and Perr they've twenty minutes to meet us at the door. It'll be closer to thirty, if I'm honest, but no need to tell them that. Only mention they'll need an excuse on a par with the second coming if they're not here waiting by the time I'm back."

Brando grinned, and while Janet veered to the right and cut through the armory gate that led down to the village road, he took the smaller staircase that led to the garrison room beneath the southwest tower. From there, a hidden door—left open now for the tours to access—led into the warren of tunnels that had originally been built as an escape route to the smaller harbor below the original priory on the headland. Like the castle, the tunnels had been expanded for various reasons through the centuries—for smuggling, politics, or safety—and the entire complex now served as the cellars and press for the winery that the two older Nancarrow brothers had started with their share of their father's inheritance.

The stairs were narrow but well lit, winding around to the sealed inner door that helped regulate the temperature of the cellars. Brando pressed the button on the wall beside it, and the door hissed open into the low-light, ventilated tunnel lined with barrels. Further on, a room hewn from the granite bedrock was more brightly lit, and it housed the presses and metal vats, and a laboratory at the far end. Beyond that, more storage tunnels branched off below.

The brothers stood halfway back in the large room, deep in conversation with the winemaker they had hired to manage production. As Brando approached, they looked up and smiled, but he stopped a few feet away to give them time to finish.

They were both alike and different, the two of them, Brando reflected as he watched them. Kenver, Janet's husband and the older of the two, was dark haired, with lean, aristocratic features and an aquiline nose set beneath gray eyes that kindled easily with humor. Brando had hated him for stealing Janet away, for making her turn her back on him and her family roots, for being Connal MacGregor's friend when MacLarens had been feuding with MacGregors in the glen for more centuries than any of them could count. But for all of that, through the years, Kenver had been good to Janet. Bookish and studious, he had the kindness and thoughtful, patient temperament to counteract her faults.

Perran Nancarrow, in contrast, was more prone to doing than to thinking. While Kenver was Brando's own height, a hair over six-foot and a good ten inches taller than Janet, Perr was stockier built and more easily prone to laughter. He was also less apt to feel the weight of responsibility than his brother, but they were solid, the both of them. Dependable. As Janet had already voiced the question earlier, Brando couldn't help agreeing that it was odd they'd ended up with Treave as the bump on the family tree. Then again, Treave'd had a different mother. Maybe that was what had made the difference.

The telephone rang back in the laboratory, pulling him out of his musing as the winemaker rushed away to answer and Kenver shifted over. "I take it my wife's sent you down with orders for us to turn out for inspection?"

"I wouldn't call them orders precisely," Brando said, raising his palms in denial. "At least not where Janet's liable to hear about it. But she did mention she'd be back with your brother in fifteen minutes give or take."

"We'd better get our skates on, then, hadn't we?" Perran asked, but the winemaker came back with a question that delayed them another few minutes.

When they made it up to the door at the castle

entrance, Janet had already pulled the car through the arched gate into the courtyard and was bustling around to get the trunk open. Brando and the brothers went to help with the luggage, and given how hard the rain was coming down, by the time they all ran back under the deep arch that ran between the church and the entrance hall, they were all dripping water on the pale stones and wiping it from their eyes.

Even so, Brando couldn't help being aware of the woman who'd arrived with Treave. Couldn't help staring at her.

Emma, that was her name.

It suited her.

She ducked from the courtyard into the archway, smiling faintly at everyone as though she were a wee bit shy, but assessing them at the same time, cataloging them with the careful attention of someone for whom details mattered. Something about her went straight to Brando's gut. Every bit of her went straight through him, if he was being honest, not only because she was beautiful, to him she was beautiful, but because she was also familiar. He'd seen her face in the loch at the Beltane Sighting the spring he'd come back from London, and ever since, she'd been a promise in his mind.

A promise that, until this moment, he hadn't been entirely certain he believed.

Despite having grown up in the glen and seen the damage—and the good—that the Sighting could wreak, in spite of what it had done to his own parents, it still half-shocked him to see the proof of it for himself. Living proof, standing there in front of him.

The idea that one day a year, when the veil between worlds ran thin on Beltane morning, Loch Fàil could reveal the image of one's true love was a romantic notion. One that required a leap of faith. Some people wanted to believe it. They wanted hope, or reassurance, or an excuse to follow their hearts.

Brando'd had all too much reason to know that the Sighting offered heartache more often than hope, and he'd had no intention of taking a look himself. But the Spring that he'd come back to the glen from London, he'd been weak. Then, too, he'd wanted—rather desperately—to be part of the village again. To have them accept him. Along with everyone else, he'd lined up along the shore at first light, half-afraid of seeing Simone looking back at him from the water and confirming that he'd be alone forever. Equally afraid of seeing no one at all.

Instead, a stranger had looked back at him. A single face, that was all. Not his own image reflecting back at him, not the reflections of Elspeth Murray or the half dozen other people standing right there on the shore beside him. Just one face.

Emma's.

And now she was here, pale from the boat ride and soaking wet, her dark gold hair clinging to her face in a way that made his fingers yearn to brush it away, her brown fawn's eyes flecked with amber and looking nervously back at him while he stared.

Brando needed to stop staring.

The others were noticing. Janet frowned at him in warning. Treave scowled at him even while in the midst of receiving brotherly back-thumping greetings from Kenver and Perran. Emma, too, kept looking over at him as though she wondered if there was something wrong with him.

It took Christina, arriving up the staircase behind them, to break the awkwardness. Rushing straight over, she drew Emma into the kind of unselfconscious hug that Janet had never been able to manage.

"Welcome, Emma! Oh, look at you, you're dripping wet, poor thing. The storm's a sad welcome for you, but Perran and I—all of us—are so happy you're here. Personally, I'm doubly glad because I'm an enormous fan of your mother's books."

The way Emma stiffened at the mention of her mother was nearly imperceptible. Brando only saw it because he'd been staring at her again, because he couldn't seem to stop staring at her, and he found himself wanting to go over and say something to tease that stiffness away, to make her smile at him. To see him.

Then Christina leaned in and said something to her he couldn't make out, and Emma laughed in response, laughed with her entire face, her entire self. For a moment, Brando lost all capacity for thought.

"Are you kidding?" Emma was asking. "I'm so glad you don't feel like I'm barging in, but I wouldn't have passed up the opportunity. I've read so many books about Cornwall that even if I didn't adore Treave he would have had me at 'come to my Cornish castle.'"

"You're likely to be disappointed in that case. I'm afraid we can't offer the sort of 5-star accommodations you'll be used to," Janet said.

"It's magnificent and I'm not fussy—and honestly, any place on dry land feels like heaven to me right now. Put me in a cell in the dungeon, and I'll be thrilled."

"Rought trip over, I take it?" Kenver came to slip an arm around Janet, giving Emma a sympathetic nod. "We all said Treave was crazy when we heard he'd gotten Jack to bring you over."

"Jack was great—but I'll admit I fully expected to end up in the water the whole way over." Sliding over Christina's head, Emma's gaze landed on Brando then quickly darted away again.

"You haven't officially met my brother Brando yet," Janet said, gesturing him over while simultaneously giving him the kind of warning head shake she'd used the time he tried to put a worm down the back of Angus MacGregor's shirt in church. "He's visiting from Scotland—"

"I suspect the kilt might have given her a clue about that," Christina said, laughing.

Janet ignored her and continued. "And the tall one here beside me is my husband, Kenver, and over there with Treave that's Perran, Christina's fiancé."

Perran shifted closer, and there was handshaking all around, along with a squall of conversation into which Christina dropped a rapid-fire series of questions that Emma did her best to answer. When everyone was distracted, Janet sidled closer and pinched his arm. "Stop staring, you ruddy great idiot. You're making a spectacle of yourself, and Treave's none too happy about it. Which'll mean trouble, you mark my words."

Brando looked over and met Treave's eyes, which were icy cold and assessing. Janet smoothed her face into a smile and with a final elbow in Brando's ribs, turned back to Emma. "Now," she said, "we need to let you get out of those wet clothes, love. You must be freezing. Come in, and let's get you up to your room so you can get warmed up before dinner. That won't be until late, I'm afraid. Our cook usually does trays for the overnight guests as well, but with no way to get to the restaurants and pubs on the mainland, we've opened up the dining room and Gwen's got a load of extra work on her hands."

"Is there anything we can do to help?" Emma asked.

"No, of course not," Janet said. "Go on up with you and come back down whenever you're ready."

Brando reached for the two larger suitcases. "Your rooms are right across from mine. I'll give you a hand with the luggage."

"Thanks, but we can manage." Treave put a restraining hand on his arm. "In any event, I have an announcement before we go up. Give us your congratulations, everyone. Emma and I just became engaged."

TWISTING TRUTH

*"I love you as certain dark things are to be loved,
in secret, between the shadow and the soul."*

PABLO NERUDA
100 LOVE SONNETS

THE ANNOUNCEMENT STOLE EMMA'S breath. Before she could protest that it wasn't true, Treave's brothers swept in and thumped him on the back and Christina caught Emma in another hug, and then Treave was back, reaching for her hand, his expression nervous and apologetic, his eyes begging her not to contradict him while he whispered into her ear. "Please don't say anything."

Congratulations rang out from everyone at once, voices echoing sharply on the damp stone inside the castle entrance, and the moment—if there'd ever been one—where Emma could have corrected Treave slipped away.

She couldn't have said anything, in any case, without calling Treave a liar in front of his entire family. Humiliating him. More than anything, he hated to be embarrassed.

"Best wishes, Emma." Janet's brother Brando stepped in and offered her his hand with an oddly formal and solemn gesture. "Treave's a very lucky man. I hope you'll both be happy."

Brando's hands were hard, calloused, with long tapering fingers. They wrapped around Emma's, and heat curled through her blood despite the chaos of wind and rain from the sea storm that seemed to have transferred themselves inside her. The whole day had left her confused and uncertain, and her stomach churned almost as much as it had during the boat ride over. Why was the man staring at her so intently? He needed to stop. And she needed to stop letting her eyes drift back to catch him watching.

He moved on to shake Treave's hand in turn, and neither one of them smiled while they exchanged a few clipped words. Treave's jaw jutted forward, and the two of them measured each other like two dogs circling for a fight. Which wasn't a fight that Treave had a hope of winning. Both men were tall and well built, that was true enough, but Brando was broader and bulkier beneath the damp fabric of the pale blue T-shirt he wore with his kilt. And while everything about Treave was civilized and polished, there was something about Brando that was scrappy and raw and suggested he'd know his way around a brawl.

Emma shivered, more from confusion and reaction than from the damp clothes she was wearing, but Janet must have seen it. "What are we all doing, standing here letting the poor girl out to catch her death. There'll be time enough to celebrate properly later. Go on up now the both of you. Brando, give them a hand. And Treave, not knowing the situation, I've put Emma in the third floor rose bedroom and you're in the blue beside her. If you're wanting me to switch that out you can both take the tower room—"

"Oh, no. That's completely fine," Emma said, jumping at it with relief. "I'm happy to stay wherever you've put us."

Brando picked up both the larger suitcases, leaving the two carry-on bags for Treave. But Treave reached instead to take the bigger suitcases for himself.

"You can give those to me, mate. Emma and I can manage fine," Treave said.

"For heaven's sake, there's no sense having Emma carry that up the stairs," Kenver said, shaking his head at him. "She's had a long enough day already. Let the man give you a little help."

Treave's jaw jutted dangerously, but he scooped up the carry-on bags and strode past Brando.

The arched passage in which they'd all been standing led between the gatehouse and a courtyard filled with wrought iron café tables, potted fruit trees, and topiaries. Stairs led up to heavy doors on either side of the passage, the one directly into what appeared to be a church with a tall, round tower spanning its width on the left, and the door into the main part of the castle on the right. Passing through a narrow antechamber, Treave strode through a long armory lined with hundreds of muskets and swords hung along the wall and suits of armor flanking an enormous coat of arms. He pushed through a second set of doors on the far end without a backwards glance, and it was Brando who opened them for Emma when they'd swung shut again, admitting them both into a square lobby at the base of one of the four crenelated towers that formed the outer corners of the castle walls.

"It's a little convoluted, the way the castle's laid out," Brando said, "and I'm afraid it's a bit of a walk to the residence from here." He opened yet another door beyond the lobby, and led her through a long corridor flanked by a series of rooms blocked off with velvet ropes, past a library, and what appeared to be a map room, and a series of drawing rooms. Finally they reached a wide, carpeted staircase.

Treave stood at the bottom looking sheepish. He let Brando move past him before falling in step with Emma. "I'm sorry, Em. I really am. That was unforgivable of me—all of it. Losing my temper just now, saying we're engaged. I'm behaving like a fool, but I opened my mouth, and the words came out. I didn't plan them. How angry are you?"

"On a scale of one to ten," Emma said, "try incandescent. What is *wrong* with you?"

Treave swallowed and started up the steps. "It was the way Janet's brother was staring at you. It's stupid, I know, but he and I have some history from Kenver's wedding. The moment I saw him, it all came rushing back. I know I behaved like a two-year-old. I'm ashamed of myself. Can you forgive me?"

"You have to tell them the truth."

"I don't think I can." He stumbled on the steps then caught himself. "Couldn't you play along? I know it was unforgivable, but I swear I'll make it up to you."

"I don't want to lie to your family." Taking a deep breath, Emma shook her head.

"If I admit I lied, Kenver and Perran will never let me live it down." Treave's face had grown flushed, and a muscle ticked along his cheek. Ahead of them, Brando had reached the second floor, and he crossed the landing and stepped over a velvet rope with a placard strung along it that read, "PRIVATE. NO ADMITTANCE."

Emma shifted her gaze away. "I'm sorry. I'm a terrible liar, anyway. You know that."

"You've never had brothers." Treave set his jaw and climbed to the rope and waited for Emma to step over before doing so himself. "Please, Em? Save me from myself. The pair of them would make my life a living hell for the rest of our lives, and it's only two short weeks of pretending. You don't truly want to see me humiliate myself any more than I have done already, do you? It's bad enough I've embarrassed myself in your eyes."

The grin he gave her was the sweet, pleading one that had always made her forgive him for not stopping by when work had made him cancel plans, but this was something entirely different. Emma couldn't imagine spending two weeks being a guest under his family's roof while lying to them every time she opened up her mouth.

Nor would words be the only lies. Her behavior with Treave would have to change. They'd have to pretend to actually be engaged, to be *in* love.

It was a mistake to have agreed to come here with him at all, she realized. A mistake and completely unfair to him.

She didn't love him, and she wasn't going to fall in love with him to order. That had nothing to do with him. Possibly there really was something wrong with her. In twenty-four years, she'd never had more than a couple of brief, high school crushes and some fumbled experiments in college. Could it be that she wasn't capable of truly loving someone? Maybe that was why she hadn't been able to cry over her mother's death, because something inside of her was broken.

"It would be far more humiliating if we tried to pretend and then got caught," she said. "I'm sorry, but I just can't do it."

Treave's face fell, and she followed him down the corridor feeling worse and worse.

While the first and second floors of the castle had seemed to be in good order, the third floor was shabbier. Frayed and stained French-patterned rugs ran along cream walls with wallpaper that was peeling at the edges. Rain damage puckered the plasterwork on the ceilings, leaving discolored blotches of yellow and rust, and the mismatched tables and chairs and bureaus that stood somewhat forlornly in assorted alcoves and niches all had a lightly battered appearance as if the worn things had all been taken from downstairs and shifted here out of sight. She couldn't help wondering where they'd come from, who'd made them, touched them, bought them or conquered them or stolen them. It was odd to think of one family living in the same place this long, putting down roots into the bedrock of the island. But it was also a lot of pressure on a child growing up, a lot of expectation.

It had never occurred to her that Treave would have his own family baggage. He'd always spoken as if he'd had a happy childhood, and he'd always been so grounded and dependable, so certain of himself. She'd envied him having siblings, but maybe it hadn't been so easy being the youngest child.

She glanced at him walking beside her, and found him looking rigidly ahead. She couldn't tell if he was just upset or if he was watching Brando carrying the luggage ahead of them. And then she found herself watching Brando, too, the relaxed slope of his shoulders and the ease with which he carried the suitcases, the swing of the kilt that fit low over his narrow hips, the way he moved unconsciously as if he wasn't thinking about himself at all.

Stopping about halfway down the long corridor, Brando waved Emma into a room with faded rose tapestries, pale pink velvet bed hangings, and an ivory and pink Aubusson rug long past its prime. It would have been a charming room, Emma thought as she stopped in the center of it, if the lead-paned windows at the far end weren't being battered by the storm that seemed to be getting worse with every minute.

Brando snapped on the light to dissipate the gloom

then set down the suitcases on a long bench at the foot of the bed before turning to smile at her. "I'll leave Treave to show you where everything is in here, but if you need anything, I'm directly across the hall."

"I'm sure we'll be fine, but thanks very much for the help." Treave dropped the two lighter suitcases beside the others.

"Yes, thank you," Emma said, tired suddenly, and eager to get rid of them both. Crossing the room, she found a door that looked as though it might lead into a bathroom, and she paused beside it and cleared her throat. "Now, I'm frozen and dying for that bath, so I'm going to excuse myself."

Without waiting for an answer, she opened the door and ducked through, hoping it wouldn't lead into a closet or something embarrassing. It was indeed a bathroom complete with a chipped claw-footed tub and curtains and rugs in soft florals of ivory and rose. Closing the door behind her, Emma sagged back against it and closed her eyes.

The low murmur of voices from the bedroom diminished, and then footsteps approached. Emma recognized the cadence of them, the measured, even pace.

"Em?" Treave asked softly. "Are you okay?"

She tiptoed away and stood beside the claw-footed bathtub in the corner. "I'm tired, and I really do want a bath."

"You know that I'm truly sorry, don't you? Please let me in so we can figure all this out."

She hesitated. "There's nothing to figure out. I can't lie to your family—I told you."

There was a silence long enough that she wondered if he'd moved away and she hadn't heard him going. But then: "I'm putting you in a horrible, no-win situation. I understand that, believe me. I don't know how to begin to apologize enough for that. It was only . . . the way that Brando was staring at you. And you kept darting looks at him, too. Frankly, it made me jealous, I'll admit it, and a bit embarrassed, if you want the truth. I suppose I was worried about what Kenver and Perr would think with me bringing a woman home and having her obviously fancying another bloke—"

"I don't fancy him—"

"I realize that—only it was how it felt at the time. I'll plead guilty to being an utter tosser, and I'm throwing myself on the mercy of the court. Begging you. Forgive me? I should have been honest with you from the beginning, told you more about my relationship with them."

He fell silent, and Emma sighed. But she couldn't resist. "What about your relationship?"

"Their mother was older than mine, quite a bit older. She was bitter about the divorce, and she did her level best to poison Perr and Kenver and all the staff against my mother and me every chance she had. Then since Father died, we had a few squabbles about his will on top of everything else. Some things they were supposed to do that they haven't done because they've poured money into the winery and the B&B. Maybe that's why I'm fighting so hard for you not to throw away your inheritance. It's not that I'm not willing to help them, but it would be nice if they didn't resent me for being entitled to any of it in the first place. No matter what, somehow in the eyes of everyone on this island, I'll always be a bit of an outsider. Not the same as Kenver or Perran. Second class citizen. There's nothing I can do about that, and I've fought hard to get to a place where the three of us can be comfortable with each other, where I can get even a small measure of respect out of them. If they find out I let Brando goad me into lying about being engaged, we'll go straight back to our childhood patterns, and they'll treat me like nothing more than a needy little brother. Worse, they'll pity me. They don't mean to do it. I know that. Still, knowing it doesn't help, does it? I feel what I feel, and I'm going to have to find a way to get past it. I only hate that I've drawn you into all this. Please tell me you understand."

Emma slumped down onto the edge of the tub, understanding better than she wanted to after all the times Evangeline had humiliated her in front of other people. But she would still never have done what Treave had done.

"What is it you want me to do exactly?" she asked.

"Go along with it. You don't have to lie, but don't contradict it, either. And if you're worried about having to change how we are together, if you feel like that's rushing things, don't be. This may be Cornwall, but we're all properly English enough that no one will expect to see me with my tongue reaching for your tonsils. Two weeks, Em.

That's all. Once we've gone, if you still want to be nothing more than friends, I'll wait a suitable interval and tell them you and I have called things off. Not that I'm giving up on seeing if we can actually making a go of it. You haven't changed your mind about that, have you? I'll understand if you have, of course, but I hope you haven't."

Emma's hands had somehow managed to clench themselves into knots of protest on her lap. That alone should have pushed her into telling him that there was no chance for the two of them. But if she confessed that now, how on earth would they survive the next two weeks together?

Stiffly, she straightened her fingers. "Whatever else we are or might someday be, we will always be best friends," she said. "At least I hope we will."

STORM CAT

"Intuition is really a sudden immersion
of the soul into the universal current of life."

PAUL COELHO
THE ALCHEMIST

INSTEAD OF KNOCKING ON Treave's door as he'd requested, Emma dawdled in her room after she finished her bath. For a full fifteen minutes, she stood at the window watching the storm whip the ocean into madness and the sky boil overhead. The storm both frightened and fascinated her. Living in DC with only the Potomac River nearby, she had never felt the full fury of an Atlantic hurricane over water, the sea clawing at the cliffs as if it were trying to reach the castle at the top. The castle, of course, had withstood far worse, as Treave had told her: seizure by Prince John to defend against his brother,

Richard the Lionheart; the six-month siege during the War of the Roses; the coming of the Spanish Armada, where the Mount watchtower had been the first in England to light the warning beacon. Anne, the wife of the Sheriff of Cornwall, had helped to hold the castle against the Parliamentarians during the English Civil War, only to have to flee when the Royalists had finally lost the war and Treave's family received it as a gift.

Emma watched the storm outside, but it was the one within her that felt more disorienting. She wasn't naive—of course people lied. Evangeline had romanticized reality so often that Emma wasn't sure her mother had known the difference between her version and truth half the time. So what was it about what Treave had done that bothered her so much?

Shaking away her doubts, she wrapped a pale scarf around her neck to go with the teal green sweater that had been a gift from her mother before the accident. Leaving her hair loose, she let it fall in unruly waves down her back, a testament to how long it had been since she'd had time to do anything but trim off the split-ends herself. And if she spent extra time on her makeup, she told herself that wasn't for any specific reason except to give her a bit of added confidence. Still, the realization that she was doing it, taking extra care, propelled her from the room.

"You look beautiful," Treave said, smiling at her when she knocked on his door a minute later. He leaned forward and brushed his lips against her cheek. "Thank you. Again. I'll keep saying it until you understand how much I appreciate that you're willing to play along."

"The fact that I understand what you're going through doesn't mean I'm happy about it," Emma said.

He wound her hand through his elbow after he'd closed his door. "You're the best of the best, Em. I know I'm behaving like a child, and I wish I had the courage to face them. I just can't bear the idea of confrontation. I'll make it up to you; I swear I will. I'll be on my best behavior."

Emma couldn't help relenting. She knew, after all, exactly the lengths a person could go through to avoid unpleasant confrontations, didn't she? What right did she have to judge? In spite of herself, she smiled back at Treave. A small smile, but what the heck. She was going to forgive him eventually. She always did.

They descended the stairs, and he led her through a maze-like warren of rooms, lifting more velvet ropes and taking a variety of shortcuts that Emma knew she would be hard-pressed to remember on her own. Eventually, he ushered her into a robin's egg blue drawing room whose formality was softened by deep brown hardwood planks and beautiful plasterwork on the ceiling.

A black and white border collie lifted its head with a gentle *woof* and thumped its feathered tail where it lay beside a pair of twin boys of about eight or so who were seated at a card table near the fireplace. The twins' russet hair, darker than Janet's by several shades, reminded Emma of Brando and, as if she couldn't help it, she found herself looking for the man himself. He stood closer to the fire with the rest of the family, nursing a glass of amber liquid and staring at her again where she had paused just inside the doorway. The rest of the others in the room fell silent.

For a moment, no one moved, and the silence was the slightly guilty kind that said the subject of a conversation had just walked into the room. Treave's footsteps faltered and his face reddened, and even as Emma couldn't help squeezing his hand in reassurance, Christina peeled away from the group and ran toward them, her short dark hair tousled charmingly around her elfin wide-smiled face.

Jogging over to Emma, she held out both hands and drew her toward the deep damask couch. "Come and sit with me," she said. "Can I get you a glass of wine or are you more of a beer sort of girl? We do hard orchard ciders in the winery as well, and the pear is divine, if you'd like to try it. Of course there's regular liquor, if you'd prefer a gin and tonic or whiskey or something more bracing." She glanced at Treave, who'd crossed over to where the men were standing together, as she spoke.

Emma tried not to read anything into that, but her protective instincts were kicking in. Poor Treave. Maybe she'd gotten off lightly not having brothers or sisters after all. "I'll pass for the moment, thanks. If I drink anything at all," she said, "I'm liable to fall asleep into the soup."

"And you haven't even been subjected to Gwen's soup yet," Christina muttered as Janet came up behind them.

"I'd leave off complaining if I were you, Christina," Janet said with her freckled nose crinkling faintly. "You know full well that whatever Gwen lacks in imagination, she makes up for in hearing and a long, vindictive memory. You're liable to have your guests eating stargazey pie and pasties at your wedding feast, if you're not careful."

"Only because I let you talk me out of doing the sensible thing. *Stargazey pie,* I ask you." Christina sighed and gave Emma a mournful wink. "If you don't know what that is, I'm very much afraid you'll find out soon enough. Dead sardine heads poking out of the crust, staring back at you while you're trying to eat them." She gave a theatrical shudder. "Some things about Cornwall, I'll never get used to."

"So you're not from here, then?"

"Heavens, no. London born and bred, but I love it here. I only wish *some people* could change a bit faster with the times instead of being stuck in the last century for all eternity." Sinking onto the couch, she tucked her knees up underneath her and managed to look instantly as though she ought to have been painted by the likes of John Singer Sargent or Thomas Gainsborough.

"Don't you go listening to Christina, she loves to exaggerate." Janet swirled the wine around in a glass that looked too delicate for her sturdy fingers before looking up at Emma again. She gestured over to where the two boys had launched into an argument that resulted in them tugging what appeared to be a bishop back and forth. "Be honest with me now," she said. "Do you enjoy children or merely tolerate them? We eat late here because of Gwen cooking for the guests, and the twins normally eat earlier and go to bed. I've let them stay up tonight since you and

Treave just got here, but if they bother you, I can stick them on the far end of the table."

"Of course not," Emma said, appalled.

"No worries, love, either way. They're an acquired taste, these lads. I can bring them over to do the polite introduction thing now, or you can keep your distance and no one will blame you for it. Their father put the fear of God in them to be on their best behavior, but that's not a bit of a low standard, I'm afraid."

"I actually love children," Emma said, laughing. "I just haven't had much experience with them. I don't even have cousins, as far as I know."

"Well, I expect you and Treave will have kiddies of your own soon enough, then. That'll be lovely. I do hope you'll take a little time for yourself first, if you don't mind my saying so. He mentioned that you'd had to give up university to take care of your mother after the accident. It must have been hard for you, spending so much time alone at your age when you should have been out living life." Janet frowned suddenly down into her glass. "I'm sorry, that was unpardonably rude of me to say. And I was sorry to hear about her death—sorry for your loss, I should have said that sooner."

Emma wished she had something to do with her own hands—maybe she should have taken that drink after all. She gave Janet an awkward smile. "It's all a little complicated, isn't it? I feel like I should apologize to Kenver and Perran for the accident on my mother's behalf, but then again, I'm not sure whether to bring it up at all. It's been four years, but since it's the first time I'm meeting them, it feels odd to have it go unsaid. Especially with all the changes here on the island that happened because of it."

"No one's ever blamed your mother for that," Janet said.

"Of course not," Christina added quickly. "A boy chasing a soccer ball into the street—we can all imagine the nightmare of that. We can't blame Treave for swerving to avoid the boy, and by all accounts your mother had nowhere to go. It was just bad luck with the old Lord in the passenger seat. Treave doesn't talk about it much, but I can't help suspecting he takes all the blame for it all on himself. We kept thinking it was nice the way he's spent so much time with your mum these past few years. Of course, now we see you, we understand the real attraction, don't we?" She gave an impish grin and winked at Emma, lightening the mood. "In any case, the castle would have ended up going to the National Trust eventually. Or being sold to a hotel chain. All these old buildings do in the end, unless you're lucky enough to get someone to produce *Downton Abbey* in them."

"Or *Poldark*," Emma said, smiling back.

Janet rolled her eyes. "Oh, don't get Christina started on that."

"That show is actually filmed at a manor house in England," Christina said. "Shame, too. I'm doing my best to contact the film companies and see what we can arrange. Not for *Poldark*, obviously, but films could be a lucrative sideline."

"Lucrative." Janet snorted. "More jumped-up pish-posh that'll cost a fortune and make everyone uncomfortable."

Christina gave Emma an impish wink. "Don't let her fool you. She'll change her tune the moment someone offers to bring a load of handsome actors in, and she can squeeze a penny with the best of them. Give her a chance to have the Mount appear on the telly, and she'll be the first to stand in line asking where we sign."

"All depends on the terms, doesn't it? But that's enough of that." Janet turned back to Emma. "Now tell me, did Christina at least offer you a drink? I'd asked Dena to bring in some champagne to celebrate your engagement, but that girl wouldn't be on time for her own funeral."

Celebrate the engagement. Emma's smile faltered, and she had to literally push the corners of her lips upward a millimeter at a time as if she'd forgotten how to make the muscles work.

"Champagne would be lovely," she said.

"Good. Good. Then I'll just bring the boys over for a brief hello and slip out to the kitchen and see what's keeping Dena. It'll give me a chance to check how Gwen's managing with the dinner as well."

She started to turn away, but a disreputable-looking calico cat that Emma hadn't even seen until that moment suddenly jumped from a chair by the window with a hiss and every hair on its body bristling. Bolting out of the room, the cat gave an eerie yowl and disappeared down the hall beyond the door with the border collie and the two boys immediately running after it, making a pink-haired young woman in jeans and a nose-ring leap back to avoid being run over.

"Shipwreck! You idiot!" the girl yelled, barely managing to save the contents of a serving tray of appetizers and a bottle of champagne that she was bringing in.

"Penny, boys, come back here this instant!" Janet chimed in. "Dena, get after them."

The girl set the tray down on a drop-leaf table and raced out of the room. Christina jumped to her feet as well and ran for the door, narrowly beating out Kenver and Perran who were also rushing out.

"What's happening?" Emma asked in confusion. "Where's everyone going?"

Janet, who had started to follow them all as well, stopped, glanced at her brother, and shook her head. "You'll think we've all gone doolaly, but the cat can tell when a shipwreck's coming. Been doing it since he was a wee kitten before I got here, and he's reliable enough that Christina and the others always head straight out to the lifeboat station in case the coastguard calls them to go out."

"Pure, ridiculous superstition about something with a perfectly logical explanation," Treave said, wandering over to join them. "The cat simply gets upset when a storm gets bad enough, which also happens to be when the storm's bad enough to endanger shipping. It's just another of the St. Levan legends people have dreamed up for the tourists."

"Given that Shipwreck does the same thing in fair weather or foul, even you don't believe that." Janet glared at him and took another step toward the door, hesitating as if torn whether to stay or follow everyone else now that the room had emptied.

"Go see to the boys, if you need to," Brando said, walking up beside her. "Treave and I can look after Emma."

Janet sent him a grateful glance. "No telling what they get themselves up to, those two. Caught them sitting up on the sea wall a few weeks back insisting that Shipwreck wanted help singing. But you're sure you'll be all right? We might be a while. Especially if the lifeboat does go out. I'll have a devil of a time getting them to leave the village."

"We'll be fine," Brando said, nodding at her. "Don't worry."

Janet hurried out, leaving the three of them standing awkwardly together, and now Emma really wished she'd taken Christina up on the offer of a drink.

"What did she mean by Shipwreck needing help singing?" she asked, turning back to Treave.

He threw back the remaining contents of his glass of Scotch in a single gulp before he answered. "The locals in the village seem to think that there's been death after every time that Shipwreck's jumped up on the sea wall and started wailing. Why Janet encourages those boys to believe it, I can't imagine. Given their father's on the lifeboat crew and knowing he might be called out, it can't be healthy for them to have to worry."

"Lifeboats?" Emma asked.

"Sorry, forgot you don't have that in the States. They're a bit like your volunteer fire departments."

"Aye, we have Her Majesty's Coastguard, too, but the bulk of the lifesaving is down to the the Royal National Lifeboat Institution—the RNLI—who train volunteers and provide the boats and boathouses all along the coasts and inland waterways," Brando added.

Treave nodded. "The Mount's had a crew here ever since back when there were a lot more people living on the island, and it's become a matter of pride trying to keep the station open."

"Christina is on the lifeboat crew?" Emma asked.

Treave gave a bark of laughter. "That's my girl. Ignore the superstitious nonsense and jump straight to the fact a woman is the star of the show."

"Superstitious nonsense? I take it you don't believe in anything you can't prove beyond a shadow of a doubt?" Brando said. "Must be a bit hard for you around here, living on a 'placid island of ignorance' when everyone else believes."

"I do believe," Treave retorted. "I believe in math, physics, and physiology. In concrete facts, such as tests that prove cats hear frequencies even dogs don't hear, which means Shipwreck could quite well be reacting to something entirely real that we simply aren't aware of."

Brando turned to Emma. "What about you, Emma? Can you imagine there are things beyond our ken?"

"I guess I keep an open mind. But since you quoted H.P. Lovecraft a second ago, I'll admit that, like him, I don't expect my beliefs make any difference to whether something is or isn't real."

"You've read Lovecraft?" Brando gave a wide, happy grin. "I wouldn't have taken you for someone who reads horror."

"Said the kettle to the pot," Emma answered placidly.

Brando laughed. "Touché. Though for me, reading Lovecraft isn't about the horror as much as a fascination with what fate and forbidden knowledge do to people." Something shifted behind his eyes. "Is there such a thing as fate, Emma Larsen? Do you believe in destiny?"

There was something odd about the way he watched her, as though the question mattered more than it should have. "I can't say I've given it a lot of thought, but I probably fall more into the science-isn't-science-until-we-understand-it school of thought," Emma said. "I mean, until we know the right questions to ask, the things we'll consider science in the future still fall into the realm of faith or magic or wishful thinking, don't they?"

Brando cocked his head, his eyes holding hers in a way that made her find it hard to break away.

Treave stepped in. Taking Emma's hand, he twined his fingers through hers and tugged her toward the door. "I can take you down to the village, if you like. Might as well go see the cat and the excitement for ourselves. Not that there's probably very much *to* see."

"It's wet out, and Janet will have taken the car, but mine's still parked in the courtyard," Brando said. "I'm happy to provide a ride if you don't mind the company."

Treave glared at him, making it more than clear that he actually minded very much, but there was clearly no way to say so without being unpardonably rude, so he glanced at Emma and then gave a sideways nod. "Fine," he said. "Thanks very much."

SHIPS IN THE NIGHT

"With a philosophical flourish
Cato throws himself upon his sword;
I quietly take to the ship."

HERMAN MELVILLE
MOBY DICK, OR THE WHALE

DESPITE THE WATER CRASHING against the sea wall and the wind that blew the downpour of rain nearly sideways, Brando spotted the calico cat crouched just where Treave had said, wailing away into the storm. The sight raised gooseskin along Brando's arms.

He steered the Land Rover he'd driven from Scotland down the hill and turned it onto the road that led along the waterfront. Up ahead, Janet, who hadn't—much to his surprise—driven down after all, was splashing through the puddles on the cobblestones, looking even smaller than usual in her red Wellies and the long slicker she'd pulled on over her dress as she battled against the wind.

"That's a sight to give you goosebumps," Emma said from the passenger seat, gesturing at the cat. "I thought cats hated water."

"Shipwreck does, too, ordinarily," Treave said, leaning between the seats from where he sat in back, "which doesn't stop him sitting up there. He'll be washed out to sea one of these days."

"Today, judging by the look of those waves. Shouldn't someone try to get him down?" Emma glanced over at the recessed doorway of the Barebones pub where a good half of the village seemed to have gathered, none of them making a move to do anything to stop the cat.

Treave's laugh was humorless. "Ask Janet to show you the scars on her arms from the time she tried when she first saw him up there. If you do manage to pull him off, he'll only find a way to get back up again."

Looking back over at the villagers as he pulled the Land Rover to a stop, Brando realized not one of them was paying attention to the cat. He drew the emergency brake and turned in the direction they were watching, down beyond the neat row of whitewashed homes and shops to where the RNLI lifeboat stood alone on the far side of the harbor with the Union Jack and the black flag of Cornwall whipping together in the wind above it. From the front of the building, the orange rescue lifeboat was just emerging, sliding slowly down the long ramp toward the sea. Six people clung to the sides in the open back of the craft, their red life vests painting a warning over yellow waterproofs, their heads encased in crash helmets that obscured their identities.

Six out of thirty villagers. Twenty-seven, if Brando didn't count the island residents under the age of eighteen. High odds for a small community.

In the two days he'd been on the island, he'd met most of those standing in the pub doorway already. With her bright pink shock of hair, Dena Libby, the castle's maid and cleaner, was easy to recognize, and her brother Alwyn was equally identifiable, thin and vague-looking and always talking to things that weren't there. They huddled together beside their father, Harry, who ran the pub, but their mother, who was the castle's chief tour guide, wasn't with them. Brando wondered if that meant she was one of the lifeboat volunteers. Beside Harry was Gwen Nance who, with no small amount of hubris, called herself the castle chef, and Tamsyn Penrose, the housekeeper, who insisted on leaving treats out for the castle ghosts. Beside Tamsyn was Nessa Rowe, buttoned up to the chin and timid as a field mouse. Lockryn Williams, who booked the tours and kept the accounts for both the castle and the winery was there as well, looking more than ever like a stoop-shouldered undertaker beneath his somber black umbrella.

The thought of a funeral, given that the cat was singing a dirge on top of the wall and that the lifeboat was descending the ramp with an odd almost ceremonial slowness, was morbid enough to send a chill of warning across the back of Brando's neck. And he couldn't help wondering, suddenly, how often those left behind in the village thought of graves and funerals every time the cat sang and the boat went out. Was that what Janet's boys were thinking? The twins stood uncharacteristically still, the black and white border collie held by the collar between them, the dog's wet fur pressed against both their legs as if the three were providing each other wordless reassurance.

Janet shouted something, and they turned toward her, their expressions apprehensive. Brando jumped out of the car and slammed the door behind him. He'd seen that determined set of Janet's shoulders too many times on his own account, and the last thing the boys needed was her tearing into them right now. But then the twins ran to meet her, and she stooped in front of them, listening while they both talked at once. While Brando watched, she gathered her sons close and held them, their faces pressed in tight, and he released a long sigh and stopped, the cold rain sluicing down his face and the back of his neck. Penny the dog gave two sharp barks, wagged her tail, and pressed her nose into the family huddle as though she couldn't bear to be excluded. Brando didn't blame her. To his shame, he felt a twinge of jealousy over the way Janet was with the boys, their closeness.

It made him feel wrong-footed all over again.

Aye, as usual, he'd misjudged her. Hadn't given her the credit she was due. That in itself was a certain reminder he needed to get past whatever it was that was holding the two of them mired in the past. Janet might claim not to know they had bridges to be mended, but Brando knew full well there were years of resentments built up on both sides.

Standing in the rain watching her, he shook the guilt aside as Treave and Emma ran past him. Treave held one of Emma's hands, supporting her, while her other hand held the hood of her jacket to keep it from blowing off her head. The sight prompted another wave of resentment at the thought of her marrying Treave, and he quickened his footsteps, ducking in after them beneath the overhang of the pub roof to stand with the others.

Janet herded the twins in, too, and they all turned to watch the lifeboat accelerate down the ramp as it neared the water. Brando sidled closer and bent his head to be heard over the roar of the wind. "Is Kenver on the boat?"

She gestured back toward Lockryn Williams, who held a portable VHF radio to his ear, listening.

"Not that one," Lockryn said. "That's Christina, Mary Libby, John Nance, David Evans, Michael Donovan, and my own Steven. Kenver and Perran are going out on the inshore boat."

"The Coastguard's sending out both boats?" Treave asked, turning sharply to stare at him.

"There's a freighter with her engine stalled dragging her anchor toward the rocks. The other nearby stations are already out on calls with the strength of the storm, and the boat they're sending from the Lizard is having a hard time getting here against the wind. Our lot'll have to do what they can to get her towed back out to sea."

Janet had gone very still, her face turned to watch the lifeboat, her expression typically resentful and hopeful and stubborn, as if she could hold the boat poised on the last few feet of the ramp with the sheer force of her considerable will. But the boat splashed into the sea in spite of her, colliding with a wall of water that broke over the orange cabin and plowed it under.

The boys gasped audibly and gripped Janet's hands, still young enough that they weren't too embarrassed to do that. Then the lifeboat bobbed back to the surface and sped away, rocking wildly, while the crew held on as best they could in back.

"Daddy and Uncle Perr will be all right," one of the twins—Cam—said, biting his lip, his voice cracking with a mixture of fear and excitement.

At nine, Brando remembered, there wasn't much difference between the two.

Jack, the other twin, gave a nod. "And Christina. Everyone will. Right, Mummy? Won't they? Even if Shipwreck's singing?"

"Of course they'll be all right, love. Right as rain. Always have been," Janet said staunchly. "Today's no different from any other day when the boats go out. And what did your father teach you both? Everyone has to do their part." Her eyes met Brando's briefly, though, above Jack's head, and Brando knew her well enough to know she wished Kenver had never said those words, that her husband didn't believe them. Because this was Janet. Once their parents had died, she'd done her best to keep Brando locked in the house, keeping him safe when being safe had been the very last thing he'd wanted.

He wondered if she was remembering that. Wondered how she could bear having Kenver volunteer on the lifeboat crew, bear to watch him go out on one call after another when it had to kill her wondering if he'd be coming home again.

She must have seen the sympathy in his eyes, because she looked away.

"What do you say we go back up and get some supper now?" she said to the boys, then she glanced around and narrowed her eyes at Gwen Nance who, in her worn-out Wellies, long black skirt, and old beige coat, was walking toward the lifeboat station with a determined stride. "With a bit of luck, Gwen'll have left dinner nearly ready," she added with a sigh. "Otherwise, we'll have to manage on our own, won't we, boys?"

"Cam and I don't want any of your pooey mac and cheese," Jack said, dodging away from her. "We want to go to the lifeboat station with Gwen. Daddy's lifeboat isn't even out yet, and we want to wait for them to come back."

"Well, you can't wait at the station. It's against the rules."

"Gwen doesn't care about the rules," Cam said.

"Her husband is in charge of the lifeboats—"

"Our daddy's in charge of the *island*," Jack interjected with undeniable logic.

Janet seamed her lips and sent him a warning look. "That, my lad, is not an argument I ever want to hear from you again. In any event, Gwen's lived a few years longer than you have. When you're her age, you can do as you like, same as she does."

"Then we want to stay at the pub with Lockryn," Cam said.

"And I want a month's vacation in Aruba. Beggars can't be choosers, can they, my lads? Now, come along."

She reached for Cam's hand, but the second, smaller lifeboat emerged at the top of the tractor ramp and Cam, too, darted away from her. Jack and Cam simultaneously screamed out, "Daddy," and took off at a dead run toward the lifeboat station with the border collie barking at their heels.

Brando pushed past Janet, aiming to catch them, but Treave reached them first. Snatching them by the back of the collars as if he'd caught two pups by the scruff of the neck, he shook his head at them. "Nice try, you scoundrels. Listen to what your mother says and go up and get your dinners."

Cam turned to glare at him. "You can't tell us what to do. We want to stay with everyone else when they go in the pub to listen to the radio."

"So you shall—ten years from now when you're as old as they are. Until then, do as your mother says. But"—Treave grinned and glanced at Emma—"*if* you ask her nicely, you might get Emma to make you some of her famous fried ham and cheese sandwiches. She puts jam and powdered sugar on them, which makes it like eating dessert and dinner all together. And if you ask extra, extra nicely, I might even tell you the story of the Count of Monte Christo who the sandwiches are named after. Then again, maybe you aren't interested in a story about a sailor who's imprisoned on an island fortress and escapes to take revenge on all the people who betrayed him and sent him there."

Emma tried not to smile. "Oh, that old story. No, Cam and Jack wouldn't care for that. It's much too bloodthirsty and frightening for boys of—" She glanced over at the twins. "How old did you say you were?"

"Nine and one-half," Cam said.

"Yes, that's definitely too young for the Count of Monte Christo. Your mother wouldn't like your uncle telling you that one."

"I don't know," Janet said solemnly. "I might be persuaded, if they ask me nicely."

Jack and Cam exchanged a look, an entire conversation told in silent twin speak.

"He can tell us later. If you like," Jack added, as he looked at Treave. "Once the others get back. But we're going to stay here with everyone else." He folded his thin arms across his chest, and Cam followed suit, both of them leading with their chins in unconscious imitation of their mother.

Janet wanted to stay herself—Brando could see that in the way she watched the boat. There was probably a radio at the castle somewhere, but imagining Janet pacing the long corridors with it glued to her ear while the boys were forced to try to sleep, Brando couldn't see that boding well for any of them.

"What if I help Emma make those sandwiches down

here at the pub for everyone?" he asked, looking first at Harry Libby for approval and then at Emma. "That way we can all stay and wait together."

Janet opened her mouth to refuse. It was a reflex for her, saying no, a reflex as certain as the sun rising in the morning and setting in the evening behind the Balwhither hills. But then she closed her mouth and sighed.

"All right," she said eventually. "We can stay an hour, and then it'll be off to baths and beds with you, and I won't hear another argument on the subject. Is that clear?" Back straight as a flagpole, she turned and walked back toward the pub.

Maybe she'd learned a little something over the years after all, Brando couldn't help thinking. Either that or her own need to know what was happening outweighed what she saw as her duty to be that worst of all the legendary monsters ever bred in Scotland: the mythical perfect parent.

Honor and Duty

*"Life is a shipwreck, but we must not
forget to sing in the lifeboats."*

Voltaire

S HUTTERED AGAINST THE GALE, the darkened windows
made the pub as dim as twilight. Old paneling on the
walls and the oak bar at the back had all blackened over the
years, the wood permeated with the peaty scent of whiskey
and tobacco smoke and logs burned in the enormous
fireplace. Chipped porcelain pitchers and washbowls and
chamberpots hung on hooks from the low-timbered ceiling,
casting shadows across the floor.

Emma slipped through the doorway in the wake of the
rest of the villagers and removed her wet jacket while Harry
Libby stepped aside and switched on more lights. Dripping
rain from his slicker and the heavy whiskers that curled

down into his barrel chest, he gestured for Emma and Brando to follow him while he led the way to a door behind the bar and let them through into the kitchen. Clutching the wet jacket, Emma walked self-consciously, aware of Brando behind her, his stride surprisingly quiet given his size. She was aware, too, of Treave frowning, watching them both, ready to renew his offers of help she didn't need.

Or want.

But Lockryn's VHF radio crackled, offering up broken conversations between the captain of the lifeboat—the coxswain, she corrected herself, as the boys had already pointed out—and the captain of the tanker. Now and then, someone from a Coastguard helicopter chimed in. The room fell eerily silent while everyone listened, and since Janet was focused on that, Treave was the one who helped the twins take their wet gear off and hang it over the backs of their chairs. Turning back in the kitchen doorway, Emma smiled at him, partly to relieve a vague sense of guilt— unearned, she knew, but then guilt was never rational—and partly because, not for the first time, she was envious of the bonds of family.

She'd been thinking a lot about family lately, conscious of being the only one left. Her father didn't count, and Evangeline had grown up with an alcoholic mother in a trailer park with no idea who her own father had been. That was something Evangeline had never talked about, never revealed intentionally—but she'd let slip enough over the years for Emma to understand it hadn't been an easy childhood. Watching Treave as he talked to the boys, settled them in, and reassured them, Emma thought that this was what family was supposed to be, this whole village with everyone pulling together.

"You all right there?" Harry Libby asked her.

"Of course," she said and walked in through the door.

Where the pub outside must have looked more or less the same for at least a couple hundred years, the kitchen was both modern and efficient. A large cooktop with a pair of deep fryers within easy reach stood along the back wall halfway to the roomy walk-in refrigerator and the freezer. Further down, open shelves held dry ingredients, canned goods, and spices in easily accessible groupings, and copper pots and saucepans hung ready to hand from a round rack above a roomy worktable.

Brando studied it professionally, then catching her eye, he gave an approving nod. "A good setup," he said, coming to take Emma's jacket and hang it with his own on a hook behind the door. "Easy to work in."

"The missus'll be pleased you said so." Harry's grin revealed short, even teeth in the midst of the impressive beard. "And she'll have my hide if I don't take a photo of you cooking in here to hang up on the wall. Wish I had a copy of that magazine cover with you on it you could hold up. The tourists would love that, they would, and Mary's always thinking of the tourists."

"Aye, and don't we all have to in our line of work? I'm happy to help if I can." Brando picked up an apron from a hook and tossed it to Emma, his cheeks slightly flushed. "Now, about those sandwiches, tell me what you need me to do."

Emma caught the apron, feeling as though she was missing something. "A magazine cover?"

"You don't mean to say you don't know who you're cooking with? The Kilted Chef?" Harry leaned back against the counter, looking amused. "The papers lapped up the idea of him cooking in a kilt when your man here got his first Michelin star this year for his restaurant up in Scotland."

"No reason for her to know any of that. She's scarcely been here an hour yet." Brando's flush had deepened, and he busied himself tying a dishcloth around his own waist.

Harry dismissed the objection with a wave of his hand. "Janet's that proud she's told everyone on the Mount at least six times. I assumed she'd have broadcast it the moment the boat pulled in."

"She'd be the first to point out it's a team effort, isn't it?" Brando turned to examine a stack of frying pans on the nearby shelves. "And we've been lucky on the publicity front as well these past two years. Your wife's right, Harry. Every little bit does help."

"They don't give out Michelin stars for publicity, lad," Harry said.

Emma bit her lip. "Now I feel like an idiot having you help me make sandwiches. I should be the one helping you."

"Any chef worth his salt knows you can learn something from every chef you work with." Brando pulled two of the frying pans down and set them on the stove.

"Seeing as how I've never made a Monte Cristo, much less one with sugar and jam, I'll let you take the lead. Especially if it gets me out of sitting in that room in there watching poor Janet worry herself into a dither."

"She does do that, doesn't she?" Harry said, heading toward the door. "On which note, I'll leave you to it and go have a listen to the radio myself. Take whatever you need, and give me a shout if there's anything you can't find."

"I'll settle up the cost with you later, if you'll put it all on my tab," Brando called after him.

"No need. You're the ones doing the work."

Once Harry had gone, the room seemed to have shrunk so that Brando filled it to overflowing. Emma had never cooked with a Michelin-starred chef before. She'd never cooked with any chef before, other than Julia, who had worked briefly as a *sous chef* in a hot start-up Spanish restaurant that had vanished as quickly as it had risen. Looking around the kitchen, Emma tried to decide where to begin. Cooking here with Brando was going to be a series of firsts. She'd never worked in anyone else's kitchen before either, or worked with copper pans like the ones he'd set down on the stove. Nor did she believe he'd have any problem making the sandwiches, anyone who could make French toast and a ham and cheese sandwich could make a Monte Cristo. Which meant that he was generous—and kind.

Well, she wanted to be a caterer, didn't she? Wanted to see if the little bit of talent she thought she had for making people happy might multiply and possibly even spill over onto herself. That wasn't an unreasonable hope. Or so she told herself. So why, then, did her palms feel clammy?

Slipping past Brando, she ducked into the walk-in refrigerator to rummage for ingredients. He followed and stopped behind her in the doorway.

"Tell me what you need," he said, his voice low and rich with that lovely Scottish accent.

He always seemed to take up more space in the room than his body allowed for. Emma felt herself shrinking away, as if her body wanted to make itself smaller to make up the difference. She snatched up ham and currant jelly and mustard, and kept her back to him while she searched the cheeses on the shelf, hoping for a nice Jarlsberg or an Emmental, and settling for plain old Swiss instead.

"We'll want custard ingredients," she said, "nutmeg not cinnamon, and bread—something with a good, cakey crumb but not a lot of crust. And confectioner's sugar. Oh, and make the bread as dry as you can, obviously."

"For French toast, essentially."

"Yes." With an inward sigh, she forced herself to turn, and found he was even closer than she'd thought, blocking the exit so that she had no way to go around him. "I really do feel awkward about you helping me."

She stopped, then made herself continue, because even if it was presumptuous—ridiculous—to ask, when was this kind of a chance going to come her way again? She'd regret it if she didn't seize the moment.

"I'm thinking of opening a catering business," she said, "but I'm a self-taught cook, and it's like what you said about learning—I need to take every opportunity I can to learn from other chefs. Any bit of advice."

Brando shifted backward on his heels and pushed aside the hair that still clung damply to his head. Emma chewed her lip and watched him, all too aware that a thousand people a day probably asked him for things since he'd gotten his star, the way they'd asked Evangeline for things so that she was constantly shedding little pieces of herself in a thousand directions. But Evangeline had loved the admiration so much that she'd thrived on that. Not everyone did.

"I'm sorry. Th-that was really presumptuous of me to even bring up," she said, shaking her head and stuttering with a cringing sort of embarrassment that felt all too familiar.

"Under the circumstances, it's exactly what I'd have done. Near enough what I did do to get my first job," Brando said. "I was only hesitating because I'm no expert on catering. I've only hired an events planner recently. We're expanding, but it's not a very proven track record so far. Still, I'm happy to do anything I can to help. If you've done up a business plan, I could look that over for you, if you like."

Emma released a breath. "That would be incredible. Treave was going to help me put one together while we're here. This gives me extra incentive to get on it. Seriously, thank you."

"Seriously, you're welcome," he said and smiled down at her, "but I haven't done anything yet."

Emma shivered in the cold air and added a package of butter to her armload, using her chin to keep it in place on top of the mustard jar. Edging around him, she scooted out the door, feeling like she could breathe again fully for the first time when there was more space between them. As he left to hunt the dry ingredient shelves, she separated egg yolks into a bowl and whisked them into an even creamy consistency, then poured milk into a glass and went to the sink to set both containers in hot water to bring them up to room temperature before combining.

"Your basics are good. That's a technique I don't see many cooks pick up," Brando said, setting a load of ingredients on the counter as Emma turned away from the sink.

"I have a mad obsession with Julia Childs. I must have watched all her cooking videos a dozen times, not to mention a zillion others," Emma said, ridiculously pleased.

She slid glances at him when she thought he wasn't looking as they worked side-by-side, but often she found him watching her in return. He sliced the bread and cut off the crusts for her, and she spread them with mustard and layered them with cheese and ham and cheese again, then soaked the sandwiches with the fatty, eggy custard. She added oil to the pans he'd already set on the stove, then cut in slabs of butter to melt as well and leaned down to check the flames on the dual fuel cooker. When she turned back, Brando had propped his hip against the counter, his eyes on her and an enigmatic expression she couldn't gauge. Her hands shook as she dusted the exterior of each slice of bread with flour before dropping the sandwiches into the heated pans.

"The flour's to crisp up the outside of the bread?" he asked.

Nodding, Emma listened to the sizzle of the bread in the melted butter then turned the burner down even more. "Keeps the velvety custard mouth feel like French toast on the inside that way, but you can still eat it with your hands like plain grilled cheese."

While the first batch of sandwiches cooked, Brando wiped down the countertop and Emma set out plates. She tried not to be aware that he was still watching her, his eyes serious, slate blue like the storm-dark sea outside. She told herself it was the heat from the stove getting to her, and she pushed damp curls off her temple and kept her back to him.

"Will you tell me if I do something wrong?" she asked. "Or if there's something I could be doing better? Differently?"

He cleared his throat as if it tickled and fabric rustled behind her. "I was thinking you move like a chef already, no wasted motions. And those must have been good videos. You talk like a chef."

"I expect half of America talks like a chef thanks to the Food Network and the Cooking Channel," Emma said, trying to remember when she'd ever received a compliment that had pleased her as much. Maybe she never had. The last batch of plates rattled together as she slid them to the counter.

"That'd be an improvement, then, over all the kitchen staff I interview who seem to think it's obligatory for Scottish chefs to swear and scream at them like Gordon Ramsey."

"I was wondering when you were going to start terrorizing me," Emma said, laughing. "I'm almost disappointed."

"Och, love. Disappointing people's what I do best— only ask my sister."

The door to the pub pushed open, and Treave poked his head inside. Feeling guilty, though she couldn't have said exactly why, Emma felt herself flushing, and she bent her head to hide it, which may have been the worst thing she could have done. Treave stared at her suspiciously, then stepped all the way through and stood with his arms folded over his chest. "How are you coming along?" he asked. "I could stay and help if you need an extra hand."

"We're nearly done. Has there been any news from the lifeboats yet?" Emma's voice came out too bright, and she reached hastily for the jar of red currant jelly and wrenched it open to give her hands some work to do.

"No good news. The storm's dragging the freighter toward the rocks faster than the lifeboats can tow it away. They're starting to take the crew off the freighter."

"Leaving her to run aground?" Brando asked, turning to stare at him.

"It's not as though there's anything else that could be done unless another lifeboat can get there quickly. They'll take the freighter's crew off in increments to buy some time, but the captain's got his wife and daughter on board, which makes it even more complicated."

Emma tried to imagine a child caught up in this situation. Pausing with a spoonful of jelly poised above a plate, she couldn't even picture how the logistics worked, trying to get someone from an enormous freighter into one of the much smaller rescue boats. Did they use a ladder? Lower the freighter's lifeboats?

"How old is the girl?" she asked.

"Young. Eleven," Treave said, his expression softening. "But they'll all be all right. Lifeboat crews train for this, and Kenver and Perran have each been going out since they were seventeen. John Nance, too, and he's nearly sixty-three. They've got enough rescues between them there's nothing they can't face."

Brando swung around. "Is Janet holding up?"

"She's fine. The boys are fine."

"Honestly?" Brando studied Treave's expression.

Shrugging one shoulder, Treave propped a fist against the edge of the counter. "Your sister's never very happy when Kenver goes out by all reports. He teased her about it a bit the last time I was here, and she tried not to let him see she was upset, but I remember thinking she was holding it in a bit. Same as now."

"Aye, that's our Janet. Won't ever admit there's anything she can't handle. She's been afraid ever since our parents died that the people she loves will leave her and not come back. Holds on so tight it makes you want to pry her fingers loose."

"Couldn't stop Kenver from going out even if she tried," Treave said. "We've been rescuing shipwrecks from this island since before the priory was built. Our grandfather funded the RNLI station and our father fought to keep it going when the population shrank and a full crew was hard to find. Kenver and Perr both see it as a family tradition. An honor."

Brando pulled the first pan off the stove and slid the sandwiches, crisp and golden brown with the cheese just bubbling around the edges, off onto the plates. "You don't see it that way, I take it?"

"We're not ship captains with a duty to go down with a sinking ship. At any other RNLI station, there'd be thirty or more volunteers to man two lifeboats. No one would feel they had to answer every call. Is it any wonder Janet worries? We could have closed the station long ago. Sold this whole place off, locks, stocks, and illuminated manuscripts. Let a developer take it. But our father gave it to the National Trust instead and took back a 999-year lease to keep the family stuck here and try to save the village. I hate seeing Jack and Cam raised with the responsibility of that instead of being free to be whatever they like. Much as I loved growing up here, I wouldn't wish that on anyone."

The words were a bit different from what he'd always let on, all the stories that had seemed to Emma like an idyllic childhood: crabbing in the tide pools, playing hide and seek in the tunnels, sneaking swords off the armory walls to play knights with his brothers, racing them across the causeway before the tide came in. Hearing him now, hearing him earlier after he'd lied about the engagement, Emma wondered how many of those stories included a good dose of wishful thinking. Maybe no one had quite the childhood they would wish for.

She dropped a bright dollop of jelly beside a sandwich and pressed the back of a spoon through it, swiping it across the plate to leave a fading streak of color. The spoon skittered as someone screamed out in the other room.

Someone else shouted "No!" and then everyone seemed to be yelling all at once.

Treave's face went pale. Emma's heart thumped and her head jerked up, and she and Brando looked at each other briefly. He switched off the burners on the cooker.

Out in the pub, chairs scraped back and feet pounded toward the exit.

"That'll be the rescue gone to hell," Treave said, and he ran through the pub and out into the night after everybody else.

DROPS OF HOPE

"Waiting is painful. Forgetting is painful.
But not knowing which to do
is the worst kind of suffering."

PAUL COELHO
BY THE RIVER PIEDRA I SAT DOWN AND WEPT

T HE LIMBO BETWEEN KNOWING and not knowing was
a special kind of hell. Emma hadn't had much time
for uncertainty the night her mother had died, only minutes
while the paramedics tried and failed to revive Evangeline,
but it had been long enough that she could imagine the
terror that everyone on the island had to be feeling now.
Waiting for news and fearing it would come.

She ran through the storm, fighting to keep up with
Treave and Brando. The twins were up ahead of everyone
else, racing out to the point of the island beyond the

lifeboat station while Janet ran after them, carrying their slickers. Everyone else must have decided it was as good a place to watch from as any because they followed, too. By the time Brando, Treave, and Emma caught up, just about the entire village was standing or pacing on the rocks in the spray and the rain, waterproofs and coats billowing in the shearing wind, eyes stinging with salt and rain and worry.

"What's happened?" Treave demanded.

Everyone turned to look at him, but the explanation seemed to be beyond them. It was Lockryn who pulled them out of earshot of the others.

"The all-weather's gone over," he said. "Capsized."

"The all-weather?" Emma asked. "That's the bigger one?"

Lockryn nodded, rain sluicing down his cheeks and drops clinging to his eyelashes. "She's self-righting, but the storm pushed her up against the hull of the freighter as she went over. That trapped the crew between the two and kept her from coming right a while."

Emma went cold with dread, and she was glad when Treave asked the question she was afraid to ask. "Is everyone all right?" Treave demanded. "Do they have everyone back on board?"

Lockryn's hands hung helplessly at his sides. "Mary Libby and Michael are all right, but the others—There's no word yet. It's a lot of people to find and rescue in a heavy sea, with the freighter still moving toward the rocks and her crew still on board."

It was all too easy for Emma to imagine the boiling

sea, six people fighting to swim in the crushing waves while the two boats had to avoid both each other and the freighter as they searched.

Christina, John Nance, the little girl and her mother, Lockryn's son, and David Evans. All missing.

"I'm so sorry," she said.

"Perran's switched boats so they'll be able to use them both. They're sending another Coastguard helicopter out. Lifeboat from the Lizard's nearly here as well, and they'll get every available boat they can from nearby stations. This island was founded on miracles, and there are plenty of them all the time," Lockryn said, his eyes fixed on the ocean as though it were possible to see more than a few feet in the rain, as if seeing through the darkness and distance was another miracle he'd have liked to ask for.

Emma felt like an intruder. "What can I do?" she asked, turning to Brando and Treave. "How can we help?"

Brando glanced over to where Janet was struggling with the boys. "Someone should help her with them. You want to go, or should I?"

Treave stared at him a second then glanced over at Emma. "I will."

"Maybe some tea or coffee," Emma said. "People will be cold. And I could wrap up the sandwiches and bring them over here."

"I'll give you a hand." Brando turned and headed back toward the pub as though it was a relief to be moving.

Emma wondered if he felt the same way she did, as though he couldn't bear to do nothing. Everyone had to be feeling the same way, because that was the worst thing about a tragedy: you couldn't fix it from the sidelines, you couldn't change anything except your own tiny corner of it, like the rain falling into the ocean was barely noticeable now. There was too much ocean.

Too much to search for six people. So much to search.

She started the coffee and tea while Brando wrapped sandwiches in cellophane and searched the kitchen shelves for styrofoam cups. They poured the drinks into an assortment of Thermoses, everything from a child's *Beauty and the Beast* lunchbox Thermos with a pink lid to a sturdy green one topped in stainless steel.

"I can't even imagine what it must be like for everyone out there. The waiting. Not knowing," Emma said, packing the cups into a plastic bag along with packets of sugar and napkins.

"I can imagine it." Grimly, Brando stooped to pick up a cup that had fallen on the floor. "The night my parents were killed, it was hours of waiting for news and then getting the worst. That's what Janet will be expecting now."

"Do you want to go to her?"

"It isn't Kenver who's missing, which won't stop her from worrying about him. She'll be out there thinking that if the one boat can capsize, so can the other, and she'll be thinking that Kenver will be taking chances he shouldn't, trying to rescue everyone. But she'll know that's not the same as what other people are worrying about now, so she'll pretend she isn't worried, and she'll snap at anyone who tries to talk to her. It's best to leave her alone."

"It's good you know her well," Emma said, thinking it would have been nice to have a brother or sister. Even if it meant worrying about them. Even if it meant having to rescue them.

She thought about Kenver and Perran fighting to save Christina, and John Nance who'd been going out on rescues for nearly half a century, and Lockryn's son, and all the others. A little girl out there alone in the black, shifting ocean, and her mother out there, too. Alone.

All of them needed to come back.

Six people missing, and every one of them was loved and needed by someone.

"Ready?" Brando asked, watching her as he picked up two of the bags in either hand. Her throat too clogged to speak, she nodded and picked up the bag of sandwiches.

Behind the storm clouds outside, night was creeping in. Someone had driven several cars down to point their headlamps out to sea, and alongside the boathouse, the slanting streams of rain and the puddles on the cobblestones glinted beneath the exterior lights.

Apart from the fury of the waves and the howl of the wind, the village was ominously silent. The few lifeboat volunteers who hadn't gone out on the shout with the others were still in the station, waiting, but even more people had gone out to the point to watch for the boats.

Janet paced back and forth, her hands clenched at her sides, Treave crouched with his hands on his knees, and the twins stood still and silent. The border collie darted back and forth between them all, her tongue lolling and her fur so drenched and plastered to her sides that she looked twenty pounds thinner, all legs and tail and ears. She bounded up to Brando and Emma, whining softly, but Emma couldn't fix what was wrong, so she only rubbed the dog behind the ears and that wasn't good enough. The dog pulled back and trotted back to Janet.

Seeing Penny made Emma remember Shipwreck, but the cat hadn't been on the wall when they'd run back out of the pub. She hoped that meant he was safely back up at the castle, not somewhere swimming for his life. And that thought made her feel sick all over again as she imagined Christina and the others desperately treading water.

Fortunately, she didn't have much time to dwell on thoughts like those. The radio reported in quick succession that they'd found the girl and her mother and Lockryn's son, all of them with relatively minor injuries. Emma and Brando handed around cups and sandwiches and poured the tea, then they helped Gwen Nance, John Nance's wife, hobble back to one of the waiting cars when she fell on a rock and hurt her ankle.

Having deposited Gwen in the passenger seat, Emma bent beside her and tried to examine the foot, but there wasn't enough light to see by until Brando came over and turned on his cellphone camera light.

"Here, how's this?" he asked.

Emma was used to massaging Evangeline's muscles and helping with the exercises the physical therapist recommended. She'd studied anatomy, even toyed with the idea of going to medical school, but she wasn't great with diagnosing a strain versus a sprain versus a fracture.

"It's swollen and getting warm," she said. "Which isn't good—and that's about all I can tell you. Can you bend it, Gwen?"

"Don't want to bend it, do I?" Gwen scowled up at Emma, wet grey hair leeched even more of its color beneath the car's dome lights and the broken vessels in her apple-round cheeks standing out in sharp relief. "If I'd wanted to bend it, I'd have done it without the trouble of walking all the way over here. And put away that bleddy light before it blinds me," she added, shooing Brando away.

"Let's get her into the lifeboat station," Brando said. "They'll be used to assessing injuries, and they'll know what to do."

"No sense bothering them when they'll be having other troubles to deal with dreckly, soon as the boats come back," Gwen said, and whether from the thought or reaction or shock, she began suddenly to shake.

Brando glanced at Emma, then gestured for her to step away. Stooping, he swung Gwen into his arms as if she wasn't nearly as wide as she was tall, and carried her easily back to the lifeboat station, ignoring her protests and the fist she pummeled weakly against his chest. "You put me down this minute. I'm not going to miss me husband coming back whilst you're hauling me from place to place."

Brando exchanged a look with Emma as she hurried along beside them. "Aye, but you were in the lifeboat station when he went out, as I remember it. So that's where he'll expect to see you when he comes back."

Gwen's fist stilled briefly then gave his chest one last thump. Inside the lifeboat station was compact, everything neatly in its place: a ladder hanging on the wall, a stretcher propped up, a yellow hose wound and hanging on a hook beside the empty bays where the boats belonged. A room with racks for life vests and yellow slickers and mostly empty cubbyholes for the white RNLI helmets stood open to the left of a staircase leading to the second floor. Three men appeared at the top almost immediately once Brando called out a "hallo."

"We've brought you a patient," Brando said. "Can we leave her with you?"

Two of the men were ancient, one so thin the suspenders on his trousers rode up against the sides of his neck and his white hair looked as soft and downy as cotton candy. The third man had a crutch tucked in the pit of one arm, but he still stepped back more spryly than the others.

"And what have you been doing to yourself now, Gwen Nance?" He crooked his finger at Brando. "Bring her up here and set her down on the bench."

Emma stayed downstairs, out of the way and listening to the radio chatter that came from both upstairs and the radio in the downstairs office. She heard when Perran, who had transferred to the bigger all-weather boat, recovered the body of David Evans from the water.

Gwen Nance gave a single cry, sharp as a seagull, and then fell silent. Silence, too, marked the cessation of any movement on the second floor, as if time had suspended itself in the boathouse while out in the storm, tragedy and the grim work marched on, recorded in crackling, adrenaline-filled voices that barked news and instructions into the radios.

Emma slumped back against the wall, legs pushed out to brace herself. All the tears that she hadn't cried when Evangeline died suddenly welled up from inside her and spilled out in great, gasping sobs she couldn't seem to stop.

Brando came slowly down the steps and stopped in front of her, looked at her silently for a moment, then pulled her into his arms and held her while she cried. She didn't object at first. It felt too much like they both needed the human contact, the warmth.

When she was calmer, she broke away, not looking at him. "We'd better get back," she said. "You'll want to check on Janet, and maybe we should help Treave try to coax the boys away in case the news gets worse. It's been so long now."

"Not that long." Brando dropped his arms and stepped back, his eyes dark and shining in the light overhead, and he raised his chin and looked straight at her. "We have to keep hoping."

"Yes, we do," Emma said, not quite sure what they were talking about anymore, the lifeboat crew and maybe something else, but there was something about Brando that made her want to believe there were things worth hoping for and believing in. Maybe when you stopped believing in them, that was when they slipped away from you a drop of hope at a time.

"They've found four out of the six already," she said,

"and three of those were alive. They're bound to find Christina and John Nance soon, aren't they?"

"Yes," Brando said, touching her back briefly as they turned to leave. "I've a feeling things are going to be all right."

INSANITY

"Insanity: doing the same thing over and over again and expecting different results."

ALBERT EINSTEIN

B RANDO WAITED AT THE sea wall with the rest of the village, watching for the boats to come in at last. Even once the rescues were complete, there had still been the required trip into port at Mowzel, the slow transfer of the rescued into waiting ambulances, the sad removal of David Evans' body.

The storm had blown out the bulk of its fury in the meanwhile. All that remained were occasional sputters and gusts of wind, like an exhausted child kicking its feet, trying to prolong a tantrum. The twins, too, fought their exhaustion as well as Janet's restraining hands. Hair and slicker gusting around her, Janet's grip was white-fingered on their shoulders while they squirmed and tried to get away. But whether they squirmed because she held them too tightly, or whether she clung so hard because they fought her, Brando couldn't tell.

He scrubbed a hand across his eyes as the smaller lifeboat started slowly up the long tractor ramp to the station. Every muscle in his own body longed for bed, and he couldn't even begin to imagine how Janet or the boys were still on their feet now that the adrenaline and worry had ebbed away. The animals were the only ones who'd given in to temptation, the cat long since gone up the hill to the castle, and the border collie sound asleep, squeezed in tight against the sea wall and protected from the wind. Unfortunately, those two were the only ones who didn't have to be up again in a few hours, too. Having been in the hotel business long enough, Brando was well aware that guests wouldn't wait for their food, or their bills, or oven clean linens for that matter, no matter what was going on around them.

He hated to bother Emma, who had turtled deeper and deeper into her coat as the night had worn on. He especially hated involving Treave, though he had to admit that Treave had done a brilliant job keeping the boys occupied most of the night while Janet had quietly panicked. Still it couldn't be helped.

Hands buried in the pockets of his coat and his shoulders hunched against the wind, he strode over to where they stood. "I've been thinking," he said. "I suspect the three of us are going to need to pitch in a bit to help."

"What now?" Treave asked, looking up. "The night's been long enough already."

Brando ignored the aggression in Treave's voice. "The guests will be waking up expecting breakfast in a matter of hours, and since the storm's blown over, more or less, the tourists'll be queuing up for the ferry, expecting to come over for the castle tours."

"The tourists can go hang, as far as I'm concerned," Treave said. "Without Christina, John, and Mary Libby, I don't see how Janet and Kenver can manage to open. Not to mention Gwen, and we won't know how long she'll be off until she can get to the hospital herself to have that ankle x-rayed. And Perr won't be leaving Christina in hospital by herself."

"That's my point exactly. None of this has hit Janet yet, and she needs to start making plans."

"What sort of plans would those be?" Treave's expression tightened. "There's nothing to be done apart from cancelling tours and future bookings. We can try to shift the guests who are already checked in to other hotels and make do as well as possible in the meanwhile with anyone who refuses to change. It's a shame about the wedding, too, but I suppose it can't be helped."

"Cancelling guests is not so easy—or so pleasant. I know that from experience." Brando kept his voice reasonable, pushing aside a twinge of irritation. "More importantly, it doesn't matter what's posted on the website or how many local hotels and caravan parks you notify, tourists won't always check to see if a place is open. They'll show up with their family in tow and have their holiday ruined, which they'll see as everyone's fault except their own. Then they'll plaster negative reviews every place they can think of. Janet can't afford—"

"It's not Janet's money," Treave said, his voice low as he drew himself up taller. "And all of this, trying to make a go of it, trying to keep the village going—it's already worrying Kenver half to death. You don't see that."

Emma caught Treave's wrist. "Brando's Janet's brother, so naturally he's worried about her—the same way you're worried about your brothers. Look, I don't pretend to know who does what around the castle, but David Evans and the gardens aside, there are three—potentially four—people too injured to work, right? There are three of us, so surely we can find a way to cover whoever's missing, at least until Janet and Kenver can get in additional help. You could run the tours in place of Mary Libby, couldn't you? All those stories you've told me about the place—people would eat those up."

"I didn't come here to entertain tourists from Hounslow while their bored offspring roll their eyes and complain they've better things to do." A gust of wind swept across the sea wall, throwing spray into their faces, and Treave steadied Emma, both hands on her arms. "Anyway, you don't want to work while you're here on vacation. You've been slaving away for four years, and I won't have you jumping straight back into that after I've dragged you all the way out here with me."

The crescent moon emerged like a grimace between

the racing clouds, gleaming on Treave's forehead and cheekbones and leaving his eyes cast in empty shadow. It struck Brando that Emma stared at Treave as if she didn't know him, as if she didn't want to know him. And Treave certainly didn't know Emma well if he thought for a moment that she could be so selfish.

She let go of Treave and took a step back from him. "You think I could lay around on the beach while everyone on the island is worried about how to make ends meet?" she asked. "Kenver and Perran are your *brothers*, Treave. I know how much it would hurt you to see them fail. You've seen me manage my mother all these years. I can handle this, and what's more, I want to help. I know you do, too. You can handle the tours—I saw you with your nephews. You were wonderful."

He stared at her as if he was working through a puzzle. Then he ducked down and kissed her cheek. "Whenever I think you can't surprise me, you do anyway. I'm sorry—it's not that I don't think you can handle this. I'm just worried about you wearing yourself out." He glanced over at Brando. "Are you all right with this?"

"Of course," Brando said.

Treave nodded curtly. "Good. Then once Kenver has a moment, I'll find out what needs doing. In the meantime, as soon as the boys have a chance to see for themselves that he's all right, I should try to get them off to bed, and you two should try to get a few hours sleep as well."

Brando had gotten to be a fair judge of people since moving back home from London. He hadn't always been, and that had cost him, so he'd made a concerted effort. But reading Treave confounded him. Just when Brando thought he'd got the man sussed out, when how good Treave had been with the boys had gotten Brando feeling guilty about having misjudged him, the man went and shifted again like mist across a peat bog.

Brando dug his fists deeper into his pockets. The first of the boats disappeared back into the building, and Janet and the boys didn't stay to watch the second boat start up the ramp. Her face pinched and suddenly furious, Janet turned to hurry toward the station, towing the twins beside her. Brando hurried to catch up.

"Kenver won't be needing a lecture from you after the night he's had," he whispered in her ear. "Hold your relief and your temper a while, woman. Give yourself time to think."

Janet rounded on him, her eyes furious and glassy. "Don't you be lecturing me, Brando MacLaren. Who d'you think you are, presuming to tell me what to say to the father of my children? The man who *left* his children over some s-stupid, misguided notion that he's invincible and n-needs to save the whole world because it's liable to stop spinning around without h-him."

She paused on a sob, and Brando pulled her into his arms, holding her as she finally released the tears she'd been bottling up all night. Treave and Emma hastily gathered up the twins and walked on with them toward the boathouse, followed by half the village. Glancing back over her shoulder, Emma sent a sympathetic smile that managed to encompass Brando as well as Janet, and he found himself smiling in return. Treave glanced back, slipped an arm around Emma's waist, and hurried her away.

Brando's fist itched with an irrational desire to deliver a quick right hook to Treave's smug aristocratic jaw.

Janet must have felt his tension. Stepping back, she dragged her thumbs across her eyes, brushing away tears that had mingled with the remnants of the rain. "Don't you dare pity me. And don't be thinking I'm an idiot, either. You wouldn't be wrong, mind, but that's for me to think, not you."

"The tighter you hold on to someone, the harder they'll fight to get away. You should know that by now."

"And you should know not to fall for women who are only going to break your heart. I'll learn my lesson not a moment sooner than you learn yours—don't think I haven't noticed the way you look at Emma," Janet snapped back at him.

Brando couldn't keep from stealing one last telltale glimpse of Emma and Treave as they rounded the corner toward the boathouse entrance, the twins jogging along in front of them. Penny, tail wagging, brought up the rear.

Janet gave a sudden bitter laugh. "And here I thought I was the one who needed saving from myself." She shook her head. "We're a pair, aren't we, the two of us? I can't let go, and you can't have what you want. It's a fine legacy our family's left itself."

She started walking toward the boathouse again, and Brando caught up to walk beside her. Light-soaked puddles shimmered at the base of the wall, trembling in the vibration of their footsteps. And maybe because his own world was trembling, shifting, Brando found himself needing to confess, to say the words aloud and admit them to the universe.

"Emma's the one," he said, his voice gone soft, as if keeping it quiet would make the fact of it, seem less overwhelming. "Emma's the girl I saw in the loch on Beltane morning."

Janet stopped so abruptly that her feet kicked up a spray of rainwater. "The Sighting?" She tilted her head and studied Brando long enough to make his cheeks burn. "You're an idiot, aren't you? All right, and what are you planning to do about it? Leave her to Treave Nancarrow? I should bloody hope not. And don't you go giving me any daft speeches about honor and sacrifice, either. I'm fit to choke on those after all I've heard from Kenver these last years. You take it from me, Brando MacLaren, I've been around Treave long enough to know that saving Emma from a life with *him* would be about as honorable a thing as you're likely to do in life."

"They're engaged."

"That's not the same as being married, though, now is it? So stop being daft and tell me what I can do to help."

OUT OF THE STORM

"When you come out of the storm,
you won't be the same person who walked in."

HARUKI MURAKAMI
KAFKA ON THE SHORE

EARLY MORNING LIGHT STOLE through the narrow windows of the castle kitchen, gilding the walls and the high arched ceiling and setting fire to the shelves of copper pots and pudding molds. On the opposite end of the long refectory table from where Emma was chopping red peppers, ham, and onions for a breakfast frittata for the guests, Treave set down his coffee cup and frowned across at Brando.

Emma gave an inward groan. For the last half hour, it had been a not-so-subtle battle between the two, and six o'clock was much too early for a test of wills.

"It makes no sense for both of you to cook for the café. I'll be needing Emma to help me with the tours this morning," Treave said, "and Gwen's always done fine with Nessa and Dena and the kitchen help. And she's had time to cook the family meals as well."

Kenver looked up from the note he was scribbling in the margin of the schedule they'd all been poring over. "Some of us would argue your choice of the word 'fine' is overly generous. And Dena won't be in, and Nessa was head-over-toes in love with poor Davy Evans, for all she never did more than look cow's eyes at him. She's not likely to be much help—if she comes in today at all, poor girl. Not to mention that Gwen didn't start on any of the cooking for today's lunch last night, so it'll all need to be done this morning, and the kitchen help doesn't come in until the ferry arrives."

"Most of the sandwiches and desserts come in from the bakery, so they'll still be delivered when the first ferry comes in," Janet said. "I can ring them and ask for more. We'll just have less hot food is all. No one will notice much anyway."

"If no one notices the food, you're not doing it right in the first place," Brando said, pouring the fresh, dark batch of Earl Grey tea he'd made into the batter for Earl Grey hot cross buns to serve the overnight guests for breakfast. "I'm here, Emma's here, and we're willing to work. It's a good chance to let us help you put together the type of menu guests will enjoy and talk about."

"I'd be all for that." Kenver nodded. "At the very least,

it'd be a new experience."

"Leave off Gwen, the lot of you." Janet slammed down her coffee, spilling it across the page of notes that she'd been making. Swearing lightly, she snatched up a dishcloth and dabbed at it while the angle of the light deepened the shadows beneath eyes already bruised by lack of sleep. "And you!" She rounded on Brando. "Just like always, complaining about the cooking. Nothing's ever good enough. Well, why should we have to tie ourselves in knots just because the whole country's gone daft over cooking programs on the telly? There's nothing wrong with what Gwen's been cooking here all her life. Plain good food," she added more quietly. "Nothing wrong with that."

Brando slowly set the remainder of the tea back on the table beside the mixing bowl and visibly tried to compose himself.

"It's more a question of profit, isn't it? Maybe that's what Brando was trying to say," Emma injected hastily. Picking up the batch of mushrooms she'd removed from the refrigerator earlier, she carried them to the sink that was installed in the converted workbench behind her. "I'm no expert, but it seems to me there's no reason you couldn't keep to the spirit of what Gwen's always made, let Brando add a modern twist and charge a lot more for it. Restaurants everywhere are doing that kind of thing. Obviously you all know more about this than I do, but I've been doing research, and all the trends seem to be mostly about adding healthier, sustainable options or a bit of gourmet flair. Or both."

"Precisely that," Brando said.

Janet sent him an exasperated glare. "Do as you like, then—as usual. I've no time to stand here and argue with you."

"Good, then that's all sorted." Looking halfway between relieved and panicked, Kenver gathered up the schedules and notes, wincing faintly as he knocked the long, fresh cut on his forearm against the table. "Emma and Brando will handle the kitchen. Janet you'll leave the bakery order as it is, and try to find an extra server, a cleaner, and a gardener to step in for poor Davy and a few extras to pick up the broken branches and make sure the trees and vines survived. Treave'll take the Insider tours that Mary usually handled herself, and the two regular guides will handle the rest. Treave, the main route for the tour's marked on the brochure and the Insider tours cover all the basics as well, so familiarize yourself with what Christina's written about each of the exhibits in the brochures. Then you'll take them up to the tower room and talk about Tristan waiting for Isolde, the usual drivel, and go from there to the dungeon and out through the secret passage to the headland overlook to talk about St. Levan and the bell. Mary usually adds in few of the ghost stories while she walks through the other rooms. Perr and I frightened you with enough of them through the years, and if you're at a loss, have a chat with Tamsyn." He gave a tired smile. "She'll be more than happy to tell you what the ghosts are up to now, every one of them. And if you find an exhibit's gone walkabout or moved out of place, ask her to tell you where the ghosts have put it."

Kenver's expression as he spoke to Treave was both hopeful and a little wary, as if he wasn't sure what Treave would say, as if he was trying a bit too hard. Watching the two of them together, it was easy to see the strain between them, and Emma wondered again what their childhood had been like, Kenver and Perran as little boys with a step-mother and a half-brother that their own mother hated. What had they done to Treave that they regretted now? And Treave as a boy, feeling like the odd man out while his half-brothers teased him. Still feeling like the odd man out. It made Emma's heart ache for all of them.

Maybe having Treave pitching in would be the best thing that could have happened to all of them. No matter how much he wanted to, he obviously didn't feel he belonged here as much as his brothers did. He'd colored the stories he'd told her, made them sound happier than they must have been, and maybe what he needed was to revisit them with a fresh perspective. She knew all too well that stories needed time and distance. No matter how many times her mother had worked and reworked something she had written, she often couldn't see the flaws in it until she'd stepped away, worked on something else, and then come back to it. Maybe Treave and his brothers needed the same thing, the chance to revisit the things they'd thought were long since settled and clearly weren't.

"So are we all set, then?" Kenver's chair scraped as he pushed back from the table. "With luck, Perran will be able to bring Christina back in a couple of days and both of them will get back to work. Until then, I'll need to get out the day's orders from the winery and then take the boat over to have a look at what kind of damage the storm's done to the orchards on the mainland. Fingers crossed it's not too bad. We can't afford to lose a harvest this year."

He and Treave wandered out together still talking about vineyards and apple and pear trees, and Janet stood looking after them with the dishtowel wrung between her hands. As if she realized finally she was strangling it, she smoothed the cloth out, folded it neatly into sixths, and set it on the table. "I suppose I had better go coax Tamsyn into helping at the café," she said darkly. "Wish me luck."

"Luck?" Emma repeated once she'd gone.

Brando grinned as though he was suddenly enjoying himself enormously. "I never thought I'd see Janet meet her match, but she's got her work cut out for her with that one." He picked up the first of the trays of hot cross buns and headed toward the oven. "The first night I was here, Tamsyn knocked on my door, carrying a pair of Kenver's pajama bottoms. When I asked what they were for, she told me that Elizabeth Randall was a modest young woman and didn't want me sleeping in the raw. That gave me a start, I'll tell you that much. I stood gaping at her like a loon whilst she headed back out the door and I tried to decide which question to ask her first."

"Which question?" Emma went to take the potatoes she'd been simmering for the frittata off the stove. "What do you mean?"

"For starters, there's 'Who the devil is Elizabeth

Randall?' Or 'How do either of you know I sleep in the raw?' And finally 'Why should either of you care?' There's a fourth, too, I suppose, which would have been 'Why do you think I have a prayer of fitting into Kenver's pajamas, when I weigh a good four stone more than he does?' But I'll leave that for the moment."

"So what did you end up asking?" Emma asked, laughing as she carried the steaming pot over to the sink.

"Nothing. Before I'd gathered my wits, she turned back to me looking prim and proper as a nun in that black scarf she wears over her hair, and she winked at me. 'Elizabeth also says to tell you she likes the left side of the bed,' she said. Of course, the way she's looking at you now, I doubt she'll keep to that side before the night is through."

Emma, shaking with laughter, managed to scald herself. Dropping the pot with a yelp, she turned the tap to cool, and stuck her hand under the running water.

"Here. Let me have a look. How bad did you burn yourself?" Brando hurried over.

He wedged in beside Emma and held her hand in the water while he studied it, then he briefly pulled it out and examined it more carefully. "Shouldn't be too bad, but I've got tea made. That'll help draw the heat away and—"

"Reduce inflammation," Emma said looking up at him, feeling odd and warm. "I know the trick."

He was still holding her hand, and for a moment, neither of them noticed. Then he cleared his throat and placed her wrist back in the stream of running water. "Keep that there while I get the tea for you. I'll add in some honey to help keep it from getting infected."

"We don't have time for me to baby this," Emma said impatiently.

"You don't have time not to. I'll not be the one responsible for leaving scars on that bonny fair skin." He stopped by the freezer to get some ice, then stirred honey into the pot in which he'd made the tea and added the ice cubes one at a time, testing the temperature until he was satisfied. Bringing the pot back with him, he placed Emma's hand gently down inside the liquid.

The warmth of his skin diffused the last heat from the burn as he held her hand down inside the liquid and helped her over to the table to sit down. Setting the pot on the table in front of her, he told her sternly, "Now leave that to soak in there until I say otherwise."

"Yes, chef," Emma answered smartly.

Brando stilled. "Too autocratic? Like burns and cuts, that's an occupational hazard in the kitchen."

His eyes were slate, a dark gray shifting to blue and back again with his moods, and in the bright overhead light, his hair had highlights of the same fiery copper as the pots on the walls. It struck Emma as interesting that, between Treave and Brando, it was Treave she associated with temper while Brando made her think of fire, of passion. Not only for food and cooking, but for life.

"I suspect a chef has to be a general in his kitchen as well as a first class cook," she said. "It's a skill I'd better learn. Now finish the story. Given what Kenver said, I'm assuming Elizabeth Randall turned out to be a ghost?"

"Unfortunately, no one had warned me about Tamsyn, and I didn't find that out until the following morning," Brando went back to slide another tray of the buns into the oven. "I locked the door and spent half the night wondering if one of the panels in the walls was going to slide open and reveal some brazenly horny young B&B guest from Manchester who was hoping to get a bonus for her money."

Emma giggled, and he laughed with her, a deep laugh that rolled through the kitchen while he turned his attention to the potatoes she had abandoned earlier. The sun through the windows that had already been bright earlier intensified, bathing the room in gold, fire, and amber, and Emma felt light suddenly, light and free with an edge of wildness like she'd felt in her first moments of arriving in Cornwall on the edge of the storm and wanted to dance on the cliffs with her hair loose and breathe in the danger and the salt-edged air.

When the laughter died, she found she didn't want to lose it.

"So how did you sleep last night, once you knew she was possibly floating around the bed with you?" she asked.

"Elizabeth wasn't the woman I was thinking about last night," Brando said. His back was to her, his knife moving with rapid-fire thumps. "Nor was she the woman I'd have wanted in my bed."

The smile faded from Emma's lips, and the air squeezed out of her lungs to dance around in her stomach along with a kaleidoscope of butterflies. The arched walls of the kitchen drew a breath, closing in.

Brando's knife went still, though he kept his back to her. "I'm sorry, I shouldn't have said that. I'm used to teasing—" Shaking his head, he didn't continue.

"It's fine, and that's ten minutes, I think. Time I got back to work." Emma jumped up and took the pot back to the sink to wash it.

Brando scraped the sliced potatoes from the cutting board into a sizzling pan and came over to check her hand again. "Let's have another look first, shall we?" he asked, lifting her wrist to the light. "How's it feel?"

"Perfectly fine," she said, torn between trying to impress him and wanting to keep him close. Neither of which was what she should have wanted. She pulled her hand away, and her skin burned where he'd touched almost as much it did where the scalding water had landed earlier.

That touch of skin, that smile when he looked down at her . . . The way he made her warm and awake . . . Was she really that needy and susceptible to attention? The fluttery way he made her feel could, she suspected, become as addictive as any drug. And that was all it was, her brain high on dopamine from the strength, warmth, and kindness of him. Then, too, there was the mortifying fact that she couldn't seem to block out the mental image of him sleeping naked in a canopy bed with the moonlight spilling through the window and a woman standing over him, watching him, then slipping in beside him.

The woman's face was familiar. Not Elizabeth Randall's but Emma's own.

It was the kilt, Emma decided, coupled with the cooking. A chef in a kilt with a smile that knifed right through her needed to come with a warning label so a girl could run away when she saw him coming.

HAUNTINGS

*"I believe in ghosts, but we create them.
We haunt ourselves."*

LAURIE HALSE ANDERSON
WINTERGIRLS

TWENTY MINUTES BEFORE THE first passengers were
due to disembark the ferry onto the island, the Black
Sails café was quiet save for the hum of the overhead fan
and motors in the display cases. Heat and humidity had
begun to shimmer above the steam tables that held the
freshly prepared soups and stews, making the murals of
Tristan and Isolde that were painted on the café walls
appear to move.

Emma recognized each scene, for she knew the story
well: Tristan receiving his shield from his uncle, Mark the
King of Cornwall; Tristan sailing to Ireland to bring back

Isolde to be Mark's bride; Tristan and Isolde mistakenly drinking the love potion intended for Mark's wedding night; Tristan breaking Isolde's heart by refusing to betray his uncle and his own honor; Tristan fighting the brother Isolde sent to avenge her and being wounded with the Irish knight's poisoned blade; Tristan in the tower of St. Levan's Mount nursed by the lady Morgana who comes to love him, slowly dying as he waits for a sight of the white sail that signals Isolde has come to save him. Tristan dying of despair when jealous Morgana tells him the approaching ship bears the black sail that signals Isolde's refusal. Isolde dying of grief at the sight of his lifeless body.

Emma had always thought the story was a little morbid, but in the café with its dark trestle tables and heavy benches, and with the glaring presence of Tamsyn, the housekeeper, dressed in black from head to toe, it seemed more morbid still. Tamsyn Penrose resembled a nun long past due for retirement. The kind of nun who slapped fingers with rulers and instilled the fear of God in anyone who transgressed.

Apparently, changing the menu in the Black Sails café counted as a dire transgression.

Standing in front of the display case with her arms crossed over her black-clad chest, Tamsyn read off the hand-lettered identification tags as Emma set them out in front of each white serving dish. "Chicken curry pastie, cheeseburger pastie, cheese and pickle pastie . . . " Tamsyn gave a disgruntled sniff. "What's all this, then? A Cornish pasty's meant to be a Cornish pasty—beef, swede, potato, and onion. None of this jumped-up rubbish. If the emmets wanted a curry, they'd have gone to see the sights in India instead of Cornwall. And a cheeseburger pastie? What's the point of serving that when it's easier to buy packaged buns?"

"Buying packaged buns is expensive, and tourists will appreciate more variety," Emma said. "Not to mention that the pasties taste better. Here, try this." Extending her gloved hand, she offered one to Tamsyn.

Tamsyn curled her nose and waved it away. "The old Lord'll have a fit when he sees that jumped-up rubbish being served."

"Oh, leave off with your useless ghosts, woman," Nessa snapped at the housekeeper, her eyes tearing up all over again. "The *old Lord*'s been dead four years and no one but you has ever seen him since. No such thing as ghosts."

"But you're wishing there was, aren't you?" Tamsyn gave her a pitying look and shrugged her wizened shoulders. "Ask me what you want to ask, my girl. Young Davy'll come calling on me soon enough, leaving me a message to bring you."

"Don't." Nessa, for all she looked meek as a mouse with her narrow face and pointed nose and grey clothing buttoned up to her chin, rounded on the old woman with her eyes flashing. "No games, old woman. Not about Davy, I couldn't bear it."

Tamsyn sniffed again and her eyes narrowed. "Might be he's got no reason to come back anyway, innit? Seeing as you never told him how you felt."

Nessa's mouth fell open in slow motion and the tears that had been threatening spilled silently onto her cheeks. She stared a long moment at Tamsyn as though she couldn't believe what she had heard, then with a sob she turned and ran from the café and out across the courtyard. Staring after her, Emma's own emotions pegged somewhere between pity for Nessa, fury at Tamsyn, and desperation about what they would do without anyone to man the café's cash register.

Tamsyn hobbled calmly behind the counter, donned a pair of plastic food service gloves, and came back to move the remaining pasties from the cart to the display case. "You'll be thinking I'm a cruel old woman, talking to her like that. But don't you be worrying yourself. Nessa's a strong girl—stronger'n she knows—and she'll be needing a good hard cry this morning, then a bit of fury to carry her through the day. Without that, she'll be no use to anyone at all."

Emma paused with a curry pastie in either hand. "You made Nessa cry *on purpose?*"

"Needed to be done. Mind, Davy's ghost'll be coming around soon enough. He'll have unfinished business, too, that one, seeing how he never found the mettle to tell Nessa how he felt about her any more than she told him. Take an old woman's advice, my girl. Don't you go letting yourself make the same mistake as those two. Life goes by faster'n you think—live it hard as you can. Give that man your heart and trust him to keep it safe."

Emma refused to lie to Tamsyn. She didn't want to lie

146

to anyone. "Treave's a good man," she said, "but I think I'd rather keep my own heart safe."

"Not Treave Nancarrow." Tamsyn spat as though she'd tasted something foul. "The Scot with the daft name is who I'm talking 'bout." Straightening with a creaky motion as though her back hurt, she dusted off her hands and pushed the cart over to start loading the displays with scones, eclairs, and tarts. Emma stood in stunned silence watching her, and Tamsyn flapped a hand, shooing her toward the door. "Well, don't stand there like a goat, girl. Go on back to the kitchen with you. We'll be needing more food as soon as the doors open, but I can finish setting out the rest of this. Meanwhile, I've told Janet to send those two useless girls from the village over. They'll help until Nessa's collected herself, then I'll sort out who'll do what. If we need anything sooner, I'll give you a ring." She gestured toward the telephone on the cradle beside the register.

At a loss for words, Emma crossed the courtyard to the steps that led down to the kitchen. Brando looked up from the worktable as she entered, smiling that broad smile that seemed to light him up inside, and she tried and failed not to think of all the things she should have said back to Tamsyn.

Brando's forehead creased in concern. "You all right, love?"

Had she really been staring at him so hard or so often that even the housekeeper had noticed? But of course she had been. He was a Michelin-starred chef, a kind one, one who'd offered to help her learn, and she was star-struck and eager. And that was positively all it was, Emma told herself with a mental shake.

"Emma? Did you hear me? Did something happen?" Brando came toward her, looking even more worried.

Emma forced herself to give him a brilliant smile. "Nothing. Tamsyn's finishing the setup, and she sent me back."

"Then I don't blame you for looking traumatized. She scares me—I'm not ashamed to admit it."

Emma laughed faintly. "Is Brando short for something?" she asked to change the subject. "It doesn't sound particularly Scottish."

"That's because my mother was a fan of American films. Old ones."

"Marlon Brando? That's who you're named after?" Emma went to the deep niche in the wall above the ovens where, earlier, she'd set bread dough out to proof. The dough was always better the second day, even better if a little was left to preferment before that. But beggars couldn't choose. Emma lifted the cloth and checked to make sure the first batch of dough had risen.

"Aye, Marlon Brando. The very same." Brando's voice held a hint of laughter, but the smile dropped away as he returned to the stove with his back to her. "She regretted that decision once I was old enough to look the man up, believe me. Did you know he'd been expelled twice from school? The first time was for riding a motorcycle down the hallway. Being that I was much younger, I couldn't get my own hands on a motorbike, so I nicked the head's bicycle and rode it past his office, hoping he'd turf me out. Apparently, I wasn't subtle enough about my motivations. He told me I could stay after school every day for a week and clean the hallway until it shone, because he wasn't about to give me the satisfaction of expulsion."

Laughing harder, Emma removed the bowl to the worktable, where she rubbed more flour onto the clean surface and tipped the dough out on top. "Sounds like you were a handful."

"Aye, and that was when I was only nine. I didn't get any easier to manage over the years, I don't think. Training to be a chef's the only thing that managed to teach me discipline."

"Did you always want to be a chef?" Digging her fingers into the dough, Emma started kneading.

"Lord, no." Brando switched off a burner and turned with a saucepan in his hand. "I wanted to play professional football. Only my parents were killed in an accident when I was ten, and Janet was too afraid I'd get hurt to let me play. I paid her back for raising me by being a proper, useless git. Left school without skills or a hint of a plan for how to support myself. Then she married Kenver when I was nineteen and left for Cornwall, and I pitched a selfish fit. To be honest, Treave probably had as much to do with my becoming a chef as anything else, now I come to think of it. We hated each other on sight at the wedding, and the way he sneered at the farm and the glen made me realize how much I loved them. Then I saw a program on the telly about gourmet restaurants and boutique hotels cropping up in remote places a few nights after Janet left, and the idea took root from there."

He made it sound so simple, but Emma could imagine him, wounded and scared after losing both his parents. He could so easily have lost his way and never made it back.

"It's a long way from a farmhouse in the Scottish Highlands to a Michelin star," she said, thinking for the first time that maybe her own dreams were a little small. Did the size of the dream limit the scale of the result? She thumped the dough down hard and split it into equal parts.

"Aye, but not so long as that. I talked my way into a dishwashing job at a three-star restaurant in London to help pay for culinary school, and worked my way up from there." His voice had gone low and thoughtful, but Emma couldn't see his expression, only the long, graceful line of his back and way he moved without any wasted motions, the kilt low on lean hips and the fabric shifting around his knees.

She told herself to concentrate on shaping the dough into loaves, making them look professional. "You still don't care for Treave much, do you?" she asked more quietly. "Tamsyn doesn't like him, either. Is it just the past you can't get over, or is there something else you have against him?"

"Well, he's engaged to you for starters," Brando said with a faint smile in his voice. "That's a strike against him. Then there's the fact he was cruel when I met him the first time. Cruel and uncaring about anyone except himself. I have a hard time forgetting that—"

He cut off mid-sentence as Treave strode through the

kitchen doorway wearing a murderous expression. "You're accusing me of being uncaring in the midst of making a pass at my fiancée? What do you call that, then, if it's not being selfish? And I don't suppose you happened to tell Emma that you broke my nose and threw me face first into the mud?"

POACHING

"What is honor compared to a woman's love?"

GEORGE R. R. MARTIN
THE GAME OF THRONES

T HE POT OF POTATOES threatened to boil over on the stainless steel industrial Aga, and Brando took a breath as he reduced the heat. By the time he'd turned back around, Emma had stepped past him, wiping her hands on her apron before reaching for Treave with a placating, palms up motion of her graceful hands.

"Brando wasn't talking about you," she said to Treave. "At least, not intentionally. I'm the one who asked him. I was only curious because you two don't seem to get along."

Instead of telling her she was entitled to ask whatever questions she liked, of whomever she liked, Treave looked down at the hand she'd rested on the sleeve of his shirt as if was something vile, and Emma hastily dropped it away. Treave picked off the stray bits of bread dough left behind on his shirt, which at least slowed him down long enough to keep him from storming over to Brando and picking a fight. Brando had mixed feelings about that. The thought of breaking Treave's nose a second time held a certain inherent charm.

Not that he would do that. He'd sworn off breaking noses unless absolutely necessary.

Sighing deeply, Brando removed the pans of ground beef and onions he'd been browning from the front burner and set it to the side to keep it from burning while he headed over himself to soothe Treave's wounded ego. Emma gave him a barely visible shake of her head and subtly waved him away. Then she drew Treave away into the corner by the great stone fireplace where the spit looked as though it could have cooked an ox, leaving Brando watching, worried.

Whatever she was saying to Treave was too soft to overhear, but Treave's stance was belligerent and Emma's was defensive—a dangerous combination Brando had seen too many times.

He was back, suddenly, in the kitchen of his family's farmhouse, the kitchen he'd torn out since with his bare hands so that no brick or stone or mark on the wall remained as a reminder. His father was screaming with a half-empty bottle in his hand, and his mother was screaming back. Until a fist was raised. Then her shoulders slumped and her eyes dropped, and the moment she showed weakness, that was when the first fist let fly. His mother cried, and Brando stepped in front of her, and Janet screamed at all of them and coaxed their father back into the bottle, because it was only at the half-empty moment that he was mean as a rabid dog, and at the three-quarter point he was meek as a lamb himself.

Remembering was a thorn in Brando's heart, but seeing Treave looming over Emma, that Brando couldn't bear. He told himself she wouldn't thank him for going over. That she was old enough and strong enough to make her own choices, to defend herself. Still his knuckles itched, and his heart pumped adrenaline through his veins.

He told himself he'd promised Janet he'd stay out of trouble, but it was the squeak of a rubber-soled shoe in the doorway more than his own willpower that likely saved him. He shifted his attention and took a calming breath.

Two young women came in, wide eyes absorbing the situation in the corner. Against the stark background of the three stone fireplace arches, Emma and Treave looked both larger and smaller in contrast, and though Brando hadn't thought about it before, he realized this was the first time that Emma had struck him as anything but at home in a kitchen, in her element. With Treave, she looked like a roe deer taking stock of where to run.

Seeing Brando, one of the women nudged the other and they both came toward him, their cheeks faintly red. Both were short and broad-featured with lively, snapping eyes and faces that even in their twenties were beginning to show evidence of the habitual Cornish frowns that masked naturally happy natures. They were also alike enough to suggest they were sisters, but though he'd been hoping for the kitchen help, they had dressed themselves for service in dark trousers and crisp white shirts. The one who'd noticed him first had long hair pulled back in a ponytail, exposing a small tattoo of Winnie the Pooh and a pot of honey beneath her ear.

"You wouldn't be the junior cooks, would you?" he asked. "If so, you're a sight for sore eyes, I'll tell you that."

The first girl nodded warily. "I'm Winnie, and this is my sister Bren."

Brando's grin was a little wider than he'd intended, and both girls blinked at him as if he'd startled them. But they knew their way around the kitchen, and as he went over the menu with them, he was relieved to discover they'd be able to handle enough of the café prep to leave him to plan out dinner while Emma did the more delicate desserts she'd already demonstrated she could handle. He started Bren off with another batch of the curry pasties and sent Winnie to load a cart with additional food to take back to the café. In between he kept an eye on Treave and Emma.

What the devil was taking so long to explain? Seeing Emma looking increasingly defensive and apologetic made Brando itch to grab Treave by the scruff of the neck, kick him in his tailored trousers, and send him sprawling. Not that Emma would likely thank him if he did. The whole situation made Brando's blood boil, the reaction so visceral he closed his eyes and took a breath. Partly because of Emma, and partly because Treave had been a conniving little stinkard from the moment they'd first met.

It was only with that thought that the pattern clicked. Funny how connections eluded Brando until suddenly they were so obvious he couldn't understand how he'd missed them.

He'd been nineteen when Treave had roared into the glen with his brothers and father as though he owned the world, Treave's lip curling from the moment he'd gotten out of the car as if the farmhouse that Janet had kept spotlessly clean were some flea-infested hovel beneath his dignity. Brando had written Treave off then as a prat who craved attention, the spoiled, only offspring of a second marriage with two older half-brothers to compete against. Even so, he'd seen how Treave could twist every situation to his advantage as nimbly as a dancer.

That type didn't have to resort to physical violence to gut someone. And they only got better at lying and manipulating people as they got older. Brando's own experience in London should have had him seeing the warning signs much sooner.

Thinking of Simone brought up a shadow of the old pain and anger even now. Brando hadn't been much younger than Emma, twenty-one to Simone's twenty-five. But Simone had always known exactly what to say, exactly how to hold back her kisses and approval until he was ready to do whatever she wanted of him. He'd nearly thrown away his idea of having his own restaurant and converting the farmhouse to stay with her in London instead, because Scotland wasn't ambitious enough or exciting enough for

Simone. Because it was his dream, not hers, and her own dreams had been all that mattered. He'd been love-blind, wrapped up in the spark of her, the fire and temper and creativity, the curves that had left his brain too lust-soaked to process a coherent thought. He should have seen her for what she was, realized that she hadn't given him a second glance the whole year they'd worked together in Andre's kitchen, not until he'd talked Andre into giving him a try as sous chef and he'd managed to earn the position permanently. He'd earned the job, and he knew it, but it had taken Simone only six months to nibble away his confidence and get him fired. To get herself the job instead.

Thinking about Simone was a good reminder. Simply because you wanted to see the best in people didn't mean there was anything good to find.

He watched Treave and Emma closely until Treave left the kitchen, and it was only once Treave had gone that he allowed himself to go to the refrigerator and fill a pot with spider crabs for the crab and leek terrines. He didn't trust himself to speak to Emma—he didn't know what to say to her. Partially because he wasn't sure exactly what Treave had said to her. And when it came down to it, what proof did he have that Treave was doing anything wrong? Gut instinct and his own past experience, and a powerful motive to undermine Emma and Treave's relationship.

Was he being selfish? Quite possibly.

On the other hand, something about what he'd just seen between Treave and Emma did make him feel like ramming his fist into the wall.

He avoided eye contact as Emma came back to work, giving her time to gather herself, to decide what and how much to tell him. Giving her space.

Any chef worth his salt knew to keep his head down in the kitchen. That was a lesson Brando'd learned the hard way, but working with Emma, it was easy to forget. She slid into place at the worktable beside him, her bonny face even paler than usual and her eyes red with recent tears. He wanted to take her in his arms, and at the same time, he wanted to beat Treave Nancarrow so he'd never go near her again.

"I'm sorry about taking so long," Emma said, smiling at both him and Bren, clearly embarrassed. "Treave wanted to tell us that Christina and John Nance are out of surgery and doing well, and Mary Libby's on her way home already. They're hopeful that Christina can be released tomorrow or the next day. The shoulder and arm should be fine in a month or two, but she lost a lot of blood, and they want to keep an eye on her concussion."

"And John Nance?" Bren asked from where she was cutting puff pastry for another batch of pasties.

"Still touch and go," Emma said. "They've removed his spleen and stopped some internal bleeding, but the broken hip was a bad break and apparently he needed a second surgery and possibly a third. Then, too, Gwen's ankle has a hairline fracture, so she won't be much help when he comes home."

"Kenver and Janet'll see they're both taken care of," Brando said. "I've no doubt."

"Of course." Emma bit her lip, making Brando think even more of kissing her. But he suspected she was weighing whether or not to say anything else—whether she needed to say anything else about what had happened between her and Treave.

To save her the embarrassment, he beckoned Bren over and made the introductions. He outlined a plan of work for the afternoon matter-of-factly, as if Emma hadn't only just spent fifteen minutes apologizing for his own careless remark and for an innocuous question that any man who cared about her would have pretended he hadn't heard. That any man who sat confidently within his skin wouldn't have cared a toss about.

Thinking it through, watching Emma settle down to her baking, Brando came to a decision. He'd been treading lightly, flirting half-heartedly, testing the waters with Emma when he should have been launching an all out offensive. The more time he spent with her, the more time he wanted to spend with her and the less time he wanted her spending with Treave Nancarrow. Even if he hadn't seen Emma at the Sighting, he'd have wanted to see what they had together, and he only had two weeks. Two weeks to win her or prove fate wrong.

Maybe it wasn't strictly honorable to set out to poach another man's fiancée, but whatever might or might not happen between himself and Emma, it didn't take a genius to see that Treave would be the last man to make her happy. Was it honorable to leave her to a man like that simply because Treave had beaten him to proposing? Brando glanced at Emma's long, slim, and empty fingers as she shaped the bread dough into loaves. Treave hadn't even given her a ring yet, which was a measure right there of the man's stupidity. If a man was daft enough not to announce his intentions to the world when a woman like Emma agreed to marry him, he didn't deserve her in the first place.

HANGING GARDENS

"Happiness is elusive—coming perhaps
once in a life-time—and approaching ecstasy."

DAPHNE DU MAURIER
FRENCHMAN'S CREEK

THROUGHOUT THE LUNCH RUSH and the preparation of the pastries for afternoon tea, anger was a lead weight in Emma's stomach. It slowed her footsteps and made her exhausted, and with her mind and hands both flying to keep up, she couldn't afford to contain all that inside her. Halfway through buttering the molds for a fresh batch of cocoa bean *financiers*, she decided that—whether or not Treave agreed—the pretend engagement had to end.

That's what she had told him earlier. She'd tried to explain that forcing her to lie to everyone was making her doubt him as well as herself. But instead of listening—

instead of hearing her—he'd kept asking her to repeat what Brando had said about him, kept asking her to tell him who had been talking about him behind his back. His eyes had been furious and cold, more insistent than she'd ever seen until, while he went on and on about loyalty and disrespect, she'd felt nervous and disloyal enough to apologize in as many different ways as she could think of.

But she'd spent her whole life apologizing. Saying she was sorry had become a reflex. One that was inevitably followed by resentment and regret.

That wasn't how she wanted to spend the rest of her life. Wasn't it time she grew a backbone?

No more apologizing, and no more lying. Not even to herself.

She set the brush aside and poured the dark chocolate almond batter into the fluted molds and set the molds on the baking trays. While the delicate pastries baked at a high temp for the first few minutes to give them the rich crust that needed to be as crisp as an eggshell, she wrapped the remaining batter and carried it to the cooler to bake up fresh the following day.

By the time she'd turned the oven temperature down again to keep the interior soft and springy, she'd made up her mind. She should have told Treave from the beginning that there was no chance of anything more than friendship between them. That was the first thing she needed to tell him now, and then she needed to insist he find a find a way to tell his family the engagement was off. She didn't care whether he admitted it had never been *on* in the first place, so long as she didn't have to keep on lying. If that made his family want her to leave immediately, so be it.

Sliding a look at Brando, she hoped it didn't come to that.

She loved watching Brando work. When the sun had dropped below the high kitchen windows, he'd lit the hurricane lamps that hung on chains suspended from the ceiling. The lamps swayed gently in the convecting heat of the stoves and ovens, sending gold flecks of light playing around Brando while he went back and forth between the pantry and the cooler and stooped over the worktable devising the rest of the dinner menu and the dishes for the following day.

"Tired?" he asked, smiling at Emma as he caught her watching.

"Energized," she said, feeling lighter, as though she could float up and swing on the swaying lamps or dance with the dust motes that drifted in the slanting light. "The *creme brûlées* and *pots de creme* are cooling, and I just put the last batch of pastries in the oven. I feel like we've accomplished something."

"You have—rather a lot, as it happens."

"What else can I do?"

He glanced around the kitchen, his eyes resting briefly where Winnie and Bren were prepping the last of the dinner vegetables. "Come with me," he said to Emma, then turning back to the other women, he added, "I'm dragging Emma out for a coffee break, and you two have more than earned one, too. We've a couple of hours before the dining room opens. Why don't you both take some time and put your feet up?"

Winnie and Bren exchanged a look and shrugged. "Our feet are fine as they are," Winnie said, then went back to work, chatting with her sister as the two of them had been doing all day, happy without smiling in the opposite way that Americans so often seemed to smile without being happy.

Happiness wasn't something that Emma had ever spent much time considering. Some people seemed to have a gift for it that had passed her by. Passed Evangeline by, come to that, though Evangeline'd had brief glimpses of it throughout her life that left her perpetually trying to find it again.

"Hold up just a tic," Brando said, and he moved to the coffee machine and poured out two cups of coffee with a quiet competent confidence that was a kind of happiness itself. The kind of happiness that had grown beyond caring what other people thought, or being afraid of what would happen if you didn't make *them* happy.

Leaving his own coffee black, he filled Emma's a quarter full with milk, just the way she'd been fixing it for herself. Then carrying both cups, he nodded for her to follow him and led the way down the back steps to the cellar and out again into the walled kitchen garden that sat beneath Tristan's tower. This was a true kitchen garden, with box-edged beds full not only of herbs but leeks, onions, carrots, parsnips, beets, cabbages, lettuce, and every variety of vegetable, not to mention tomatoes, pears, apples, and lemons in espaliered tiers. Seeing it, Emma suddenly missed her own garden, missed burying her fingers in the rich, dark earth, missed pruning with the sound of the fountain in her ears. Missed knowing every inch of the ground beneath her feet.

Brando led her along the path to the far side of the garden and set both coffee cups on the wall. He offered her his hand. "Are you afraid of heights, then, Emma Larsen?" he asked. "Because if you are, you won't enjoy this."

"I'm only afraid of boats," she said, and so many other things—but heights wasn't one of them.

Brando drew her closer, then caught her by the waist and raised her up. When she was seated at the top of the wall, he pulled himself to the top beside her, and swiveled his legs to face out over the sheer long drop.

Emma's feet dangled high over terraced gardens of fruit trees, hedges, and ornamental flowers that provided a visual patchwork, like the hanging gardens of Babylon, as they descended to the village. They were beautiful and clearly old, lovingly tended, and she wondered who would take care of them now that David Evans was dead. She wondered, too—thinking of Tamsyn Penrose's dire pronouncements—how Nessa was holding up without David. How someone recovered with so many things they had left unsaid.

She shook the thought away. Down in the harbor, toy-sized boats swayed as the tide came in, and the long strip of causeway to the mainland had vanished already. The last of the day's visitors were emerging from the village shops carrying bags of mugs and woven goods and hard ciders from the castle winery, or lining up for the ferry that would whisk them back to Mowzel.

The view was as perfect as a postcard, as perfect as a memory, all of Mount's Bay stretched out peacefully beyond the harbor, delicate whitecaps breaking here and there against hidden rocks. Sipping her coffee beside Brando, Emma had the odd sensation of waiting for something momentous to happen, like the day before her high school graduation or the moment when the acceptance envelope had come from Stanford and she'd been too excited to open it, knowing that as long as she held it sealed in her hand, she could still imagine what it would be instead of being certain. Imagining possibilities was too often better than reality.

Which was another thing Emma needed to change. If reality didn't measure up, then wasn't she doing something wrong?

"You did well today," Brando said, sitting beside her so quiet and still that she could almost forget that he was there. "All three of you lasses did well, but you in particular. You've developed technique, that's certain, and you've got the creativity, eye for detail, patience, passion, and the palate of a chef. Most importantly, you can cope with whatever's thrown at you and still turn out a professional dish."

Emma glanced at him sideways, afraid to look too long. "You're only saying that because you don't want me sleeping in tomorrow and leaving you with all the work."

"I'm saying so because it's true," he said with a laugh,

"and because it's rare enough that it's worth the saying." The smile faded, and he looked out across the bay. "So tell me, Emma Larsen, why do you want to be a caterer?"

"What made you want to be a chef?" she countered, uncomfortable talking about herself. "Apart from Treave being obnoxious, there has to be something that made you think you could do it."

He considered a moment, sitting silent so long that Emma thought he wouldn't answer. "My mother was a brilliant cook," he ventured finally. "At least, that's how I remember her. After she died, Janet took over the housekeeping and kept the house spotless, like she enjoyed beating the dirt back, mind. She never had the patience that's needed for proper cooking, though. Still doesn't. I took over the meals in self-defense, and it turned out I was good at it. But working for a restaurant, making the same dull food over and over? I never had any interest in doing that."

"So you went straight to opening your own restaurant?"

"I went to culinary school because I thought bringing in a small hotel and locally sourced eatery would help keep the community alive, at least if I could do it well enough. Having something to save helped me save myself."

Emma studied the clean, strong lines of his profile and tried to ignore the stir of something that was expanding like a balloon within her chest. "Wanting to be a caterer isn't that selfless. I suppose that for as long as each job lasts, I get to be part of making people happy instead of being a disappointment."

Once the words were out, she couldn't quite believe she'd said them. How did she go from holding too much back to spilling out her every thought?

"I can't see you disappointing anyone," Brando said, studying her with those storm blue eyes.

Emma should have looked away, or explained how often she did let people down. She was about to let Treave down, after all. She was letting him down right at that moment, being out here with Brando.

She drained her coffee cup with long, deep gulps, then raised it toward Brando in a brief salute. "Thanks for this. And for bringing me out here. It was good to clear my head, but we should probably be getting back."

Brando watched her another long moment, then nodded briefly. After swinging himself down gracefully and dropping to the ground, he reached up to take her hand, catching her at the waist as she jumped and lowering her slowly. She felt the warmth of his hands through her shirt long after he'd released her, but she told herself that didn't matter. She couldn't afford to let it matter.

WHITE FINGERS

"Gradually white fingers creep
through the curtains,
and they appear to tremble."

OSCAR WILDE
THE PICTURE OF DORIAN GRAY

W ITH THE WATER TAXI available for the guests again, the dinner service was light and over quickly. The family ate on the terrace on the far end of the castle overlooking the sea and the headland, where the ruins of the old abbey were outlined by the descending sun. After dinner, they lingered over coffee while the boys and the dog ran off to chase each other with sticks, the way that small boys and large dogs were meant to do.

Emma smiled, watching them, grateful for something to steal her attention from the others. Seated across from

Treave with Janet kitty-corner, she'd felt prickly and too exposed through the meal. They'd both watched her too carefully, casting assessing glances at her and Brando from beneath their brows until she'd found herself chatting too brightly. Even now, she babbled in response to Kenver's effusive gratitude for all her help.

"I loved every minute of it—honestly, I should be thanking you. Getting to see Brando orchestrate the kitchen is fantastic practice, and I already feel a thousand-times more eager to start my own business."

"All you're missing is confidence and," Brando said, cutting into a *financier* and raising it on his fork, "you should have bushel-loads of that. I've eaten *financiers* in Paris that weren't half this good."

"You didn't tell me you'd been to Paris," Janet said dourly, casting another glum assessment over the remains of the crab and leek terrine, the salad of pear and Cornish blue cheese, and the confit of pork belly with braised cabbage and black pudding bon bons. "London and Paris and who knows where learning to cook like this, but it took you ten years to come to Cornwall."

"Which was only because I wasn't sure I'd be welcome, not because I've anything against Cornwall." Brando sighed. "Look, what Emma and I have done is try to show you it's possible for you to serve food that pays homage to the area without being the same thing you'd find in every second pub. As it is, you're giving your dinners away, and wasting time and energy only doing them for the overnight guests." He waved his arm over at the ruins of the abbey and the tower, at the sunset that was just beginning to lend color to the low-flying clouds. "In a setting like this, with this kind of a meal, you could charge £40.00 a plate and sell out the dinner service every night. A proper dinner service would bring in overnight guests as well—and let you charge more for the rooms."

"To guests who'll expect the moon. No, thank you," Janet said.

"It would mean more business, which means more income for the village—and maybe some in Mowzel as well," Kenver said hastily, eyeing Janet's dark expression. "And I can't remember when I've had better food."

Treave pushed his chair back, the wrought iron sparking against the flagstones. Coming around to Emma's side of the table, he stopped beside her and offered his hand. "On that note, though, I think Emma's earned a break, don't you? If you'll excuse us, I'm going to steal her away to see the sunset from the abbey ruins."

It was hard to gauge Treave's mood, but even if he intended to lecture her about Brando again, Emma didn't care. She needed time to talk to him anyway. Straightening her spine, she mentally rehearsed what she was going to say as he led her out a side gate on the upper terrace and up a narrow set of stone steps to the top of the island where the wind was gusting.

Safeguarding access to the castle from every side, high stone curtain walls led all the way around a narrow heath. On the westernmost tip of the headland, a cemetery and the stone ruins of a bell tower marked the remains of the original priory built on the spot where a vision was said to warn sailors about impending storms. As they approached it, the bottom edge of the sun dipped below the mainland, and above the horizon the shredding clouds had turned amber and bloody red.

Treave wrapped his fingers around Emma's hand, pulling her toward the base of the tower where an odd-shaped stone about four feet high and two feet wide had been incorporated into the foundations of the tower. Placing his other hand on top, where the rock had been worn smooth, he briefly closed his eyes, and when he opened them again, they danced with mischief. His smile was the same Treave she knew, the one who had kept her company so many nights while Evangeline was in one of her furies, and when Evangeline lay spent and finally slept, he'd brought her take-out Chinese and ice cream and watched soppy, feel-good movies with her until two in the morning with the volume low.

"This stone is the best-kept secret in my family," he said, still smiling down at Emma.

Some of her tension eased away. She shook her head, squinting against the light as the wind kicked dust off the heath and whistled through the stones. "It's the original St. Levan stone, isn't it? The stone that marked his grave and the place where his spirit appeared as a warning when a storm was coming. The start of the island's lifeboat tradition. I've read the guidebook."

"This isn't in the guidebook. Well, some of it is. One of the ships that was saved carried Xerxes, the son of the *shahhanshan* of the Sassanid empire, and in gratitude, the shah sent the priory a bell cast in gold and silver, with proportions so perfect that it made a sound like the angels singing. The bell was lost in the Civil War, stolen by the Parliamentarians and melted down or taken with King Charles II to the Scilly Isles."

His voice was fervent with the rush of excitement that could keep him talking for hours, but Emma had no patience for it. She'd spent too long rehearsing what she had to say. "Treave, I need to tell you—"

"No, wait, Em. Please. Hear me out." He caught her hand again. "There's a legend in my family that we don't talk about, a tradition that says if we make a wish with a hand on this rock, St. Levan's bell will ring if the wish is meant to come true. Nancarrows have been making wishes here for centuries, for every important occasion. Wars and births and marriage proposals."

Emma's heartbeat slowed and the ocean was a roar in her ears. Her throat constricted. "Treave, don't."

A gust of wind threw dust along the path and swallowed her words, and Treave's head came up and he went still in concentration, then he smiled slowly, his eyes gleaming. "Did you hear that? Listen."

Emma's heart dropped in her chest, because he looked so relieved—and happy. And she was going to destroy all that. "Treave—"

"Quiet. Please."

They both stood and listened, and eventually he shook his head, but he was still smiling as he pulled something

175

from his pocket. "I heard the bell. I know I did. I couldn't have imagined it." He grasped her hand again and before she had a change to pull away, he slid a ring onto her finger. "This was my grandmother's, but the stone once belonged to Eleanor of Aquitaine, and it's about all I have left of the Nancarrow legacy. Will you wear it?"

The stone was a clouded emerald set in heavy silver, and before Emma could choose the words to let Treave down gently, he dropped to one knee in front of her and pushed the ring onto her finger. "Do me the honor of marrying me, Em. I swear I'll make you happy. We'll be happy together, and everything will be all right."

Tears pricked in Emma's eyes as she drew her hand away, but the ring was harder to get off than it was to get on. Her knuckle hurt with the motion, though not as much as her heart hurt watching the happiness ebbing from Treave's face when he realized what she was doing.

"I can't." Feeling miserable, she held the ring back out to him. "I'm so sorry, but I don't feel that way about you, and I know I couldn't make you happy. We'd end up ruining a friendship that has come to mean everything in the world to me."

"It's him, isn't it? Just like that. I've waited four years, and you threw yourself at him in four *hours*—"

"It wasn't—isn't—like that." Emma tried to press the ring into his palm.

He snatched his hand away and lurched, slowly, stiffly to his feet. "You think I'm blind? I saw the way you were looking at him. I heard the way you were talking about me to him. What exactly did he tell you—what lies has he been telling you?"

"Brando hasn't said anything about you at all—he isn't like that."

"You're standing here defending him."

"Because he hasn't done anything wrong! It's me. Maybe I can't love anyone. Or maybe love's an illusion and I don't know how it's supposed to feel. Maybe there's something broken inside me; maybe some people don't have the capacity for that kind of love. Whatever the reason, it wouldn't be fair for me to marry you when I don't love you in that way."

"You'd come to love me. I know you would," he said, reaching for her. "I *heard* the bell—"

"I didn't hear anything, Treave."

He caught her waist, jerked her up against him, and bent to kiss her. Her hands trapped between them, she flattened her palms against his chest and shoved him away. "Stop, Treave. I'm not going to change my mind."

"You will. You love me; I know you do. You've only to give us a chance."

"Telling me I don't know my own mind isn't going to make me think any better of you." She shoved even harder.

He drew back, his eyes dark and dreadful, flat in the moonlight. Shaking his head, he dropped his clenched fists to his sides.

"I'm sorry," Emma repeated, suddenly nervous.

He drew his head back on his neck, a motion somewhere between a turtle and a snake coiling up to strike. "What about your inheritance? You'll lose everything. Where will you get the money to open your business?"

"I'll find it somewhere else. I'll do the cookbook, I don't know."

"Marry me. Just marry me, and you'll get the money. Let me help you get it. If you aren't happy, if I don't make you happy, the marriage doesn't have to be forever."

She wondered if she knew him at all. Wondered if he'd always been like this and she hadn't seen it. Wrapping her arms around her waist, she shivered in the cold wind as the sun fell beneath Land's End and left the sky and sea streaked with the last red remnants of the day.

"What is going on with you, Treave? Since we got here, I feel like I don't know you. Sometimes, I'm not even sure I want to know you," she said, and there was a high note in her voice, something akin to fear.

His head rose slowly, as if he'd heard it, too. His expression went blank, unreadable, and he looked off into the distance as if he couldn't bear to see that same fear written on her face.

"Maybe you're the one who hasn't been the same," he said, his voice shaking. "Have you ever thought of that?" He strode away, his steps were long and his fingers balled up again into furious fists.

Emma stood and watched him go, and found that she was shaking, too, shaking harder and harder, though she couldn't have said exactly why. Regret, fear, anger, sadness . . . Maybe all of those emotions ran so close together in the nerve center of the brain that at times like this they blurred together.

Stumbling back against the ruined wall of the priory, she leaned against it, unwilling to face the thought of seeing Treave again until she knew what to say. Unwilling to face his family or anyone else.

WISHFUL THINKING

*"Very often a change of self is needed
More than a change of scene."*

A.C. BENSON

T HE SKY HAD FADED to lavender, and the first wishing star winked in and out between the wind-laced clouds. If she wished on two things simultaneously, would it increase the chances of the wish coming true?

Not that Emma's wishes had ever done much of that. Three Christmases in a row, she had spent the entire year wishing for a kitten and being extra good, dropping hints and writing to Santa, even though that last year Evangeline had told her sternly that Santa wasn't real. But even at six, Emma had been smart enough to realize that *someone* had to have brought the presents that appeared like magic beneath the tree on Christmas morning, either Evangeline or her assistant, and since at least some of the presents she'd gotten the previous year had been on her Santa list, it meant someone had read her letters. All that June, until Evangeline had yelled at her to stop, Emma had left a dear Santa note on her mother's chair. Then finally giving up on Santa, she had wished on the first star every night, and wished on every tooth she lost the rest of that year, but wishes didn't matter. On Christmas morning, there'd been a new Cabbage Patch doll, and a Breyer horse, and a gold bangle bracelet and a matching gold necklace with a sparkling heart, and Evangeline had been furious that Emma was disappointed, telling her coldly that some children didn't get anything for Christmas. Some children were lucky to get a sandwich to eat, so she needed to be grateful for what she had. And when Evangeline wasn't looking, Emma had crawled under her bed and cried herself to sleep so that her eyes were red for Christmas photos and Evangeline had gotten mad all over again.

Thinking about seeing Treave again felt like that. Only Emma wasn't sure whether, this time, she was the little girl hiding beneath the bed so no one would see her cry, or whether she had reversed roles so that now she was Evangeline who'd gotten mad because Emma wasn't happy with something she had never wanted.

If Emma could have had one wish in that moment, it would have been that she had never agreed to come to Cornwall in the first place. That Evangeline had never written that stupid clause into her will. That Treave had never changed.

But that was three wishes already. She was getting greedy.

With a sigh, she loosened her hand where the ring she'd retrieved from the grass was digging into her palm. She pushed the ring into her pocket. She needed to take it back to Treave and try to talk to him. Figure out whether she was leaving or staying—no. She needed to figure out how quickly he wanted her to go.

Rising, she dusted herself off and headed back. In the darkness, the path was lost, but the lights from the castle were a beacon. As was the figure who mounted the steps before she reached them.

She hesitated, but there was no way to avoid him. She walked forward and he came to meet her. "It's getting late," she said, trying to skirt around him. "I was just heading in."

"Treave stormed back a while ago, and so I came out to see if you needed anything."

"I don't," she said, turning away as her voice trembled. Kindness always did her in, and she didn't want to cry in front of Brando.

He caught both her arms and turned her toward him, peering at her in the velvet dimness as if he could, like Shipwreck the cat, sense things no one else could see. Maybe he felt her trembling. He peeled the light sweater he was wearing off and, before she'd registered what he was doing, he settled it around her head.

"Come here," he said, tugging her into it, drawing her closer.

The sweater was still warm with his body heat, and it

smelled like him: warm man and spicy aftershave with a combination of delicious cooking smells. He smelled like kindness and safety and danger, which made her tremble even more.

"What did that bastard do to you?" His voice went hard. "He didn't hurt you, did he?" She shook her head, and he breathed out a long sigh. "Are you sure?"

"I'm the one who hurt him. I said I wouldn't marry him."

She couldn't see Brando's face, but she felt the way he released, like a spring that had lost its tension. "Don't feel guilty for that. You haven't done something wrong."

She hadn't, but she only shook her head and the rest of her shook as well. Brando went even more still, then as gently as if she were a soufflé fresh from the oven, he pulled her into his arms and let her rest her cheek against him. "You can't help the things you feel, love," he said. "Or the things you don't. Sometimes, our best intentions don't work the way we meant them."

The fabric of his T-shirt was cold in the wind and soft against her skin. Beneath it, the hard muscles were still bunched with tension, but as she let go a sigh, he released one, too, ruffling her hair as he held her. Only held her.

She couldn't have said when it changed, whether it was her or him. His arms shifted gradually through the spectrum from tension to comfort to a different kind of tension, and she became aware of his breathing, and her own, and theirs together, and then her heart was quickening and his hands edged up to her arms, brushed her shoulders, cupped her face.

Her chin tilted up to meet him, slowly. Slowly. He waited. She waited, barely breathing, and finally his lips descended, firm on hers and warm, drawing heat from her and want. She *wanted*. More than she'd ever wanted anyone.

The wind gusted, raising goosebumps, and she seized the excuse to shiver closer, to stumble into him and wrap her hands around his neck to keep herself from falling. Only she felt the opposite the more she touched him, as though she were plunging from a cliff into deep, deep water that was going to drown her—and she didn't mind. Because wasn't that what it was supposed to be between a man and a woman? Was this the feeling that Evangeline had craved? Had written about? This knife-edge out-of-control sensation that made Emma feel as though anything were possible? She felt outside of herself, lost in him. Maybe people had to step out of themselves before they could feel each other, find each other. Maybe that was what she'd been doing wrong all her life, not letting herself drown in life enough to live.

She forgot to breathe at the thought. And she pulled away.

"What's wrong?" he asked. "Did I frighten you?"

"I frightened myself." She drew back another step. "We really should go in."

"Only if you tell me what you're thinking first," he said, looking down at her.

With no moon and only the castle lights in the distance, she had to rely on memory to see his face, yet she had no trouble with that at all. She could have closed her eyes and seen him, seen all the small details of features and coloring and expression she hadn't even realized she had memorized.

"I have Treave's ring in my pocket, and I have to give it back to him. I can't be out here with you."

"Until you give it back?" Brando asked.

"He'll want me to go. He won't want me here."

"What he wants isn't the only thing that matters. Gwen won't be able to do the cooking for Christina's wedding and that'll be ten days out by the time she gets back from the hospital."

"With her arm in a cast and stitches on her face, she'll probably want to cancel."

"Janet says she won't."

"Then you can handle the arrangements."

"Not on my own, but that's not the point. After all you've done for the family already, she'll want you to stay. Janet will want you to stay. Of course it'll be a little awkward, but Treave can set his feelings aside for his brother's sake."

"Why are you assuming that I want to stay?" Emma said.

"Because I hope you will. Because you strike me as the kind of person who likes to see things through. Because it's an opportunity for you to learn, to discover things about yourself, and for you to help people you like, people who need your help. I may not have known you long, Emma Larsen, but I know you. You haven't got it in you to walk away from someone when you're needed."

EMMA KNOCKED ON TREAVE'S door and waited, then knocked again but he didn't answer. He must have gone to tell Kenver that she was going, or to get a drink.

The light flickered at the end of the hallway—Brando's shadow moving—and she froze, determined not to look at him. The floor creaked, and then Brando's door groaned as he opened it. Then she heard him close it gently.

Thinking of Brando sleeping across the hall from her, knowing that he was across the hall all night . . . Cold with guilt, she felt the heavy weight of Treave's ring in her hand, and she didn't want to keep it a second longer.

She pushed the door open and slipped inside. The lights were on, but Treave's bed was still made. She was halfway across the room, ready to set the ring on his nightstand, when she heard his voice from the bathroom where the door stood ajar.

"I need more time, that's all, another month. I already have a lead on additional funding options."

Uncertain whether to continue or retreat, Emma stopped a few feet into the room and listened. A brief silence was broken by Treave's voice again, and it wasn't until then that she realized he was on the phone.

"Three weeks, then. That's nothing, and I told you I have a solution. What's the alternative? You don't want this getting out. It won't do anyone any good. Your reputation's at stake every bit as much as mine."

The slap of bare feet sounded on the bathroom floor, Treave's familiar certain stride, and Emma, panicking though she couldn't have said why, searched for somewhere to hide. Finding nothing close enough, she ran back toward the corridor, then whipped around as the bathroom door creaked open wider.

"Anyone here?" she called out, as though she'd only just come in.

Treave emerged from the bathroom in a thick white robe, his hair wet and a towel hanging around his neck. His face reddened on seeing her. "Hold on," he barked into the phone before looking back at her again. "What are you doing here?"

She held the ring up. "I brought this to give it back, and I wanted to know what you want to say to everyone in the morning. We can tell them that you ended the engagement. Or that we're putting it off because of my catering business—or whatever reason you want to give. Then like you said before, we just let it die, the way things do."

"Are you sure that's what you want?" He leaned against the wall and studied her.

Of course it wasn't what she wanted. What she *wanted* was for everything to be the same between them, but that was not an option. Maybe it never had been. Maybe friendship had been an illusion on her part. How could she not have realized what he'd felt?

"I want you to be happy," she said gruffly.

He rubbed a hand across his eyes. "That's what I've always wanted, too. Seems I've spent a lifetime chasing happiness, and look where that has gotten me." He stared at a point somewhere over her shoulder as though he couldn't bear to look at her. "Just set the ring over there. I don't want to touch it." He gestured toward the dresser, and then went back into the bathroom and shut the door with a determined click.

Emma set the ring down, then rushed back to her room. Something about Treave's behavior worried her, a manic edge to his bluntness that had left her unnerved. But going back, trying to talk to him, wouldn't that only make things worse?

She peeled off her clothes and threw them on the chair, then took a long hot shower that somehow wasn't hot enough. For a long time after she'd crawled between cool sheets in the drafty room, she lay awake thinking. Trying not to think.

Well after midnight, with only hours left before she wanted to get up and at least help Brando get a start on the day's baking, sleep still eluded her. She needed warm milk and a change of scenery, so she plucked up the sweater from the wad of clothes to pull on over her thin pajamas. There was a thud in the room beside hers. A door closing. Something scraping.

She stood with the sweater in her hand and listened,

imagining Treave pacing restlessly, sleeplessly. The way the doors creaked, if she tried to leave the room, he'd likely hear her. Seeing him now, talking to him now—they would both be useless in the morning. Anyway, she wasn't ready to face him again. Somewhere in the long empty hours of staring at the ceiling, anger had taken hold of her again, anger and determination.

She wasn't going to slink off the island to try to salve Treave's ego. Janet and the family needed help in the kitchen, and Treave had offered to help her set up a business plan. That wasn't likely to happen now, but Brando had offered, too—and why should she pass up the opportunity to work with a Michelin-starred chef? She'd be stupid to do that. Why should everyone—everyone—suffer because Treave had chosen to tell a lie to salve his ego?

She wasn't going to do that. She threw the sweater back onto the chair. It slithered down onto the floor, landing in a pool of moonlight, and it was the first time she had a good look at it. The first time she realized it was Brando's sweater and not her own. How could she have forgotten that's what she was wearing when she'd gone to return Treave's ring?

No wonder he'd been bitter. If she'd been deliberately trying to hurt him, deliberately trying to make him jealous, she couldn't have found a better way to do it.

These past four years, Treave had been the one who'd saved her sanity more times than she could count. If she left now, he'd probably never speak to her again, and she couldn't live with that. Somehow, she had to think of a way to ensure that she could stay long enough to fix things between them and repair their friendship.

MISTAKES

"Any man can make mistakes
but only an idiot persists
in his error."

MARCUS TULLIUS CICERO

J ANET OPENED THE DOOR at five in the morning wearing
a flannel robe that looked exactly like the manky green
one of their mother's that Brando had burned on Janet's
birthday the year he had turned sixteen. The one Janet had
worn to breakfast every morning since their mother's death.

"Do you name these robes?" he asked to cover his
shock. "Junior and Third and Fourth? Or is this your
preferred form of birth control?"

"Quiet, you great lump." Folding her arms beneath her
bosom, Janet darted a look into the dim interior of the
bedroom that remained still and quiet save for a light

snoring from the left side of the canopied bed. "Did you get up extra early to insult me or do you have a reason for pounding on my door before the sun comes up? Kenver's still sleeping. Or trying to sleep."

"I'll be needing the help you offered," Brando said more softly. "Emma's broken it off with Treave and given him back his ring."

"Already? That was quick work, I must say. But I'm no good with a gun, so if it's come to pistols at twenty paces, you'd best look elsewhere." Janet peered out into the corridor as if Treave were likely to be standing there with a loaded weapon. Then, satisfied that all was quiet, she stepped out through the door and sighed. "All right, so what is it that you need? Only don't tell me you've decided it's a mistake now you've broken them up and you expect me to clean up your mess?"

Disappointment, bitter as apples, made Brando's fingers curl. But this was the way Janet had always been. He should have known better than to come to her.

"Never mind," he said. "You offered help, so I thought—I hoped—"

"I didn't expect you to send the poor girl packing after she's only been here a day, did I? That wasn't the brightest move on your part. What are you thinking to do with her when she's clear on the other side of the Atlantic? Anyway, since when did Treave give her a ring? She wasn't wearing one yesterday."

"Can we focus on the important part? I don't want her leaving. That's where I need your help."

"No sane woman would want to stay under the circumstances. Or expect to."

"She will if you convince her we need her help with Christina's wedding. She's the type who can't say no to anyone who needs her."

"Which means we shouldn't be taking advantage of her. Not that I think there should be a wedding—or will be if I have anything to say about it."

"Why, if Christina wants to go ahead with it? What's it to you? Seems to me that another setback and defeat is the last thing anyone on this island needs. Unless you're thinking the preparations would be too much for you to handle?"

He threw out the challenge, expecting Janet's temper to take the bait, but she only arched her eyebrow at him. "Don't think I don't see what you're trying to do, Brando MacLaren. But I've no time for your nonsense now. I've the twins and the reservations and the guests to manage, and the staff and tours to oversee. These people all depend on us, and every additional chore I take on increases the chances I'll fail and let someone down. I'm not surprised that you can't see that. It was always easier for you to slope off somewhere and get yourself in trouble than to take responsibility."

Words welled up in Brando's throat, but he bit them off. What was the point of trying to defend himself? Truth was, he had done that while he was growing up. He couldn't blame Janet for thinking it. Then again, when no one believed you were worth anything, what difference did it make to confirm what they already knew? Janet's opinion and that of everyone in the glen had set against him the night his parents had died. And he'd spent a decade afterwards proving they were right. It had taken him years to understand that when he was getting himself in trouble, when he was living on the edge of fear, it left no time for thinking. For guilt. Years and hard work had finally let him come to understand why he'd done the things he'd done, and it had taken another decade to convince the glen that he had changed. They were only now starting to see it. He wasn't sure Janet ever would.

Swallowing down the disappointment, Brando studied the light reflecting on his neatly polished motorcycle boots. "Help me convince Emma to stay, Janet. Please? She and I'll handle everything. You wouldn't need to lift a finger, but you said yourself, these people all depend on you. They need something to look forward to, something hopeful. Christina's going to need it. Don't let her feel she should be ashamed to want the celebration to go ahead."

"You can't change what Gwen's already set in motion. She'd be livid if you changed it."

"I can't promise that. You've seen what Emma can do already, and she's good. We'll take our orders from Christina—and Perran. Besides, I swear I don't understand what you think you're doing, letting that old woman walk all over you. Or Tamsyn Penrose, come to that. What are you doing? Your whole life, Janet MacLaren, you gave an earful to anyone who so much as looks at you cross-eyed, and here you are letting those two tell you what to do and how it should be done."

"Exactly what I've been telling her since my father died." Wearing a pair of faded paisley satin pajama bottoms that looked ludicrously out of place beside Janet's awful green flannel robe, Kenver appeared out of the gloom in the bedroom and stepped out into the corridor. "The fact that they don't like the changes we've had to make doesn't mean they can hold back the tide by refusing to make more changes. We can't live the way we always have, however much we'd like to. I don't see John Nance coming back to work with those injuries, not at his age. And they've more than earned their pensions, all three of them. Problem is, they don't want to leave the island, any of them, and they don't want to spend their days watching grass grow, as Gwen Nance puts it. Tamysn's got a son who moved to the Lake District, but Gwen and John don't have anyone. None of this is easy."

"Getting old is never easy," Janet said.

Nodding, Kenver raked a hand through his sleep-tousled hair. "So tell me, why is any of this important enough to invade my bedroom in the middle of the night?"

Brando rubbed the back of his neck and glanced at Janet. How did he explain about fate or destiny or the Beltane Sighting? How much had Janet told him over the years? Without knowing that, nothing involving Emma would make sense to someone who hadn't grown up in the glen. Even Janet, having lived with what their parents had been through, had never dared go to the Sighting herself.

"What's the good of having the loch show you who

you're meant to love," she'd said, "when it takes two people to make a relationship? Two people choosing, and only one to get it wrong."

Brando'd agreed with that originally. Their father had seen Ailsa Murray in the loch the same year that she'd seen him, but the daughter of the Murrays from the big house up the glen'd had no interest in marrying a farmer's son— and a MacLaren to boot. Ailsa ran off with the first man willing to take her away.

Brando's own mother had been a good woman, a solid woman. Maybe in another lifetime, she and John MacLaren could have been happy together, but knowing he was meant to have something else, something he always imagined would have been better, something *more*, had left John finding fault with every little thing his wife and children had done. Maybe when you'd been promised magic, it was hard to settle for the mundane.

Brando'd felt no desire to look in the loch himself until the year he'd come back to the glen from London. As much as he'd tried to tell himself he'd only imagined himself in love with Simone, that he hadn't even *known* the real Simone, he'd needed the loch to tell him she wasn't the one fate had intended for him.

Knowing had helped him to recover, just like not knowing had allowed Janet to fall in love. But how did he explain any of this to Kenver?

And broken engagement or not, Treave was Kenver's brother. Whatever their differences, Kenver wasn't likely to help Brando steal Emma from him.

Kenver turned to draw Janet back into the bedroom. "No offense, Brando, but I've had a long couple days. Tell me in the morning when you've decided what to say."

Brando thought about Emma leaving and panic fluttered in his chest. She was likely packing to leave already, pacing in her room, waiting to call a water taxi the moment it was daylight. Who knew if she'd even say goodbye. She was the type to leave a "thank you" note with apologies on the bedside table, not wanting to disturb anyone. The idea of that had kept Brando up half the night.

"We need Emma if you want to give Christina the kind of wedding she deserves," he said, grabbing the door as it closed and putting his foot inside. "She's good at this. And I'm good at what I do—check yesterday's receipts from the café if you're not convinced. Let Emma handle the wedding, and I'll help you put together a restaurant concept that will have a month-long waiting list for tables and help you sell out your overnight bookings. And I'll help you find a chef to run it."

EMMA SQUARED HER SHOULDERS as she shuffled down to the kitchen bleary-eyed after setting the alarm early enough to get breakfast made and the baking started before everyone else was up. The rising sun had turned the tendrils of fog rising from the ocean opalescent, the island rising up like a pearl between it. She expected the kitchen to be dark and quiet, but as she opened the door, the wrought iron hurricane lamps were lit and her stomach purred in response to the scent of coffee and sausage. Brando, frying eggs at the stove, stopped and turned as she entered, and Kenver and Janet looked up at her over the steaming cups they held. All three of them said "good morning" at once, their smiles too broad and their voices too bright.

"Good morning," Emma replied, trying to keep her stomach from twisting itself into knots, trying to keep her cheeks from burning.

But of course they knew. Brando must have told them.

She felt sick when she found him watching her, his hair glinting gold in the lamplight and wearing a pale green T-shirt that made his skin look bronze. "I'm sorry," she said to no one in particular. "I know the engagement being off is going to be uncomfortable for everyone. If you want me to leave, I'll obviously understand. I'll call the water taxi and be out of your hair. But please consider letting me stay. I know you're in a bind, and I was thinking—"

"Emma, stop. First, don't you dare apologize." Janet set down her cup and crossed to Emma, holding out both arms and grasping her by the shoulders to look her in the eyes. "What's between you and Treave is between you and Treave. We're the ones who are sorry. Are you all right?"

Kindness always brought stupid tears, and Emma really wasn't going to lie to them. Any of them. "I wish I hadn't hurt him, and that's one of the reasons I'd like to stay. So I can find a way to fix things with him, provided he'll speak to me."

"I'll have a talk with him myself. I'm sure we can work things out." Kenver opened a drawer and pulled out forks and napkins as Brando brought plates of eggs and sausage and crisp fried bread to the worktable. "Actually we—Janet and I—have a proposition for you. We'd like to hire you to plan Christina's wedding, if you're willing. Dena Libby will be back to work today with Nessa, and with the ferry and the water taxi running on schedule again and things back to normal, the café should run more smoothly. But Brando has offered to help us put together a concept for a fine dining restaurant here, and we'd love to lay some of the groundwork for it with the wedding celebration. Isn't that right?" He cast a guarded look at Janet.

Janet, holding the cup of coffee between her palms, brought it to her lips and blew the steam away. "I haven't been exactly fair to Christina about the wedding, if you must know. There were things she wanted that Gwen—that I—talked her out of doing. Might be too late for a lot of what she had in mind, but if you could . . . Whatever you can do to make sure she has something special for her wedding day, we'd be grateful. It would give us all something joyful to think about instead of focusing on the tragedy."

A bubble of excitement swelled in Emma's chest. She managed to squelch it down. "I'd love to help, and of course you don't need to hire me. Pay me, I mean. I'm only starting out with the catering, and you're friends."

"Nonsense." Kenver's smile didn't quite mask the gray tiredness in his face. "The fact that we're friends only means we're not going to take advantage of you. Janet can find you Christina's notes about plans and guests and so forth, and I'll have Perran ring you so you can have a good background before you speak with Christina. Maybe throw together some ideas to get her excited again, if you would. I know she'd wanted to use the tower or the winery for the reception instead of the banquet hall. See if you think that might work? Of course, we'll give you whatever help you need."

"So will I," Brando said, bringing Emma coffee with the perfect amount of milk.

It had to be his doing—all of this, and the bubble in her chest pushed up into her throat. She met his eyes, and they were warm and serious and full of questions.

"Thank you," she said, intending the words to encompass far more than caffeine and breakfast.

"You're welcome." He smiled down at her, offering more warmth, more kindness.

Emma's thoughts swirled suddenly in her brain like alphabet soup until she couldn't pull out a single coherent one. Except the fact that Brando had kissed her, and she had kissed him back, and if she was completely honest with herself, which she really didn't want to be, she wanted to kiss him back again. Right that moment.

Which absolutely could not happen.

Brando cleared his throat and picked up his own plate from the worktable, and Emma swallowed her discomfort and cut a piece of sausage. While Janet and Kenver smiled and lapsed into an animated conversation with each other about wine shipments and the number of guests arriving that night, Emma allowed herself to start thinking about what a wedding at the castle could look like. Not the kind of wedding that might grace the society pages with a bride in an expensive dress going down the aisle in St. Levan's chapel. The kind of celebration that was as fun and fierce and brave as Christina herself.

There was no sense letting herself get excited about any of it, though, not yet. She still had Treave to think about, and whatever Kenver had said about talking to him, it wasn't up to Kenver. Emma needed to be the one to tell Treave herself that she was staying.

BURIED WOUNDS

*"When you wish to obtain some concession
from a man's self-love, you must avoid
even the appearance of wishing to wound it."*

ALEXANDRE DUMAS,
THE COUNT OF MONTE CRISTO

E MMA MADE TREAVE'S FAVORITE *kouign-amann*, the
caramelized, puffy Breton pastries he'd once brought
back for her from a New York bakery. She'd called him in
desperation after a sleepless night with Evangeline, not
knowing that he was out of town. But he'd hopped on the
first train to DC and taken a cab straight from Union
Station, then sat with Evangeline while Emma ate,
showered, and changed into fresh clothes. Somehow, he'd
even coaxed Evangeline to sleep. It was those moments, so
many of them over the years, that Emma thought of as the

hours ticked by in the kitchen and Treave didn't come down to eat.

Forty minutes before the first ferry was due, she poured a cup of coffee and arranged three of the pastries on a plate. Penny the border collie bounded toward her on the stairs carrying a half-chewed sneaker, followed by twin pairs of pounding feet. Emma jumped aside, trying to keep the coffee from spilling over.

"Catch Penny," Jack called out. "Don't let her get away."

"Penny, sit," Emma ordered, debating the merits of stepping in front of the dog. But the stairs were carpeted, and the shoe was clearly dead already. She wasn't surprised when Penny gave her an almost amused "are-you-kidding-me?" look and barreled past without so much as slowing.

The boys were less amused, and she mumbled "Sorry" as they darted past her.

"Mum'll throttle her," Cam said over his shoulder as he raced past wearing one shoe and a dirty sock.

"You mean she'll throttle *you*," Jack said. "That's the second pair of shoes this month."

Having seen Janet in action, Emma wasn't entirely sure the boys were joking, but she found herself smiling as they disappeared around the corner. Shaking off a drop of warm coffee from her hand, she climbed the rest of the way to the third floor where she found Tamsyn beating a threadbare brocade curtain in the window alcove with a stick and coughing in the resulting dust. Nearly tripping over the old fashioned vacuum cleaner sprawled like an octopus of hoses and tubes along the floor, Emma paused to ask if Tamsyn had seen Treave come by.

"Haven't seen him all morning," Tamsyn said with another hard whack of the stick. "Must be sleeping late. Or sulking. Ridiculous either way, and making work for them as got no time for extra work."

"Maybe he's not feeling well," Emma said. "I know he was up very late."

Worried now, Emma continued to Treave's door and knocked. "Treave? Are you in there? The ferry'll be here soon, so I brought you breakfast."

Beyond the door, there was silence, but it was impossible to tell if it was the silence of an empty room. With Tamsyn watching her from down the hall, looking like a demented nun in her black scarf and clothing and the long beating stick in her hand, the whole third floor felt brooding and more ominous. Even the temperature had dropped enough to make Emma shiver.

After knocking a few more times, she stooped to set the plate and cup beside the door. "I'm leaving the food out here for you since I need to get back," she said. "Will you please come and see me later, Treave? There's something I need to tell you."

"What did I tell you?" Tamsyn asked, nudging the vacuum cleaner over with her foot as Emma came back toward her. "You ask me, you're well rid of that one. Take my advice and leave here while you can. He's never taken well to being crossed."

"He's not like that," Emma said.

"He's exactly like that. People don't change," Tamsyn said, pushing a loose strand of iron gray hair beneath her scarf. "Not in their essentials, down deep in the parts they try to hide. They only get better at hiding what they really are. You ask Kenver about his electric car, or Perran about that fancy computer building block set he got for Christmas. Found them both at the bottom of the well, didn't we? The spirits told me, and he said I was a crazy old woman. Said I'd put them there myself. You tell me what it says about a lad who'll do that to his brothers' things because he's not old enough to play with them himself. 'Course, there's worse as well, innit? You ask Perran when he comes home. He'll tell you."

Feeling itchy beneath her skin, as though disloyalty were a rash she wanted to brush away, Emma still couldn't manage to keep Tamsyn's warning words from echoing in her head. She'd seen already that rumors flew around the island at the speed of light, so it wasn't surprising that the news about the broken engagement had gotten around so quickly. It was possible, too, that Tamsyn already knew about Emma catering the wedding. With Tamsyn and Gwen Nance apparently friends and staunch allies, the warning might have been nothing more than a way to keep Emma from changing what Gwen had already set in motion. Or there could have been a hundred other reasons. Anyway, Treave had told her himself that there'd been competition between him and his brothers.

It worried her more that no one had seen Treave that morning. But as the family trickled in for lunch later, Janet mentioned that he was taking the tours around the same as he had the day before.

"Does he seem all right to you?" Emma asked, leaning her hip against the table in the kitchen garden where Janet had taken a few minutes to eat with the boys while Penny thumped her tail against a chair leg.

"Surly," Janet said, "and full of himself. Which is to say the same as always."

Jack, who was busy spearing the tips of two cooked baby carrots on his front teeth to pretend he was a vampire, rolled his eyes. "He said he vas vanting to learn to fly."

"You saw him this morning, too?" Emma asked.

"Not this morning," Cam said, kicking his brother beneath the table.

Emma studied them both suspiciously, but Jack threw one of the carrots to Penny and the other behind the nearby topiary where Shipwreck lay on his side in the shade with only the tip of his tail moving faintly.

Cam rolled his eyes. "Cats don't eat carrots, stupid."

"Do so. Shipwreck does."

"Does not."

A tour group cut through the kitchen garden on the way to the terrace overlook, but it wasn't one of Treave's "Insider" tours, merely one of the regular groups, thirty-odd visitors who'd paid the cheaper fares. A few elderly couples soaked in every word the guide was saying, while parents attempted to keep young children corralled as they tried to scatter down the paths. A few noticed the private table and turned to stare, so Janet gave a slightly flustered smile while the boys waved enthusiastically, scattering crumbles of cheeseburger pasty filling for Penny to hunt out among the gravel.

Emma made a concerted effort to stop thinking about Treave after that, because thinking about it wouldn't change the facts. Either everyone else was wrong about Treave, or she was. She hoped they were wrong.

Walking back into the kitchen filled with the warmth of bread baking and the sweetness of the honey balsamic beef filling and creamy chicken and artichokes bubbling on the stove, she set herself to work, determined to earn the chance that Brando was giving her. To take advantage of that chance and soak in as much as she could learn.

Treave was icily polite at dinner, edgy and nervous as if he couldn't bear to look at her. He was short-tempered with everyone else as well, and after she'd finished the last of the preparations in the kitchen before going to bed, Emma stopped one more time by his door and knocked.

"Treave?"

"Go away, Emma. I'm not in the mood," he said through the door.

"I just wanted to say that I'm sorry. I'll go if it's too uncomfortable for you—"

"And if I say yes, then I'll look like a proper tosser, won't I?" There was a brief silence before he continued. "Look, just give me a while. I'll get over myself eventually. I'd just spent a lot of time imagining how things would be, and nothing's turning out the way I'd planned."

There wasn't much Emma could say to that apart from

another brief, "I'm sorry," and over the next day as they all settled into a routine, she watched him, trying not to push too hard, but also trying to get back to something close to their old friendship. He just seemed more and more tired, less like himself.

Worried, she brought it up to Brando as they were sitting together and going over the menu for the next day's lunch. "Do you think I should try to talk to him again?" she asked. "I hate seeing him like this."

Brando clicked the pen several times before he answered. "What do you think you could say that would help at this point?"

"I don't know." She'd been wrestling with the idea that she'd have to reconcile herself to *not* being friends with Treave, to possibly never seeing him again once she left the island. To having him continue with the rest of his life resenting her and to having the last four years of her life vanish with no trace at all, nothing good to show for it.

"You can't make anyone forgive you, love," Brando said, brushing a finger gently across her cheek. "As much as we'd all like to have a magic wand to make that happen. Half the time, being able to forgive someone isn't about what they've done to us anyway. It's something we can't let go inside ourselves. Treave will be all right, or he won't. There's nothing you can do to change that."

Nodding glumly, Emma put her head down and for a day and a half, she made herself concentrate on the things she could control, wedding plans and making notes about the recipes Brando showed her, making notes about all the things he did without explaining: the way he lined his worktable with plastic wrap, the way he seasoned and tasted a dozen times through the cooking process, the way he finished tomato sauce with butter and cream sauce with a hint of acid. He shifted between the cutting board and the stove in a choreographed dance, every movement graceful and deft, entirely comfortable within his skin.

It made her feel even guiltier to realize how much she enjoyed watching Brando work. Guiltier because, as much as she told herself her interest was entirely professional, the way he made her feel reminded her too embarrassingly much of the feelings Evangeline had written about. The feelings Evangeline had chased like a mirage all her life. Somewhere, wherever she was, Evangeline was probably laughing herself sick over this, preparing an entire book-length treatise of I-told-you-so's.

For Treave's sake as much as her own, Emma squashed the feelings down. Or she tried to. Somehow, they must have been visible, because Treave watched her and Brando during meals with a wary, sullen expression that made her feel even more self-conscious. And he wasn't sleeping. She heard him pacing, moving around his room late at night and early in the morning restlessly. Hating the idea that she had done that to him, she told herself the kind of hungry excitement she felt around Brando didn't—couldn't—last anyway. It didn't matter. Hunger and heat were only hormones. Her own hormones responding to the fact that Brando was the most *male* male of the species she had ever met. And probably every human female on planet Earth responded to him in the exact same way. She'd seen Winnie, Bren, and Dena all watching him moon-eyed behind his back.

Sending her knife flying with satisfyingly emphatic thumps through the slabs of butter she was cutting to make a Swiss buttercream meringue for Christina's coming home on Thursday, she told herself she didn't mind that at all.

"Easy there with the knife, love," Brando said, coming up beside her, cradling a spoon with a bit of the sauce that he'd been cooking. "What'd that butter ever do to you?"

Emma glared down, as if it was the butter's fault that it was too weak to stand up to aggression better. She finished the last slices more gently and scraped them back into a bowl. "I want to get this frosting done for Christina's welcome home cake and check the carriage house again before dinner."

"Taste this for me first. What do you think?" Brando asked.

"Another of the signature dishes?" Emma asked, stepping closer.

"Potentially. I don't know why, but this Angevine white has been harder than any of the other wines to work with."

"You don't like it?"

"It's fine. A good wine. Not stellar yet, mind, but the winery is young yet. The ciders are better actually, really good." Brando cupped his hand beneath the spoon, watching Emma as she leaned forward and took a sip.

It was professional interest on his part, and she was a professional. Or trying to be. Only it was hard to concentrate on the flavors instead of the disconcerting fact that Brando stood toe-to-toe with her, watching her lips as she tasted. And it was only in the professional sense—absolutely—that the sauce left her yearning for a little bit more than the delicate flavors of mussels and cream and wine and leeks.

"It's good," she said.

His mouth quirked. "Good like the wine good? Or good *but...*"

"Very good, only not—maybe—good enough for a signature dish. Can I say that?"

"Aye. You can, if you'll tell me what you think is missing."

"More citrus. Something to kick up the lemony notes in the wine, but not juice—it doesn't need more acid. Something unexpected." She grinned suddenly, because she loved those moments when inspiration came like magic. "There are marigolds in the garden, and the petals would look spectacular with the mussel shells."

"They would." He held her eyes, smiling, and it felt like there were two conversations going on, one about food and a wordless one in a language she didn't speak.

He walked her as far as the garden later when she went out to the carriage house, and as he stooped to pick a few frilled saffron-hued heads of marigold, she glanced up at the square tower at the far side of the castle.

"Do you think people can change?" she asked. "Deep down in their essentials?"

Brando stood up quickly. "Changing for the worse is

easy. People slide into that without realizing they've done it. Changing for the better requires the desire to change, and understanding why you need to. Understanding why you have to for survival, sometimes. Even then it's hard."

"And selfishness? Self-absorption?" She bit her lip. "Are those born in you?"

"In me in particular? I hope not."

"You know what I mean."

He sighed, stepping closer. "Tell me, what did Treave say to you in the kitchen the other day after he overheard us? Is that why you broke up?"

She turned and leaned her hands against the wall that overlooked the terraces and the surf-topped sea while the wind at her back whipped the hair she'd caught back in a ponytail against her cheek. "It was hard for him, growing up with two older brothers and not feeling like he belonged here."

"The way he's always talked, he thinks he belonged here more than anyone. None of us had perfect childhoods. I don't imagine you did either, but I don't see you nursing old wounds and hoarding grudges."

Emma fought down the sensation of standing at a dizzying height, about to fall. Because in some ways, wasn't that exactly what she was doing? "Maybe we all have to nurse old wounds when a parent dies," she said. "First we have to recognize there are wounds we've tried to bury. I imagine that takes a while for some."

"Could easily take a decade," Brando said, speaking very quietly. "And it could be, it makes a difference if the parent had old hurts themselves they'd allowed to fester. The wounds we inherit are the hardest ones to heal."

SCARS AND GRACE NOTES

"Blemishes on the beauty of a person one loves
are like grace notes adding something to a piece of music."

WINSTON GRAHAM
THE BLACK MOON

THEY DIDN'T DISCHARGE CHRISTINA until late in the afternoon, but since it was a special occasion, Janet let the twins stay up to eat with the family in the small dining room behind the banquet hall. So long, she said, as they were on their best behavior. The way Cam and Jack interpreted that instruction included using mussel shells as improvised slingshots with Penny playing catcher.

Treave, his mood oddly brittle, egged them on instead of discouraging them, which Emma didn't understand. Then again, she hadn't understood a lot of what he'd been doing lately.

"Boys!" Janet emerged from the conversation about wedding guests to give them a threatening look. "That's enough! If I have to tell you again, you'll go to bed without the rest of your dinner. *And* there'll be no boat, no beach, and no electronics tomorrow. Are we clear?"

"Yes, Mum," Jack said, dropping the mussel shell back beside his bowl and trying to hold back a cheeky grin.

Janet glared at them both until Cam, too, picked up his fork and made an exaggerated show of eating quietly, then she turned to Treave who sat across from her. "I can't send you to your room," she hissed, "but I wish I could."

"They're boys, Janet. I'm only keeping them entertained. Where's the fun in having all of us talking about the wedding?"

"Not everything in life is fun. You're a grown man, not a child."

A draft invaded the room as if the temperature responded to Treave's anger, but he only sat still a moment and then smiled at her. "Point taken. I'll leave them both to you."

He dipped his chin and Emma felt torn between sympathy and anger—at him and Janet both.

Kenver placed his hand over Janet's and turned back to the twins. "Find anything interesting in the tide pools today, boys?"

"There's still nothing from the shipwreck. There was only a mermaid's purse with a dead cat shark in it," Jack said. "A big one. I split the sack open."

"Tell me it was already dead before you did that," Janet

said.

"Already stinking. But it would have been ready to hatch. Nearly."

Cam made a face. "I saw a *live* blue shark swimming off the far end of the cove."

"It was only the dolphin," Jack said.

"You don't know. You didn't see it."

"Boys," Janet said in a warning tone, watching them until they settled back down, then returning to the wedding discussion while they kicked their chairs and nudged each other through the turbot course and meat. They were half asleep by the time Emma and Dena brought in the cake, and the staff and family gathered around Christina's chair.

Christina clapped as Emma set the cake in front of her, three tiers of pale icing that Emma had rimmed with yellow satin ribbon and a cascade of fresh pansies and carnations that she had brushed with egg whites and dusted with decorating sugar. "You made this? This afternoon? Emma! It's brilliant."

Emma handed her the knife and slid the stack of dessert plates closer. "Perran told me you like lemon and raspberry, so I thought I'd test out the recipe in case you might like it for the wedding. But if you don't like it, we can do a different flavor. And a totally different design and decorating style. Whatever you and Perran want. This was just simple to put together."

"Simple?" Christina said, laughing. "I'd love to see what you'd consider complicated." She winced and put her hand to her face as the laughter pulled at the stitches that ran from her hairline across her eyebrow and down the temple nearly to her ear. "But look, it's utterly perfect. The fresh flowers look magical the way you've used the sugar. We could do that idea with roses for the wedding, couldn't we? And maybe some of the rock sea lavender that grows up on the headland?"

Tamsyn sniffed loudly. "No one wants a mouthful of weeds they can pick up between every rock in St. Levan parish. All this mucking 'round, changing things." She sniffed again, even louder. "You'll make the spirits teasy and where will that leave us? A nice iced fruit cake's always been good enough for St. Levan weddings. And getting married on the headland? What's the point, when you've a perfectly lovely church where every good Nancarrow bride's been married?"

"Not every Nancarrow bride." Kenver's jaw hardened. "Not mine, certainly. And for this particular wedding, there's only one bride that matters. It's Christina's day, her and Perr's, and for all you are family, Tamsyn, and you always will be, it's time you worried less about the dead and more about the living."

The light from the electric candles in the chandelier overhead revealed every line and crevice in Tamsyn's face as she raised her chin. She looked old and tired, but she straightened her shoulders and took a deep breath, filling out the shapeless black clothing momentarily as though she'd filled them up with air. Then she released the breath between her teeth. "I worry about those need worrying about, and don't say I didn't warn you."

Turning abruptly, she walked out of the room with her back and shoulders stiff. Perran cleared his throat. "Wish I knew what to do with that woman. I love her, but I'd as soon throttle her half the time. Now you'd better cut that cake, hadn't you, Christa-belle? Looking at it's making me hungry all over again."

Christina gave him the knife and shook her head. "You cut then. Left-handed, I'd make a proper disaster of it."

Perran leaned over her, but instead of taking the knife, he helped to guide her hand as they cut the cake together. When the first slice was on the plate, he brought a forkful to Christina's lips. "I don't care about cakes or menus or where or when we get married," he whispered. "You're what matters to me. Having you home. Safe, smiling at me, and beautiful."

She pressed her palm against his cheek and kissed him. Fiercely. Tenderly. Which was how love was supposed to be, Emma thought. Christina hadn't tried to hide her stitches or minimize them, and she hadn't tried to postpone the wedding because of them.

Emma's throat tightened, full of admiration and a little envy as she passed around the remaining plates of cake, and she didn't look at Brando as she handed his serving over. She told herself the way her heart fluttered upward, nervous as a bird, when their fingers touched was purely because she wanted him to like the cake. Because she didn't want to disappoint him professionally.

He looked down at his plate while he chewed, then he raised his eyes and lifted his empty fork to his temple in a salute that made her feel lighter than the sponge in the cake. She picked up the last two plates smiling, and turned to hand one to Treave.

Something dark and desperate slid behind Treave's eyes, and he glanced at Brando then walked toward the door.

"Treave, wait." Emma set the plates down.

Janet caught her elbow. "Leave him. Don't let him spoil things with all his brooding."

"That's not fair," Emma said.

Janet crinkled her freckled nose. "Since when is life ever fair? Ask Christina—or Gwen and John, or Tamsyn. Or Nessa—anyone on the island. Hard is relative, and we all do the best we can."

"Speaking of which," Kenver said. "Treave, I've been thinking. Emma was right about using the carriage house instead of the tower for the wedding, but why couldn't we make the tower work as part of the restaurant? You tell me. You go to all the posh places. Can you see it?" He quirked an eyebrow at Brando for support. "I was thinking one or two tables per level, very exclusive. Private dining in Tristan's Tower. We could open the tunnel underneath that connects to the cellar by the kitchen, and we might need to put in cameras and figure out some logistics for the wait staff—"

"Far too expensive." Treave paused beside the door. "Take my advice and get the winery and the B&B running smoothly before you go haring off into the restaurant business. I'll happily look over the marketing you've done already—"

"Marketing's Christina's job. You want to offer up a business plan or find us a way to get some additional funding, we'll be grateful for your help. But marketing's not your expertise," Perran said, his hand tightening on Christina's shoulder.

"I have a degree—"

"So does she. In marketing. Not international whatever the devil it is that you do."

"Stop it. Both of you." Christina reached up and squeezed Perran's hand. "It's the result that matters, not who does it. Marketing's one of the reasons I thought we might use the tower for the wedding. Tristan and Isolde are always good for the romantics, and I thought if the photos turned out, we could put together some wedding packages. And anniversaries, and mini-breaks. That would work perfectly using the tower for special romantic dinners."

"You could get four tables of two in, eight at most. And even if you filled every guest room at package prices, there wouldn't be enough overnight guests to fill two seatings, let alone three. You couldn't afford to hire the staff, never mind paying for renovations. On top of that, you'd have tables in the way of the tours through the tower."

Emma looked around at all the faces watching Treave: the twins, Dena and the staff, avid and horrified and gleeful as they drank the argument in. "The photos will be gorgeous up on the headland with the heather and the lavender in bloom," she said, trying to defuse the tension, "and we can find a way to include the tower. There are lots of ways we could incorporate marketing opportunities in the wedding, if that's what you want."

"Why not?" Treave scrubbed a hand through his hair. "Add even more work for you—for everyone. And more people milling around."

"What is it with you?" Christina spun in her chair to face him. "Either you see we need more marketing or you don't."

Treave stared back at her, his jaw working as if he couldn't choose what to say. Then with a last glance at Emma as if she'd betrayed him all over again, he slipped out through the door.

Christina heaved a sigh. "I'm sorry. We shouldn't have said that," she said to no one in particular. "Any of that. After the fuss he's made about wanting to sell this place over the years, it just makes me mad to hear him telling us what to do. I do realize he's only trying to help."

"He is. I think it's . . . Well, the headland is where he tried to give me his grandmother's ring. By the wishing stone," Emma said quietly, as thought that was an excuse as well as an explanation. "That's where I turned him down."

She said it hoping to make them understand, but maybe she was trying to understand herself. The way he was behaving made her keep forgetting that the engagement had never been real. For all that he'd thought—he'd seemed to *feel*—like it was real enough, she'd never agreed to marry him. She had to remember that. He wasn't being fair to her any more than she'd been fair to him. It was time to stop making excuses for him.

"I should go have a talk with him. Apologize to him." Perran squeezed Christina's good hand and bent to kiss her.

Kenver put an arm out to stop him. "I've done that—tried talking. All he did was work himself into more of a self-righteous snit like he always did. You go after him now, you'll end up yelling at him and only make things worse. It's growing up he needs. Time to realize he's not the only person on this island."

But Emma had given Treave time, and instead of helping, it was clearly making him feel more isolated. "I'll go," she said. "I'm the one he needs to yell at, and I'll yell back at him, and maybe when he and I have cleared the air, all of us will be able to breathe more easily."

She climbed the stairs to the third floor and found Shipwreck, tail lashing as though waiting for a mouse, crouched in the corridor outside Treave's bedroom. "What are you doing out here?" she asked, stooping to scratch the cat behind the ears. He straightened and rubbed himself against her shins, and she picked him up and rubbed his cheek while she knocked on the door.

"Treave? This can't go on. Let me in or I'm coming in without an invitation."

There was a long silence, then something banged beyond the door and Shipwreck's ears swiveled and his whiskers quivered. Eventually the door creaked open, and Treave stood there, half-dressed in dirty-streaked jeans and an equally dirty T-shirt, looking more disreputable than she'd ever seen him.

"New look for you?" she asked.

"I thought I'd walk down to the tide pools. I need to burn off steam."

"In the dark?"

"It's not that dark quite yet. Kenver and Perran and I used to go down with flashlights. I haven't been in eons, and the tide's still fairly low."

"Then I'll come with you. We really need to talk. Seriously talk."

He hesitated, staring at the cat instead of looking at her, and then he shrugged. "Fine. If you like. But you'd better change into something else. Knock again when you're all set."

He closed the door before she could answer, and she was left with the uncomfortable feeling that when she knocked again he wouldn't open. Setting the cat on the floor, she whispered, "Watch him, will you? Yowl or something if he tries to get away."

She threw on sturdier loafers, jeans, and a light jacket to break the wind. Not having had the foresight to bring a flashlight to Cornwall with her, she settled for her phone. Within five minutes, she was knocking on Treave's door again, not sure why her chest was tight while she waited for him to emerge.

"Are there many sharks around here?" she asked as she followed him down the stairs.

"None that are a danger to people," Treave said. "We see basking sharks and porbeagles occasionally, and the blue sharks migrate through here this time of year. Mostly it's smaller sharks. The egg cases—the mermaid's purses—from skates and dogfish sharks or cat sharks wash up sometimes, especially after a storm when the rough seas break them off the seaweed."

He led the way past the main stairwell along another long corridor, circling around to the square tower nearest the steps that led out to the headland. Halfway to the wishing stone, he unlocked a gate in the curtain wall and followed a narrow path along the top of the cliff, turning on a powerful flashlight as the trail began to descend toward the sea. Where the going was steepest or clambered over slippery rocks, he hung back and took Emma's hand, helping her navigate. But the wind blowing off the ocean ripped words away, and neither of them spoke much. Emma concentrated on keeping her footing until they had reached the narrow cove beyond the point of the island where a single tide pool large enough to swim in was surrounded by dozens of smaller ones.

"Janet and Kenver let the boys come down here by themselves?" Emma asked, more than a little shocked.

"Janet?" Treave laughed, and laughing, he looked suddenly like himself. More relaxed as he stood on the edge of the rocks while the incoming tide lapped in rising moonlight below him. "My brothers and I practically lived here in the cove and no one thought a thing about it. But times change. Janet would have kittens if anyone suggested the twins didn't need supervision. Alwyn Libby's not good for much with his head in the clouds half the time, but he's steady with a boat, and he swims like a fish so Janet trusts him. He's good with the boys. I've seen that myself."

"You're good with them, too." Emma climbed up to the rock beside him.

The sea shimmered, soft waves winking at the moon, while the lights of Mowzel and Penzance and Marazion glowed along the long arc of the bay. A handful of ships' lights dotted the horizon, distant and tenuous as mirages, coming and going from unknown places above the depths. It seemed endless to Emma at that moment, the sea, the sky, the future.

"Is something wrong, Treave?" she asked. "Something besides me, I mean. You haven't been yourself since you got here, maybe even before that although I was too wrapped up in myself to see it."

He turned to face her. "It's nothing. Your mother's death hit me hard. That and losing you. Losing everything."

"You haven't lost me, Treave." She sighed softly and then refilled her lungs. "You can't lose what you never had."

"In my mind, I was going to have it. Had it already. And then it was gone."

"Not all of it. We can still be friends, if you want to. I hope you want to."

"Wanting won't fix things this time." He shifted over and took her hand, his fingers cold against her skin. "You don't understand. I've spent my whole life looking ahead, looking for something better or different. The eternal optimist, that's me."

"You've never been an optimist."

"Only about the things I'd no right to be optimistic

about. I've made mistakes, Em. I can't come back from that. You don't know how much I wish I could."

"Now you're worrying me."

"Don't. It's not your fault. None of it. I really did love you, though. I didn't realize how much until it was too late already."

Turning away as something large jumped and splashed out in the cove, he shone his flashlight along the water then shrugged and turned the light onto the smaller tide pools, catching the scurrying of crabs along the rocks and the bright yellows and reds of starfish stranded by the tide. A small octopus slunk around the edge of the pool, trying to find darkness again among the rocks. He scrambled down to crouch along the edge of the pool, the back of his neck exposed and oddly vulnerable, and Emma stood and watched him, trying to decide just how worried she should be by what he'd said. But then he smiled up at her, looking entirely normal and unconcerned, and he gestured for her to join him.

"Forget I said anything just now, will you?" he asked when they were crouched side by side. "I was spouting nonsense. You and I will be all right. The one thing you know about me by now is that I always land on my feet somehow. Always do."

THIEVES IN THE NIGHT

*"We struggle to climb, or we struggle to fall.
The thing is to discover which way we're going."*

DAPHNE DU MAURIER
THE SCAPEGOAT

O N THE CLIFF ABOVE the tide pools, Brando stood
watching Treave and Emma. The wind blew his kilt,
and he huddled deeper into his sweater. Climbing slowly,
the moon wasn't full enough to do more than cast the gorse
and heather and bare, harsh rocks to shadow, but on the sea
the light was brilliant. Too much light.

Jealousy was one of the few knives he hadn't yet
wielded against himself, and it surprised Brando to discover
the depths to which it pierced into his chest. The way it
tore at him and twisted. The need to run down the cliff
path and drag Emma away was a physical ache that made

his hands clench. Wrestling with himself, he didn't hear the footsteps on the path over the sound of the waves beating at the rocks and the rush of the wind. Not until they'd nearly reached him.

Fists raised, he whipped around.

"Easy there." Kenver backed a step and put his hands up in surrender. "It's only me."

Brando dropped his guard. "Sorry. Wasn't expecting anyone."

Turning slowly, he went back to watching the two figures at the tide pools, and Kenver stepped around beside him. For a moment, the two of them said nothing more, only stood and watched together.

"You've fallen for her, haven't you? Don't envy you that in this situation," Kenver said eventually. Burrowed deep within the hood of the dark sweatshirt he'd put on since dinner along with a dark pair of jeans, his expression was impossible to read. Still there was an urgent tension about him that made it clear he wasn't out for an evening stroll.

"I don't suppose you came all the way out here dressed like a burglar to discuss my love life," Brando said. "What's going on?"

Kenver gave a surprised bark of laughter that quickly stilled. "Burglar's not too far off the mark. Don't suppose you've seen one wandering around the place?"

Now he had Brando's full attention. "A burglar? You're serious?"

"Possibly. I followed you when I heard you come

downstairs, but you seem to have been following Treave and Emma. Half the castle is creeping around, apparently, and I'm left no closer to catching the bloke than I was before."

"Isn't this better left to the police, then?"

"Don't know that anything's been taken yet." Kenver stepped back, out of view of anyone looking up from the rocks below, and swept back his hood with an impatient gesture. "I loathe this. Feel like an idiot creeping around my own home dressed like a second story man. Detest the whole situation."

"You do realize you're not making sense, don't you?" Brando stepped back as well and turned to face him. "No offense intended, mate, but if you've been drinking, you'll be wanting to ease up or Janet will skin you by slow, painful inches. After the time we had with our father, a drunk's the one thing she'll never tolerate."

"I'd guessed as much—not that she's ever come out and said anything. Doesn't talk about your parents much. Don't suppose you'd care to tell me about it."

It wasn't Brando's place to step into Janet's marriage. Not when it didn't seem to be broken, or at least, not very broken. "He drank, and he got mean, and he blamed everyone but himself for that. Janet, she tried to keep the family together," he said. "So tell me about this burglar? How can I help?"

Kenver turned his head sideways to look at him, considering in a way that clearly said he hadn't thought of asking Brando for help. But the moonlight only made the telltale signs of worry clearer on his lean, long face, and Brando could nearly see the mental gears grinding to a halt and shifting direction. "Wouldn't mind your opinion, to tell you the truth. D'you mind?"

"Not at all."

"We'd best get off the cliff anyway, before Treave spots us. He'd be livid if he thought we were spying on him."

"We are, though. *I* am."

"I'm not, thank goodness. The burglar's been here for three weeks, apparently. So that leaves both you and Treave safely out," Kenver said, and he turned and strode back up the path the short distance to the headland.

He swung himself over the gate without opening it. Brando followed suit, and as he landed on the other side, his eye caught on the prior bell tower and the wishing stone at the corner of it. If he'd thought there was a hope of any of them coming true, there were too many wishes he'd have wanted to make. About the past, most of them, more so than about the future. But that was the nature of wishes. A man could make his own future by working hard and dreaming hard and refusing to give up. As long as you were dreaming, there was always hope. When it came to the past, though, no amount of hope would change what you had done or hadn't done. No amount of regret could erase mistakes.

Kenver led the way down the steps to the garden, across the courtyard, and through the darkened kitchen. Instead of heading around toward the staircase, he wound through the narrow dimly lit corridor that led alongside the church and through to the rooms that were part of the public tour. When he reached the Map Room, he snapped on the lights and gestured for Brando to go in first.

The room, true to its name, held a collection of maps displayed on two of its walls, as well as additional rolled maps mounted on an antique rack tucked away in the corner. Bookcases that covered the full length of the far wall housed some of the more valuable books in the Mount's collection, and a pair of cabinets held valuable silver pieces and curios accumulated by eleven generations of Nancarrows at the Mount, including an Egyptian mummified cat in a gold sarcophagus. Velvet ropes kept visitors from getting too close to anything except the sealed display case that housed an illuminated Bible that pre-dated the Civil War, the sword that Lady Anne had carried while defending the castle after her husband was captured by Parliamentarians, and the dagger that Charles II had presented to the captain of the Mount before fleeing to the Scilly Isles to avoid being beheaded like his father.

"Looks like a burglar's paradise here," Brando said mildly, "if you don't mind my saying so. Lots of expensive things that wouldn't take much to hide. But you said nothing was missing?"

"Definitely nothing missing from here. It's not as vulnerable as you'd think, though. Which is why this is so odd." Kenver crossed the room to one of the cabinets and gestured at the floor, and Brando saw nothing there until he followed and looked straight down.

Stooping to get a closer view of the gleaming hardwood floor, he ran his thumb over several three-inch scrape marks so new they stood out pale against the rest of the darkly polished surface. Similar scrape marks were visible on the other end of the cabinet as well.

"Are you saying the burglar moved the cabinet away from the wall?" he asked, straightening to his feet.

Kenver nodded. "Tamsyn swears it happened last night, so I checked the CCTV footage in the security room, and the DVR's been reformatted and the backup footage has apparently been swapped out for the past three weeks."

"There's no one on duty at night?"

"Thought that was one way to save some money. There are cameras sweeping all the public areas and permanently mounted anywhere there's something valuable. And cabinets like this are all alarmed if anyone tried to open them. Two guards come in on the first ferry, along with the tourists. One does a sweep around while the other goes straight to the security room, runs a backup of the DVR system and files it in the box by date, then monitors the system as long as the gates are open. He didn't notice the backups were taking less time than normal."

"Because there wasn't much data to copy over?" Brando nodded. "So it's someone who isn't stupid. Could it have been someone hacking in?"

"Or someone who has the run of the place. Someone we trust," Kenver said morosely. "We're still doing the inventory to see if anything is missing, so I'm keeping it quiet until that's complete. I don't want to bring the police into it if I don't have to—that would mean notifying the Trust as well and getting the solicitors and the insurance agents involved. I'd like to know what we're dealing with before all that."

Brando stared down at the floor again, then walked around the side of the cabinet to have a look. He wasn't a detective by any means, and having barely scraped by for most of his life, he'd never had much worth stealing. But even as he had the thought, an image of Emma and Treave standing together in the moonlight at the tide pools caught him unaware.

"Do you mind?" he asked.

The cabinet slid on the hardwood with relative ease, and he started to run his hand along the back, then stopped. "The back's not alarmed is it? That's why they moved it? To see if they could get access from behind?"

Kenver nodded again. "That's my guess. Looking to see what the cabinet construction was like. Screws or nails would be relatively easy to remove, but they'd have to saw through this to get through, so maybe that's why they gave up."

"If they gave up," Brando said. "Could just be making plans."

"That's what I concluded. Tamsyn swears on her life there's been other things shifted around before this, prints in the dust, things not put back in their proper places. Of course, the second I question her, it's as likely to be spirits warning us of dire retribution over wedding cake and Christina's disdain for tradition." Kenver gave an exhausted grin. "So what would you do? If you were me?"

"Something more practical than calling an exorcist, I assume?" Brando slid the cabinet back up against the wall. "I'd get in guards for the night shift, get a more tamper-resistant CCTV system for at least the DVR portion of it, and I'd keep it all as quiet as I could."

"First two are already sorted," Kenver said. "It's that last bit that worries me. I don't want to risk spoiling things for Perr and Christina and the last thing Janet needs is anything more to worry about. But the extra security will be hard to hide."

He stepped back over the velvet rope and onto the narrow red strip of carpet where visitors were meant to walk. Crossing back into the darkened hallway, Brando couldn't help being aware of the weighted silence of stone walls that had stood against outside enemies for centuries. It had changed hands only when someone betrayed it from within.

"You should tell Janet," he said. "I didn't mean keeping it from her. She won't thank you for keeping her in the dark."

"Janet's both stronger than she knows and more vulnerable than she thinks. She's already got too much on her plate as it is." Kenver stopped inside the door of the armory, beside a suit of medieval armor that stood a half-foot shorter than himself and beneath the oversized family crest that loomed above him on the wall. "I know you resented us both for marrying so quickly, and you resented me for taking her away, but I love her. I make her as happy as she's capable of being. She couldn't bear thinking that she needs to suspect everyone she knows, every person staying under this roof. If I can spare her that, I will. That's what you do when you love someone. You trust and you protect, and you give them room to fly while doing everything you can to make sure that they don't fall. In her own way, she's done the same for you."

IN THE PRE-DAWN HOURS, the castle held a stillness that Emma had never experienced anywhere else. A waiting stillness, as if the structure held its breath in anticipation of the sleepers within it coming awake again, as if the walls themselves were lightly sleeping. The sensation put her on edge, and she jumped when Shipwreck slunk out of the shadows beyond her door as she let herself out into the corridor. She picked him up and carried him with her past the pools of light cast by the darkened lamps.

She wasn't sure about the rules about cats in a British kitchen, so she set him down in the courtyard and went back to look around for something to feed him. For lack of kibble, she brought him a scrap of fish and a bit of cream. "Don't get used to this," she told him. "I'll ask where they keep the regular stuff as soon as everyone comes down for breakfast."

The cat sat politely, tail curled around his legs, until she had set the two small saucers down in front of him, then meowed inquiringly as though asking for permission. Emma laughed. "It's all yours. Go ahead."

She went back in, put on a pot of coffee, and started baking. Humming out of mingled nervousness and excitement as she pulled the dough she'd set to proof the previous day out of the refrigerator, she wondered if she was crazy to even think of mentioning the idea she'd had in the middle of the night. And insane to want to try it. When Brando came in forty minutes later, though, she was glad of the sticky buttermilk cinnamon dough she was working into rolls as it gave her a chance to try to breathe away the feeling that hundreds of fluttering moths had taken up residence in her chest.

"You're down early," Brando said, smiling at her as he moved to the coffee pot to pour himself a cup.

His hair was still damp from the shower, the faint curl long enough in back to have wicked a damp streak between the shoulder blades of his T-shirt. Emma had seen plenty of shirtless men on the covers of her mother's books, had even slept with a couple in college on a semi-experimental basis, but she'd never particularly considered the shape of a man's back, or how deeply satisfying it would be to run her fingers over the ridges of a man's shoulders, slide her thumb down the length of his spine, trace her palms over the sides of a ribcage that tapered down to narrow hips. She'd never much considered the appeal of a kilt, but the way it moved as Brando moved, the way it suited him . . . She shook her head and chalked her thoughts up to another night of little sleep.

"Yes," she said. "I wanted to talk something through with you before everyone came down—I hoped you'd be down early."

He turned and leaned back against the table, nursing the cup in both hands as he brought it to his lips and blew on it. "Here I am, so—"

Yes, here he was, and it was harder to think with him there in front of her.

She scraped her courage together and took a breath. "I was talking to my mother's editor after the funeral, and she asked if I'd consider doing a cookbook featuring recipes related to Evangeline's books. Christina bringing up photos yesterday and her idea about wedding packages got me thinking. This whole place—everything about it—is romantic. A cookbook centered around the wedding could be great publicity for the castle and the B&B, even for the winery. We could do it together. Mix the recipes for the wedding with some of the recipes from my mother's books and some of the signature dishes you're working on with the castle wines and combine them all together. You'd get credit and royalties, obviously. We could call it 'Cooking up a Romantic Cornish Wedding.' Or something like that."

"It would be a lot of work." He'd paused with his head still tilted over the cup, watching her from beneath his lashes so that his thoughts were veiled.

Emma wiped her hands on her apron and came over to him. "As long as we get the photos as we prepare for the wedding, we wouldn't have to do the work on the actual recipes until after. We could work through email after we both go home. What do you think?"

She couldn't bear to look at him while she waited for his answer, and that in itself was a revealing fact. Funny how the mind played tricks, heaping motives on top of motives. Emma had pictured it all in the night, how much the cookbook could help Christina and Janet and the others, everyone on the island. How it could make the wedding business take off, bringing jobs that weren't dependent on tourism. Jobs for local seamstresses and cake decorators, carpenters even. But even as she had told herself that was why she liked the idea, she had felt an easing in her chest at the idea of not having to let this go, at least not yet. Simmering on the back burner of her mind was the small hope that she might keep hold of all this a little longer, the work, and Treave's family and yes, Brando, too, even after she flew back to Washington and an empty house that was no longer even home. That never had been home.

"What do I think?" Brando asked. "Come here." He set down his cup with a thump and reached for her. Hands at her waist, he drew her toward him, then cupped her cheeks in his palms and kissed her. "That's what I think. It's brilliant."

It was a kiss-and-run kiss, a brief, celebratory smack of lips to salute a good idea. Emma knew that even as he dropped his hands and drew back, but even as she was still registering the sensation of his mouth on hers, the same awareness flared in his eyes. He reached for her again, pulled her against him, lifted her up, spun her around so that she rested against the table and he could slide his hands along her back, along her sides, his thumbs grazing her breasts and setting her on fire so that she groaned and tugged at his T-shirt, freeing it from the waistband of his kilt until the soft skin beneath it was exposed and she could push upward to touch the bare slope of his shoulders, pull him closer. It was impossible to get close enough.

Then he went abruptly still. Footsteps scraped on the stone floor, barely audible over the thump of Emma's heart. Someone cleared a throat, and a male voice asked, "Mind if we interrupt?"

Relieved that it was Kenver's voice, not Treave's, Emma was able to breathe again. Momentarily. Because what on earth was she thinking? She buried her face briefly in Brando's chest, and he kissed her hair. Then he turned to face his sister.

HIDDEN DEEPS

*"Strange sometimes how easy bitter
words came, how hard the kind ones."*

WINSTON GRAHAM
DEMELZA: A NOVEL OF CORNWALL

L
UST AND SHAME WARRED in Emma's chest along with
something else, something softer and more crippling, a
feeling she suspected people invited into themselves in
place of lust, mainly because it seemed less shameful.
Because throughout history, that feeling had provided the
excusable excuse for so many, many sins.

She wasn't falling for Brando, she told herself sternly.
She couldn't be.

He excited her—of course he did. She had only to
look at him to realize he would have induced carnal feelings
in a nun on her deathbed. But falling for him? That was the

height of insanity, the sort of lunacy into which Evangeline had leapt headfirst her entire life, meeting someone and convincing herself she was in love, turning a succession of men into the heroes of her novels only to fall out of obsession just as quickly as she'd fallen in.

Pushing the word firmly away, Emma managed to keep her confusion tamped down while Brando had her explain the cookbook, first to Janet and Kenver, and then again later when Perran had come down to get a tray. Christina was supposed to have breakfast in bed and take it easy that morning, but she came downstairs the moment Perran told her, sweeping into the kitchen in a paisley satin pajama top that had obviously belonged to him and had one sleeve cut off to allow for her cast to slip through. The top was long enough that a pair of her own shorts barely peeked out from underneath, leaving her legs and feet bare on the cold stone tiles. Her short curls stuck up all directions.

"Do you mean it?" she demanded, stopping a foot from Emma and looking from her to Brando and back again. "Would you two really do a cookbook about the wedding?"

"If you want me to, I'll call the publisher and see if they'll agree. But I think they will. My mother set three of her books in Cornwall. We could come up with scores of recipes and include photos of table settings and recipes for a wedding breakfast and the rehearsal dinner, a bridesmaid's tea—all sorts of occasions. Then we take the photos in a way that will let you incorporate them into your wedding packages."

"Good as your pastries are, you're wasting your time cooking." Janet raised the pastry she was eating in a mock salute. "What did you say you studied at university?"

"Pre-med. Chemistry."

"Well, no wonder. Clever as you are, you should think about going back."

Emma froze. Feeling a familiar pressure building in her chest, she glanced over at Brando who'd gone stiff and red. She turned away, and it struck her all over again how a thoughtless word from someone you loved could cut with more speed and precision than the sharpest knife. How many times had Evangeline made the same sort of insidious belittling comment as Janet had made just now? After the funeral, Emma had wished she had stood up for herself with Evangeline, defended herself. Only now it suddenly hit her that it shouldn't have been necessary to defend herself. Why should you have to justify yourself to the people who were supposed to understand you? To support you? Why was everything about judgment and dismissal?

Her stomach twisting, she whipped back around to Janet. "There's nothing wrong with cooking—nothing *less* than being a doctor. Medicine is art as well as science and cooking is science as well as art. There were medicinal recipes cooked up in the kitchen long before there were drugs or surgeons."

"Still are in many parts of the world," Christina said.

"People think cooking is easy, but it takes understanding thousands of different ingredients and their properties, knowing what happens when you heat them, or cool them, or combine them. Cooking is chemistry and physics and psychology and pure backbreaking work done at breakneck speed, and your brother's here doing all that to help you. Because he loves you."

Janet set the unfinished pastry back on her plate. "Believe me, we all appreciate what you and Brando are doing. I didn't mean to offend you."

"I'm not the one you just offended."

In the light of the hurricane lamps and the sunrise that was coloring the sky above the window, every freckle on Janet's nose stood out as she went pale. She glanced at Brando and then slid a hesitant look at Kenver as though to gauge his reaction. He folded his arms and watched her.

Janet's hair was brighter than her brother's mahogany, but it struck Emma that while she had a redhead's temper, she didn't come close to having Brando's depth of passion. Not that Emma could see. Janet had the perfect life, two beautiful children, a husband who clearly adored her, a fairy tale castle to live in, and yet she seemed scared and bitter all the time, as if she was afraid that at any moment everything would be snatched away. And just like that, Emma's anger deflated as surely as if the thought had popped it with a tack.

Janet raised her chin. "I am sorry. Honestly, I didn't mean that the way it sounded, and Brando knows how proud I am of him."

"Do I?" Brando asked.

Janet's chin rose even higher, a pale, freckled battle

standard. "Of course you do—or you should. I am proud of you, but I'm not about to say it all the time, you great daft idiot. It'd go straight to your fat head and turn it."

Brando grinned. "You always did have a knack for flattery, didn't you? But I suppose we've both done all right for ourselves. Thanks to you."

"Is that a compliment from you? Well, I never thought I'd live to see the day." Then her expression shifted, went sober. "I should have done better by you," she said gruffly. "I could have."

He went over and wrapped his arms around her, dwarfing her like a bear. "You couldn't have. I gave you bloody awful raw material to work with—I was like aged beef; I needed time to rot, then the mold had to be stripped away."

"There's plenty of rot left on you," Janet said, laughing as she pulled away, "and that's enough of that now. We've all got work to get on with."

Christina pushed back from the table. "Yes, and Emma needs to make a phone call the moment her editor hits the office, don't forget."

"Slave driver," Emma said.

"Isn't that part of being a bride? I'm embracing my inner zilla."

Everyone laughed as they were meant to and the moment passed, leaving Emma uncertain whether she was more happy for Janet and Brando than she was embarrassed about having blown up like that. But at least she no longer felt guilty about having been caught kissing

Brando. Someone needed to kiss him. Someone needed to kiss the hell out of him.

Heading over to get another cup of coffee before she went back to work, she slid her fingers along his palm as she walked slowly past him, caught his hand and held it for an instant. Long enough to let him know . . . What? That she wasn't ashamed? That she wanted more? That she wanted *him*? That he was wonderful just the way he was? She wasn't exactly certain what she wanted to tell him, so maybe it wasn't words that needed to do the talking.

THE MORNING FLEW BY, partly because—at least as far as the work went—Emma felt less out of her depth with every passing day. Knives thumped against cutting boards, steam clouded the air above the stove, heat poured from the ovens, and the scents of pastry baking, meats roasting, and vegetables caramelizing filled her with warmth and a calm sense of certainty. The kitchen was the one place she didn't question herself. There wasn't time for it, and there wasn't any need, not when she could see the results and take pride in the way the food looked on the plate, the way it smelled and tasted. Brando stopped by to check what she was doing, smiling or offering a bit of advice, but just as often he called her over to taste something for him, or ask her opinion about a dish. He did almost the same with Bren and Winnie, a subtle way of teaching designed to instill confidence.

Bren and Winnie barely noticed. They chattered nonstop while they worked, sharing stories that Emma half-tuned out, then lapsing into an argument about the relative uselessness of Bren's latest boyfriend.

"He's better than Geoff, I'll give you that, but if he was a fish I'd throw him back," Winnie said.

"You only say that because you haven't been *fishing* since Christmas," Bren retorted. "Might be your standards could use some lowering."

"Good thing I like my own company fine, then, isn't it?" Winnie said, and she flounced off to deliver a cart of sandwiches and pasties down to the to the café.

The kitchen was pleasantly peaceful when she had gone so that it was almost a shock when the empty cart clattered suddenly back through the door and Winnie came running in behind it.

"Is it true?" She wedged the cart back into the corner behind the walk-in refrigerator. "Are we going to be in a cookbook?"

"A cookbook?" Bren's eyes widened, and she wiped her forehead with the back of her hand, leaving behind a streak of flour.

Brando looked up from where he was stacking cod fillets flesh side up into one of the large oven roasting pans. "Aye, it's true, if by *we* you mean the food we make for Christina's wedding will be in it. Provided you both want to

251

help with the food, that is."

"As if we'd miss it." Winnie washed her hands and went back to pick up a freshly-caught cod from where it lay on ice in a tray beside the small table that Brando had brought in beside the worktable. "Did Christina tell you she'd invited all the regular staff to sit down with her and Perran? We'll only be helping with the cooking early on, then she's bringing in wait staff and extra hands so the rest of us can be there for the toasts and dancing."

"That's lovely of her," Emma said, "and yes, although I'm going to call and confirm everything with the editor in a bit—there's a five hour time difference to deal with. Which is why I didn't realize we were breaking the news already."

Winnie heaved the fish down onto the newspaper-covered surface and picked up a heavy cleaver. "But Dena said they're sending a photographer."

"I'm *hoping* they'll send a photographer."

"And we'll be making up recipes to photograph for the café and overnight guests?"

"How does Dena know more about this than we do?" Emma blew a stray strand of hair out of her face. Then she caught Brando's eye and they both sighed simultaneously. "Tamsyn."

"Of course." Winnie nodded. "And did you know we have a burglar?" Her voice grew hushed, but no less excited than she'd been about the cookbook. "Tamsyn says he's been breaking in nights and 'casing the joint,' and any day now, he'll be murdering someone in their beds."

"'Casing the joint?'" Bren gave a whoop of laughter. "Been watching too much telly, that woman has. Burglars, is it? Are they alive or dead?"

"They're not good news either way, if it's true," Emma said, reducing the heat on the plum and rhubarb sauce she was making for Brando's cider-roasted pork belly. "What was taken?"

"Don't know, but Kenver's brought in two guards to patrol at night so it must be true," Winnie said. "Saw the guards arriving myself just now, and one of them's a handsome devil. Near as handsome as our own kilted chef."

Brando snorted and ducked his head. But he didn't ask any questions, and he hadn't commented at all.

"Did you know about this?" Emma asked him.

"Guards, huh? Excuse me." He rushed off to fetch more eggs from the cooler without looking at Emma, or anyone. Looking guilty. No, not guilty, because Brando wasn't a burglar, so if he was evasive it meant he knew something. A burglar? That had to mean one of the guests from the second floor. It had to.

Or so Emma told herself.

Except she couldn't help remembering Treave moving around in his room in the night, and the scrape of furniture, and Shipwreck sitting in front of Treave's room and staring at the door. Treave not wanting to have people milling about. The dirt on Treave's clothing.

Her fingers shaking, she forced herself to concentrate on getting the lid back on the saucepan without scalding more of her skin in the steam.

She needed to know what Brando knew.

Moving mechanically through the rest of the lunchtime preparations, she waited, debating what to do. Then finally Winnie set off to the café with the last of the hot food, and Emma and Brando finally had time to grab a bite themselves. She made up two plates and dragged Brando out to a bench in a far corner of the kitchen garden and sat him down, but he leaned forward and dropped a kiss on the tip of her nose.

"I haven't thanked you properly," he said.

"For what?" Emma pulled back, startled.

"For giving Janet a taste of her own medicine. I'm big enough to fight my own battles, but it was nice to have someone want to do it for me."

"Some battles you shouldn't have to fight on your own."

"True." He smiled. "But the shoulds and shouldn'ts of the world would fill entire libraries, and none of them change how people behave. Don't judge Janet harshly, though. If she's hard on me, she has her reasons."

"I shouldn't have said half of that to her."

He waved that away. "Now what is it that made you bring me out here?"

Emma handed him a ham and tomato chutney sandwich. "You weren't surprised about the burglar, and you said you didn't know about the guards, but you weren't surprised about them, either."

"It takes a bit to surprise me," Brando said, frowning at her lightly.

"That's not an answer."

Brando glanced up at Tristan's tower and seemed to be weighing what to say.

The day was full of sparkling light, light limning the tower, catching on the bits of quartz in the castle's stones and cobbles to make them shine, light reflecting off the metal of strollers and sunglasses as visitors explored the courtyards or picnicked at the tables set out on the pillow soft lawn of the upper terrace. Below, brightly colored boats moored in the harbor bobbed on the gentle waves, and beyond the sea wall, light glinted on the shallow water that hid the snaking causeway to the mainland that lay just beneath the surface.

Light and shadow and hidden depths. Too many hidden things.

"Brando, please tell me," Emma said.

He stared hard at his sandwich. "Why does it matter? The guards are here now."

"They weren't last night. I hate to think we could have been murdered in our beds."

"I'm five steps straight across the hall anytime you need protection. Or anything else."

His smile held mischief as well as something else. Hope and a sudden flaring of desire. Emma's breath caught as she looked back at him. Her cheeks heated, and for a moment, she saw herself taking those steps across the hall, stealing into his room in the middle of the night. It wasn't the first time she had imagined that, she remembered suddenly. Envisioned herself standing over Brando as he lay in bed, reaching for him, touching him. She wanted to touch him, to explore him. She shook her head as if that could shake the thoughts away.

She forced herself to concentrate. "Can you at least tell me if anything was stolen? Or why they think there's a burglar at all?"

He gave a sigh of resignation. "Look, they were still checking inventories, last I heard. It's possible nothing's been taken and Kenver's only being cautious. And now that I've told you that, tell me why you're so interested to know?"

"No particular reason." Emma bit her lip and glanced away. "Obviously, I hate the idea of someone creeping around here when everyone else is working so hard," she said, which was no less than the truth. That fact alone made it hard for her to suspect Treave, because he was working, too, and the things in the castle were all things he'd grown up with. This was his home.

Or maybe that was the problem. What if Treave was looking for things he felt entitled to take? Things he cared about, because it didn't feel like it was home for him any longer.

"What will the guards do if they catch someone?" she asked. "What does Kenver plan to do?"

"I don't know, but whoever it is has been clever up until now. The extra cameras and security will change all that, so there's no need for you to worry."

APPLES FALLING

"I am afraid you're some deceiver
That have come to charm me here
By the braes of Balquhidder..."

ROBERT TANNAHILL
"THE BRAES OF BALQUHIDDER"

I T TOOK EMMA FOUR phone calls and three times that many emails to set the cookbook plan in motion, and there would be more paperwork besides, including a partnership agreement between her and Brando that was going to require a lawyer. Or so Evangeline's agent warned her.

"Can't you just send over something standard? I don't care about the money."

"It's a lot of money. You should care, and *he* will, believe me. If not now, then down the road, and there are other things besides: who is going to do the bulk of the work, who is going to get first billing, how quickly you each have to respond to edits, how the recipes are tested. You'll need waivers from the principals at the castle, too, and all the staff."

Emma groaned. "Joanie, couldn't you just handle that?"

There was a hiss of breath across the line. "All right, I'll see what I can do. I do have another cookbook client who works with a partner, so let me see what they've come up with, and I'm sure I can find some standard waivers."

Sitting at the table in the kitchen courtyard, Emma hung up the phone and drew her knees up to her chin. It was all both simpler and more complicated than she'd envisioned, and despite what she'd said to Joanie Eldridge, a part of her—a small, vulnerable part—was petrified at the prospect of tying herself to Brando like this, of doing a book that relied on his reputation as well as her mother's. One impulsive decision, and she was working from the shadows again, lost in between like the filling between two slabs of bread someone had cut too thick.

"Penny for them," Brando said, coming up behind her as the kitchen door swung closed.

"I've never understood that phrase," Emma said, dropping her feet back to the cobblestones. "It's been around since the sixteenth century, so you'd think there'd have been some adjustment for inflation."

"Ah, and who's evading the question, then?" Brando sat down beside her. "Phone call not go well?"

"They want a legal agreement between the two of us."

"You know I don't care about that."

"Neither do I, but the agent and the publisher want to make sure we've settled all the possibilities in case something comes up later."

"That's not what's troubling you, though. Is it?" Brando half-turned and held her eyes. "Are you having second thoughts?"

"No, I want to do this—I'm going to. Only it'll be you and my mother . . . "

"And you've been wanting to stand on your own feet," Brando finished gently. "Prove something to yourself."

Emma barely breathed. "Yes."

"It's times like this when I wish I was better with words, or that fingers could reach beneath the skin. Trees do that, fuse their roots together and become one, but being only human we're alone even when we're with the people we love, and we can't make the insides of us naked down to the eight- or nine-year-old wounded child that's still there hiding away, afraid to come out and grow up and face the fact life isn't always fair or easy. And as long as that child is there hiding, it won't forgive the world for having hurt it, and it won't forgive us, either. So we can never forgive ourselves."

"I was twelve." Emma's voice came out steady, but inside she was shaking—with recognition, with truth, with fear. With the need to be a tree.

Brando's hand rested against his thigh, and her fingers slid over of their own accord, not quite close enough to touch, but close enough to feel the warmth. She let them, because it was impossible to stop, impossible not to need.

"It was stupid, really. I brought home a kitten a girl from school was giving away, and my mother told me to take it back. She was married then, husband number two, but she had one foot out the door already. Or maybe he did. Anyway, I was up in my room sobbing, and that kitten seemed like the most important thing in the world, like the one thing that was mine. Luz, our housekeeper, found me like that and told my stepfather, and he told my mother to let me keep it. I remember the way she turned to look at him, like he was dust she could blow off her shoe."

"Cats are filthy," Evangeline had said. "They poo and pee and eat and meow at you, wanting attention, that's all they do. I've got enough of that with Emma."

"Think of her happiness for once, can't you? She's your daughter," Mike had said.

"Happiness?" Evangeline had laughed. "What does she know about that? She doesn't have the capacity for it. Some people don't have a talent for living, and she's one of them. But you know what? You care about her so much, you keep her. Keep the cat for that matter. Keep them both." Then she'd calmly gone up and packed a suitcase and left, and when she sent for her things, she hadn't sent for Emma. Not until seven months later when she'd met the man who was going to be husband number three.

"She filed for divorce and left me with him until she decided she wanted me again, and I had the cat for seven months then had to leave her."

Brando turned his hand over and folded her cold fingers in his warm ones. "So you always felt like you had to be good or she would leave you again. Only you could never be good enough."

"And you?" Emma asked, shifting so that she could see him and satisfy the sudden need to memorize his features, the hollows of his cheeks, the pillows of his lips, the sharp, hard jawline, and the wide, kind eyes etched with smiling lines so that years from now if she thought about him, she wouldn't forget a thing about how he'd looked at this moment.

"I couldn't be good enough, so I tried the opposite," he said.

He looked back at her, and she couldn't look away. Goosebumps broke out on her skin, though it wasn't the least bit cold out. She didn't want to move, to take her hand away. Then he suddenly pushed back the wrought iron chair that looked too delicate to hold him. "Come with me, will you?"

"Where?" She stood up uncertainly.

"Anywhere. Out of the way somewhere, I don't know. I don't want to be interrupted—and that's a rare thing in this place."

THE LAST FERRY HAD gone and there was still dinner for the overnight guests to make, but Brando mentally reordered the work and was grateful Emma didn't argue. She followed him as he passed through the kitchen and snaked around the maze of corridors, but he wasn't certain where he was going, only that he wanted to get away.

The blasted place had people everywhere; Dena and Nessa still clearing up in the café, Kenver speaking quietly with one of the new security guards outside the control room in the southwest tower, workmen in the carriage house painting. He finally ducked through the entrance into Tristan's tower and, picking up Emma's hand to keep her from running off to go bury herself in work, led her up the full four flights of narrow steps.

He'd been up in that room a half-dozen times in the past days planning for the restaurant, measuring, thinking. Dreaming, though it'd been a long time since he'd allowed himself the luxury of dreaming. He and Emma were not so different in that respect, both of them running from themselves.

"I meant to tell everyone this morning," he said, "that I've had a few nibbles back already about potential chefs for the restaurant."

"Good ones?" Emma asked, stepping through the doorway.

"Could be."

He watched her as she turned to look around the room. It had been everything from a belfry to a lighthouse to a wartime lookout post, and now it was both empty and full of light. Full of enduring stone, wild air, and the legends that were whispered there for tourists. It suited Emma with her calm surface and her churning hopes, and the wild tangle of curls she tried to tame into a ponytail for cooking. Brando longed to pull her hair free, see it fan itself out around her as she danced with him, see it spread across a pillow. His own pillow. She made him feel possessive, uncivilized. Hungry.

Did he love her? His mind tempered the word even as his heart embraced it. He had no experience with love, he was coming to realize. Nothing like he felt for her, which was new, tentative, and so all-consuming that he was tempted to dismiss the burning heat of it as infatuation. But knowing that didn't make him want her less.

She turned to face him, and there must have been something of his thoughts written across his features. She blushed suddenly and, turning, crossed to the window at the far end that overlooked the sea. The windows were built to release the sound of the bell, high and wide and arched at the top. They were more vulnerable than arrow slits, but this high over the cliffs, an arrow couldn't reach them. Emma stood on her toes and leaned into the recess that was so deep her elbows outstretched on the cold stone width couldn't reach outside. He lifted her so she could look down into the gardens, and she caught her breath.

It was beautiful, all that sparkling water. Her.

"Makes me feel small being up here," he said, feeling the heat of her against his chest. "I've been fighting for and fighting over things that'll be gone in the blink of an eye, while all this rock and water will still be here long after the last footsteps on earth have faded into the dust. When Janet asked me to come to the wedding, I came thinking I could make peace with her, but I'm finding it's myself I've been at war against."

"Does that make it easier to find peace?" she asked.

He stepped back and let her down, keeping hold of her until her feet touched the floor again. "Makes it easier to see that the things that matter are the ones that we can't touch. Or buy. Love, responsibility, kindness . . . honor."

"What about happiness?"

"Happiness is an excuse too often. People chase it because they haven't got the pieces to make it for themselves."

"And are you happy, Brando MacLaren?" She turned to look at him, and he was still close enough that he could feel her breath warm the fabric that covered his chest, close enough that he could smell the jasmine in her shampoo and see the light catch the silk strands of escaping curls.

He tipped his head and smiled at her. "Could be I'm closer to that today than I've ever been. Will you come back to Scotland with me, Emma? Prove yourself there. With me. We can work on the cookbook easily, and I'll help you as much or as little as you like. My events manager is arranging bookings for the hotel, and you can take over the catering for them. Make that grow. Also Edinburgh's not far, and there's Glasgow and Sterling besides. Other hotels. Conventions, that sort of thing. And the glen would suit you. It's beautiful the same way you are, the kind of beauty that grows deeper the longer and closer you look at it."

Emma stared at him, studied him, then ducked beneath his arm and leaned against the wall. "Why?" she asked. "Why would you want me to come? I don't delude myself that I'm that good a chef, and you haven't known me long—"

"That's precisely why. I want us to have time to get to know each other." He looked down at his hands, and they suddenly seemed too large and clumsy. Hamfisted. His heart beat like bird's wings, churning blood and oxygen and thoughts so fast he felt like he was in danger of losing everything.

"There are things I could tell you," he admitted. "Things I probably should tell you, but whatever I feel, whatever I hope you're starting to feel, we ought to take it slowly. Without pressure. I want you to be certain of me. I'm no saint, Emma. I've done things. Some I've paid for and some I haven't, but my father was a drunk and a cheat, and when things were hard, he'd settle the blame on others. Apples don't fall far."

"Some do," Emma said, watching him from beneath her lashes. "If they want to."

The way she looked at him, as if she had no doubt,

unmanned him. Gave him hope. Because doubt was the one thing—sometimes the only thing—he'd always had in abundance.

"Aye, well," he said, shaking his head faintly. "Like I told you, you don't know me yet. I was eight the first time I got pissed enough to fall into the loch, and there was the smoking and the fighting besides. Never did have much sense. And I already mentioned the bicycle, right? Then the night before my parents died, my cousin Brice and I decided to see if it was possible to tip a cow—he'd only just seen *Tommy Boy* on the telly, and we argued because I said he was daft to believe you could tip a cow."

Emma laughed, and the sound rang through the room that had been made for sound to ring. It was a sweet sound, and it warmed Brando, made him want to make her laugh.

"And can you tip one?" she asked.

"Don't know." Brando turned and dropped down to sit beneath the window. "We might have found out that night, if it had been an actual cow we tried to tip instead of Davy Griggs' prize Highland bull." He gave Emma a sheepish grin, but that faded quickly. "One concussion and a broken arm later, my parents argued all the way home from the hospital, and then Dad got to drinking and Mum said she'd had enough. And Janet, because she'd always been the one who tried to keep the peace between them, talked them both into seeing a marriage counselor. Coming back from Edinburgh in the rain on the dark, slick road—well, they didn't come back. That's the long and short of it."

Emma's expression had gone still with shock. Then

she knelt down in front of him and took his face between her hands. "That wasn't your fault, the fact that they were killed. You know that by now, don't you? You were ten— and Janet was nineteen. She probably blamed herself, too. And neither one of you was responsible."

Her hands were as soft as her eyes, and Brando couldn't resist. He pulled her down and kissed her the way she was meant to be kissed, the way he'd been wanting to kiss her. Loved her the way she was meant to be loved. Her fire seared his lips, and he drowned in her response, the sweet, trusting openness that reached for him even when sanity intruded and made him think to stop. He laid her on his kilt, her hair tangled and fanning around her face, and when he rested on his elbows above her, spent and alive and filled with joy, she smiled up at him.

"Come to Scotland with me," he said to her. "Come and remind me that I'm better than I feared, and I'll remind you that you're better than you hoped. And when you're ready to hear it, I'll tell you that I think I'm falling in love with you. If fate is kind, you'll love me back someday. I can be patient until then."

LEARNING TO FLY

*"My will had gone and I feared
to be alone, lest the winds of circumstance,
or power, or lust, blow my empty soul away."*

T. E. LAWRENCE
SEVEN PILLARS OF WISDOM: A TRIUMPH

E MMA PULLED TREAVE ASIDE as everyone left the dinner
table. "Can I talk to you a minute?"

She held back while the others filed out of the room,
and Treave turned to her, frowning. Still frowning, still hurt
and angry because, no matter how carefully Emma and
Brando had tried to hide what had happened between
them, Treave had seemed to sense it almost the instant
they'd all sat down together at the dinner table. Everyone
had sensed it and pretended that they didn't.

Treave waited until they were alone before he spoke.

"What do you want, Em? I'm tired, and I have calls to make. Clients. Work."

"Just give me a few minutes, that's all I need." She shook her head. "It's not about us, that's not all of it. Whatever you're doing, it's dangerous."

"What I'm doing?" He stepped closer and lowered his voice to a whisper, "What are you talking about?"

"I've heard you moving around in your room at night," she whispered back. "I haven't said anything to anyone, but if you're the one who's been sneaking around, you're going to get caught. You have to—"

"I have to what?" Treave caught her by the shoulders. "It wasn't enough for you to humiliate me, reject me—for *him*? Now you're accusing me of trying to steal from my own family?"

"I never said that. I don't know what you're doing, only that I'm worried."

"So you're accusing me of something without even knowing what that is." With a humorless laugh, he bent down to her. "Keep to cooking, Em. You're not cut out for intrigue. And for what it's worth, I can smell him on you. Not looking at him, not talking to him? That was a dead giveaway. Did you think about me at all while you were . . . While the two of you—?"

His hands shook on her shoulders, and he dropped them to his sides. As if he couldn't bear to look at her, he stared past her to the painting on the wall. "Just leave me alone, Emma. Mind your own business and leave me alone. You don't have any idea what you've done to me, and believe me, I've had about as much as I can bear."

Emma slumped against the wall as her legs gave out. He strode out of the room and she stood looking after him. "I'm sorry," she whispered, though of course he couldn't hear her.

Except she wasn't sorry. She couldn't be. Not for everything.

Maybe it was illusion, but now that Treave had said it, she imagined that she could smell Brando on her skin. Her cheeks went hot at the memory of his hands, his lips, of spinning out of control on his kilt, her nails buried into his back as though she could fuse herself into him as close as she needed him to be. She'd never felt that before, never suspected she *could* feel it. Letting go, letting herself feel and breathe and touch and *be*, losing herself . . . She'd felt free for the first time in her life, as if in letting go, she had finally found herself.

None of this was fair to Treave; she knew that. And none of it was simple. Brando was anything but simple. He was two hurricanes dancing together, all wrapped up in that body. That strong, gentle, beautiful body that made her have feelings and hopes, that made her set aside common sense and caution.

Scotland? Even thinking about *that* was madness. How could she not think about it?

First, though, she had to set things right with Treave. She had to keep him from doing anything stupid and hurting the people who loved him. She'd hurt him enough already.

BRANDO DUCKED BACK IN the doorway at the end of the corridor as Treave emerged from the dining room. He needed to get back to the kitchen to finish the prep for the next day, and there was baking they'd left undone while he'd dragged Emma away. He didn't regret a moment of that, but he hated that she felt responsible for hurting Treave. Hated it more because guilt weighed on him, too. He'd set out to steal her away, and now that he'd won, he could imagine all too easily how it would feel to lose her. The thought of losing her was a sharp knife to the chest, and it kept him standing in the doorway, waiting for her to emerge from the dining room so that he could see her expression and make sure she was all right.

No matter how much she'd tried to reassure him, he didn't trust Treave's temper. He didn't trust Treave with Emma.

She stepped into the corridor. Her face was as pale as the moon in the dim light, and she paused on the threshold as Treave disappeared around the corner down at the far end of the corridor. The lost way she looked after Treave, the hunched, defeated set of her shoulders, balled Brando's hands into fists and pushed him from the doorway.

"You all right?" he asked, hurrying toward her.

She startled, her brown-amber eyes enormous and vulnerable as a doe's. "I should go after him," she said. "I knew I'd hurt him, but—I really hurt him badly, Brando. I didn't realize how badly."

"Going after him won't change that, and blaming yourself won't change it, either." Brando pulled her against him and laid his chin against her hair, trying to stop her shivering. "People can't love to order. The human heart isn't made for that. You've been friends a long time and that friendship means a lot to you both, but you can't force him to forgive you, and he shouldn't blame you for the way you feel."

"He can blame me for what you and I did. He knows we did it, and it hurt him."

Brando felt the knife of guilt dig deeper. "Aye, and I'm sorry for his pain, but not for making love to you. I won't apologize for that."

She drew back and smoothed her hair. "I need a few minutes. I'll meet you back in the kitchen."

"What are you going to do?" he asked.

"Try to clear my conscience, if I can."

TREAVE DIDN'T ANSWER WHEN Emma knocked on his door. Shipwreck was crouched in front of it again, his ears flat and the tip of his tail lashing back and forth, and after knocking six or seven times, Emma picked him up out of pure frustration and pulled him to her chest. "You really need to find a smaller mouse, puss," she said. "Treave is a bit outside your weight class."

Not that Treave appeared to be coming out of his mouse hole.

"Treave, you can't just hide in there and ignore me." Emma knocked again, louder this time, then tried the door and found it locked. "Look," she said, "I understand that you're upset and mad at me, and I can't blame you. You're worrying me, though. Let me in and let's talk this through. I'm not going to go away."

There was still no answer. She laid her ear against the door, but there was no sound, and she had a sudden odd image of Treave standing perfectly still on the other side of the door, listening. Refusing to open. Punishing her the way Evangeline had so often done, withholding, withdrawing, scaring, manipulating. Doing whatever she needed to do to wear Emma down until she agreed to do whatever her mother wanted. Why Emma was confusing the two suddenly, she couldn't have said, unless talking about Evangeline with Brando had blurred the lines of pain in her mind until she was projecting her mother onto Treave. Her mother, too, had hated to be humiliated, to be rejected.

The realization settled a heavy ball of ice in the pit of her stomach and made it impossible to catch her breath. She knocked one more time, more quietly this time, unwilling to call the family in case she was wrong. In case she wasn't. Oh, God, what if she wasn't? How many times had Evangeline said she wanted to die rather than suffer through the humiliation of life after the accident, the degradation?

Treave, too, had said he'd had as much as he could bear. And before, when they'd been talking down at the tide pools, he'd said something about mistakes he couldn't come back from. She'd told him he was worrying her.

Emma bent to peer through the keyhole. The key in the lock blocked her view, but it was the same large, old-fashioned key as in her own lock, and she dropped Shipwreck onto the floor as she sprinted for her room. It was too easy to picture Treave, lying in the bathtub with the water red, or lying on the bed, ignoring Emma while sleeping pills worked their way through his system.

In her room, she grabbed a pen and tore a piece of paper out of her notebook and went back to shove three-quarters of it under Treave's door directly beneath the lock. The pen popped the key out easily, and being heavy and brass, she could only hope it would fall relatively straight. Dropping to her knees, she pulled the paper out slowly, half-inch by half-inch, not sure the key was there until she saw the edge of it emerge from beneath the door. She didn't dare release her breath until it was far enough for her to grasp it and pull it free. Hands fumbling, she fitted it into the lock and turned until she heard a click.

The door creaked open and she stood on the threshold. "Treave?"

The room was empty, and the clothes he'd worn to

dinner were thrown on the end of the bed. She ran into the bathroom, but that was empty, too, and she would have wondered if he'd ever come upstairs at all if it hadn't been for the clothes. But that was also odd, because Treave was a folder, a hang-things-up-immediately kind of guy. He couldn't have had the time to change and go back downstairs or even disappear down the hall to the other stairs—she would have seen him. His head start hadn't been that large.

She shivered in the draft, and it was only then that she noticed the open window and the chair that had been moved beneath it. She ran the remaining steps, but the window looked out over the gardens along the back of the island, where the hill didn't drop so steeply to the sea.

There was no sign of Treave, no pile of crumpled clothing, only smudges on the window as though he'd used it to climb out. To where? The smooth stone walls of the castle didn't have any ledges. Leaning out over the window sill, Emma turned her head and found a rope hanging from the roof down beside the window.

The rope wasn't long enough to reach the ground or jump from safely—and there was no other window close beneath it. That ruled out Treave having used the rope to climb down anywhere, which left the roof.

Emma's brain spun furiously. Was Treave stealing? Or suicidal? If he hadn't stolen anything yet, and she called the family . . . But if she didn't tell anyone and he jumped . . .

She pulled her cell phone out of her pocket, and not having Brando's number, she looked up his hotel in the

Balwhither glen and dialed. A cheerful voice picked up on the second ring. "Braeside Hotel, how may I help you?"

"This is going to sound crazy, but my name is Emma Larsen, and I'm staying with Brando MacLaren at his sister's house—castle—in Cornwall until the wedding. I don't have his number, but it's an emergency. Could you please give it to me?"

There was a pause, and the sound of something rustling. "I'm afraid we can't do that. I'm sorry."

"Then can you please phone him. Just phone. Tell him I'm in Treave's room, and Treave's gone up to the roof, and I'm afraid he's—I'm not sure what he's doing up there. Tell him I'm going up. Tell him to tell Kenver."

"I'm sorry, could you repeat that?"

Panic was ticking like a clock against Emma's ribs, the sense that she was wasting time. That there wasn't time to waste. "Just tell him Treave's room, and Emma's gone out the window to the roof."

Not waiting to hear the answer, she hung up, tested the rope to see how well it was anchored, and pulled the loose end in through the window. Only after looping it twice around her waist and between her legs to make a harness did she climb out onto the thick wall of the open window.

She wasn't scared of heights, precisely. It was more that she respected them, and the distance to the ground, and the physics of what that distance could do to the human body. Still, it was only eight feet or so from the window sill to the edge of the roof, and carrying Evangeline around all those years had made her strong.

Holding the rope taut, she used her legs to walk up the wall, saving her strength until she had to swing herself across the overhang. The going was simpler from there, the angle of the roof shallow enough that she could crawl along on her hands and knees over the red clay tiles that were still warm with remembered sunlight.

Within the inner square of the castle, the courtyard lay still and empty beneath the quarter moon, a few lamps and the warm glow spilling from the windows along the residential wing twisting the potted fruit trees and topiaries into circus-strange and ominous shapes. Beyond the castle walls, the nighttime ocean darkly glimmered, the occasional whitecaps turned turquoise in the moonlight.

There was no sign of Treave. No more visible ropes, and no hint of where he might have vanished. In the four corner towers, the windows had been narrowed to arrow slits when the abbey had been converted into a fortification. Treave was too large to squeeze through them, so that left the arched belfry windows in Tristan's tower, or a swan dive to oblivion. Crouched along the roofline, Emma told herself it wasn't that. If he'd wanted to die, throwing himself out the window would have served him just as well. Except that then his nephews might have seen the body. They would have had to pass the place where he'd died for the rest of their lives. And Treave loved them too much for that.

Oh, God. What was it the boys had told her the day after Treave's proposal?

That Treave had said he wanted to learn to fly.

Acid burned up her throat, and a sheen of sweat along her skin turned cold in the wind. Carefully, she untied the rope from around her waist and, leaving the one end attached to the chimney where it was anchored, she lowered the free end back down the wall alongside Treave's window where Brando would find it. Then, hugging the roof as closely as she could, she crawled toward the southeast tower whispering small prayers to the god of tile makers and roofers, hoping they'd done their work well enough that nothing was going to break off beneath her. After a few feet, she stopped and removed her shoes for better purchase.

She grew bolder after that. Lifting her knees, she gripped with her hands but no longer scrambled on all fours.

The first tower was hard to navigate, and she had to stand and hug the wall, then step around the corner onto the roof of the other wing. But because the cliff on which the castle was built ran directly into the sea on that side, she started to slow down and search for Treave in the churning water among the rocks. She lost her footing.

Sliding, nails scraping on clay, toes digging for purchase, knees slicing on the arched tile edges, she fought. She wasn't ready to die, there was too much to live for, and all of that came flooding over her, all the bitterness she needed to release and the hope she needed to embrace so that she could live. She threw herself flat and managed to stop the slide, and she lay with her cheek against the tile, whispering prayers of gratitude and breathing, just breathing, the sound as rough as that of the battering waves below.

She couldn't look down after that.

She only wanted off the roof.

Scrambling faster, she traversed the distance to the southwest tower above the lobby more quickly, but when she stood and edged along the tower wall, ready to jump to the wing above the armory, she had to fight muscles that no longer seemed to belong to her before she could manage to take the one step over the corner where nothing lay between her and a three-story drop into the courtyard.

On the other side, finally, she crouched with her back to the tower and closed her eyes.

Someone shouted. Brando. From the roof above Treave's window, he waved his arms above his head. The wind made the words faint and indistinct, and she shook her head and pointed to her ear, then pointed to Tristan's tower, to herself, and down toward the courtyard. If he told her to wait, she couldn't do it. Without waiting for his response, she clambered the remaining distance to the bell tower and looked up at the belfry.

Unlike the battlemented towers of the later fortification, the abbey's bell tower had been constructed with ledges between each story, one level rising on top of the next to eliminate the need for scaffolding as it was being built. For Treave, standing on the roof, it would have been possible to reach the next ledge up, grab on, and pull himself up. Emma couldn't reach. On the other hand, the arrow slits weren't quite as narrow here, and as long as the width was the same on the inside as the outside, it was possible she might fit through.

She sucked in a breath, pulled herself up to the nearest window, and wiggled though sideways, moving by inches until she could reach through and try to find enough of a handhold above the inside of the window to let her pull herself free without falling on her head. Landing on her hands and feet against the rough stone inside, she felt the jolt through her entire body. After allowing herself a moment to close her eyes, she scrambled toward the door and ran down the steps.

The stairs curved back around on the second floor to overlook the gardens and the gate up to the headland. A flash of light caught her as she passed the window, and she retraced her steps to watch it bob, sweeping back and forth along the trail toward the old priory tower. Toward the path down to the tide pools or the steep cliff on the point of the island where a body falling into the sea might just as easily be swept out into the ocean by the currents.

Was that what Treave was doing? Or was he up to something else?

Emma ran the rest of the way down to the ground level, praying that the door wasn't locked. It wasn't, and neither was the gate out to the headland, as if Treave didn't care whether anyone came after him. Or maybe it hadn't occurred to him that anybody would. There was no one on this side of the castle to see the light.

The realization was like a burst of fireworks, setting Emma's heart thundering and her legs pumping while she sprinted barefoot across the lawn.

DEATH COMING

*"It seems to me most strange that men should fear;
Seeing that death, a necessary end,
Will come when it will come."*

WILLIAM SHAKESPEARE
JULIUS CAESAR

I F EMMA DIDN'T PLUNGE to her death off the roof,
Brando was going to kill her.

He swung himself back in through Treave's window
and shouted to Kenver as he sprinted past him into the
corridor. "Get up there and watch where she goes."

"Where are you going?"

"After her obviously. And call the security guards. If
she got all the way around the roof to the bell tower, it
means Treave's there or somewhere one can get to from
inside the tower."

"That'd be the courtyard or the gardens—back into the castle. He could be anywhere."

Brando didn't stop to speculate. Sprinting down the corridor, he passed Tamsyn who plastered herself against the wall, muttering, to give him room, and the twins who had emerged sleepy-eyed from their bedrooms.

"What's going on?" Cam said.

"Go back to bed," Brando snarled, because whatever was happening wasn't anything the twins were going to need to see.

What the devil was Treave doing climbing on the roof? And Emma—what was in her head to make her think she needed to go after him?

If he hadn't known he loved her before, he couldn't escape that now. The thought of something happening to her—the memory of seeing her up on the roof—he hadn't felt that kind of pain since they'd told him to throw a handful of soil on his mother's coffin and he'd turned and ran, not knowing or caring where he was going, until he'd thrown up and couldn't run another step.

The door to the gardens was open when he reached the tower. But his relief was short-lived as he spotted Emma running up the steps to the headland with her hair streaming behind her the color of moonlight. Up by the old priory tower, a flashlight appeared to be searching the ground.

What the hell was Treave up to? And what was he going to do when Emma reached him? Finding another burst of speed, Brando threw himself across the garden terrace and raced up the steps.

HER FEET ACHING AND bloody from running on the sharp granite rocks, Emma slowed as she neared the spot where Treave was sweeping his flashlight back and forth. She felt stupid seeing him like that, relieved and stupid and ready to kill him for scaring her so badly. Although to be fair, maybe she had mostly scared herself.

"What are you doing?" she asked, coming up behind him.

He swung around, the flashlight blinding her. "Emma? What—You shouldn't be here."

He lowered the flashlight, but only slightly, and though she couldn't see him clearly behind the light, there was something about his stance that reminded her of the way people tried to make themselves larger to scare away bears. She'd read that somewhere, that they did that, only she couldn't remember whether it worked. Then again, maybe Treave was the cornered bear.

Fear bloomed like ice crystals in Emma's chest, bringing the scene into cold, sharp focus. "You pretended you didn't know what I was talking about earlier."

His laugh was a hollow, manic sound. "You're worrying

because I lied?"

"I'm worried about *you*. Why you're climbing ropes and rooftops? Sneaking around? And I gave you the ring back, if that's why you're here."

"The ring?" For a moment he seemed puzzled, as if he genuinely didn't remember giving it to her, and then he laughed again. "My grandmother's ring? That's practically worthless apart from the age of the thing. The emerald's bad."

He took a step toward her and she retreated, something about him making her want to turn and run. Her foot slipped. Sand and pebbles skittered off the path, clanging with a high, pure sound after a moment as clear as a bell.

Treave listened, shifted the flashlight, his entire body stiffening with tension. "You heard it that time, didn't you?"

"I heard something," Emma said, not sure whether it was better to lie or tell the truth. Not sure if he was entirely sane.

"I didn't think it was real. All the while I grew up here, I heard the stupid stories. Tristan and Isolde—they were five or six centuries before the abbey was built if they existed at all, and experts all said the St. Levan bell couldn't have been gold and silver because the sound would have been all wrong. But I have a client in St. Petersburg who's obsessed with bells. He's spent over five million trying to raise one out of the river in Myanmar, and he says it's not the material as much as the geometric calculations for the bell itself. That this one was designed by the mathematician who built the dome of the Hagia Sofia in Constantinople. He wants it for the geometry—"

"So you're going to steal it? From your own family? Why, Treave?" Disgust dripped from Emma's voice, and revulsion congealed like beef fat in her throat. "Why would you do that?"

"What have they ever done for me? Do you know what they were like?" he snarled, then he shrugged, embarrassed, and shifted to shine the flashlight closer along the ground, bent practically double to hide his face. "There must be a tunnel here, maybe an offshoot of the one that leads down to St. Levan's Cove. That's the only thing that makes sense. The Royalists could have hidden the bell when they fled. Maybe it was too heavy for the boats, and they didn't want to leave it for Oliver Cromwell's men. That makes sense doesn't it? There was no one left on the island to remember, and our family's had the Mount ever since." He kicked a pebble and pulled his head up to listen, but the only sound was the ocean and Emma's heart pounding in her ears. He moved forward two feet, the flashlight flitting across the ground again.

Emma quietly backed another step.

"Stop," he commanded. "I'm not wrong. I'm not making this up. It has to be here. *You* do it. Kick the rocks like you did before."

"I don't know what I did before. It wasn't intentional—"

"Just do it!" He swung the flashlight toward Emma and then with a hiss of surprise pointed it past her as something moved. Sprinting so suddenly she barely registered the motion, he lunged at her, caught her by the waist, and yanked her up against him.

"Go away," he said over her head, breathing hard. "Leave us alone."

"We will. Just let her go." Brando's voice came from behind Emma, a long way behind. Too far.

Treave spun her around and caught her throat in the crook of his elbow, squeezing tightly enough that she had to rise on her toes to relieve the pressure. Brando and one of the two new night guards were walking toward them, both with their hands out non-threateningly, appeasingly. Both moving quietly. Ready to spring.

"Stop," Treave said. "I'm warning you."

The security guard kept his hands up. "No one needs to get hurt here, mate. Why don't you let her go? You haven't stolen anything, right? You can walk away."

"Walk away?" Treave laughed. "And go where? You don't grasp it, any of you." His voice was flat and weary. "I *asked* you, Em. If you'd only married me, that would have fixed everything. I told you it didn't need to be forever."

The realization and shock of that exploded through Emma, hit her with the force of stupidity, because it should have been obvious. But she hadn't seen it. "This is about money?" she asked. "*That's* why you wanted to marry me? The only reason?"

"No—yes." Shaking his head, he pulled her closer against him. "Not the only reason."

"Then I'll marry you. Of course I'll marry you," she

lied. "You can have the money, then we'll file for divorce and everything will be fine. Just let me go now, because you're hurting me."

His arm relaxed a fraction and he fumbled for something in his pocket. "He's not going to let you go. He won't."

"Yes, he will."

"Yes, I will," Brando said.

"Prove it. Get us a boat big enough to get to Scotland."

"Emma doesn't want—" Brando began.

"I'd like to get married in a nice ceremony," Emma interjected hastily. "Not elope. I'd like a reception. Food. You know how much I love food. Just give me a couple of weeks to put it all together, Treave. Please? Let me finish Christina's wedding and—"

"No!" Treave's arm jerked, and a second later, he held a knife to Emma's throat, the point of it digging into her skin. "It's all unraveling. They keep finding more—what I did. What I took. It's your fault, really—yours and your mother's. She kept saying she was leaving me something. I counted on that. I had the mess all sorted out, then she gave me a bloody *pen*. A pen."

Emma's throat was collapsing so it felt she couldn't draw in air. She told herself that was probably fear as much as it was physical. She told herself to relax, but she shrank away from the knife anyway, fighting for breath. "Just let me go, Treave. This isn't the way."

"I'm sorry, Em. About all of this," he said, not

moving.

She had to think. To find a way to reach him. He was panicking, clearly not thinking straight, and she refused to die over Evangeline's money. How much had he expected? She'd left him $50,000 and a Mont Blanc pen that Daphne du Maurier had used to write her novels. If that wasn't enough money, then he really was in trouble. And he wasn't going to let her go.

She shifted on her toes, trying to edge away from the knife even a fraction of an inch, and she looked dead at Brando while her heart shrank in her chest along with her courage. "I'll go with him," she said. "Treave, I'll go with you. It's all right."

"Good." He eased the knife back a little. "That's smart." He grabbed Emma's arm and waved the knife at Brando. "Tell Kenver to bring the cruiser around to St. Levan's Cove by the tide pools. Just him. Now you both back away and let me take Emma down."

Emma did her best to smile, to look braver than she felt. "Would you ask Janet to send me some shoes?" she said. "I hope Fate's not unkind enough to make me get married barefoot, but I won't take any chances."

THE LAST THING BRANDO intended was to let Emma get

on a boat with Treave Nancarrow. And there was no chance at all that she was going to marry the man.

Marry Treave? Even the thought of her with him, down at the cove with him, ripped through Brando, leaving his heart in shreds.

He stood at the desk in the security office, studying the paper where Kenver was drawing out locations on a makeshift map. Tunnels and the route around the island to the narrow cove where Treave wanted the boat, the path down the side of the cliff, those were the only access points for a rescue. None of them feasible. He tried to get his eyes and his tattered thoughts to focus.

"The man's only got a knife, that's the good news," the security guard was saying. "Masterson would've had him already if Mr. MacLaren hadn't been there, but if we can't get close enough to try again, you should wait for armed response to get here."

"Armed . . . No! No one will be shooting anyone. Or putting Emma at risk," Kenver snapped.

"Then we move ourselves, find a way to get close enough. Masterson and I can disarm a knife easy enough."

"A knife doesn't misfire. Or miss. He may not kill you—at least not both of you—but he can sure enough kill Emma," Brando said, his voice icing over like liquid nitrogen. "Or he can drop her off the cliff. Drown her. Break her neck. We don't know what he's going to do. I don't think he knows it himself. And there is no access. We can't come down the path without him seeing us, and he's obviously thinking of tunnels already. He's not going to ignore the one that leads to the cove—"

"He knows that was sealed off when we put in the ventilation system. It's why he must have been trying to find another way in. If we could get in through there, he might not be expecting it, only we'd need to blast through the concrete," Christina said, "and he'd hear us. Maybe we could drill through it."

"Which would still be loud and take too long." Still shell-shocked, his reactions and speech all a tick of a clock too slow as if he couldn't keep up with reality, Kenver raked his hands through his hair. "Why is he doing this? That's what I don't understand. He has a good job, and he got his share of the money when our father died. What's he want with Emma's money?"

Coming through the door, Perran waved the mobile phone in his hand. "I can answer that. Just got off with one of Treave's partners in the investment firm. Ex-partners. They've found . . . irregularities . . . in client accounts. About one and a half million worth of missing funds. They're keeping it quiet, trying to give him time to repay. Trying to keep from dragging the whole firm down."

"Embezzling? Bleeding idiot." Kenver leaned heavily against the table. He and Perran looked at each other, something unspoken and heartbreaking passing between them. Then Kenver sighed and checked his watch. "But he really is desperate, then. We'd best not play around. Where the devil's Janet got to with those shoes? Right, here's what we'll do. I'll take the boat around like he asked, and I'll try to talk to him. Buy us some time at the very least.

Meanwhile, you keep thinking and radio me if you come up with a clean solution. And ring the Coastguard and let them know the situation, there's no avoiding that. I don't know the last time the idiot was on a boat, and I can't see him making it to Gretna Green at this rate. We can't risk letting him try."

Brando looked around at the useless CCTV monitors, at the useless security guard, at the box of DVDs neatly labeled by date—also useless because apparently all it had taken was for Treave to go out the window and over the roof to bypass the cameras that led down the stairs from the residence wing and walk around searching for a hidden tunnel entrance. He didn't need to open cabinets for that, and when he was done, he simply erased the security footage, waited for the camera facing the security room door and the tower entrance to shift away, ducked back into the tower, and went back to his room across the rooftops. It wasn't sophisticated, but it was good enough that he himself would never appear anywhere on the recordings. He'd even thought to go back three weeks, before his arrival, to avert suspicion. The simplicity of it all held enough clever desperation to fill Brando with an itchy sense of urgency.

Treave wasn't likely to let Kenver talk him into giving himself up, and he wouldn't make a rescue easy. The steep path down to St. Levan's cove would be all too exposed in the moonlight. Treave would be watching that. But leaving Treave to get Emma on a boat and sending the Coastguard after them didn't bear thinking about. She'd already told him she was afraid of boats.

Brando's chest went hollow and dry as autumn leaves at the thought of Emma frightened and alone, in danger. The emptiness filled him with the sudden furious, familiar desire to inflict pain, to pummel Treave until blood splattered and bone broke. He'd thought he was over that need. He wasn't.

"I'll come with you," he said to Kenver calmly. "I'll hide on the boat; there must be somewhere. The lavatory. The cabinets in the cabin. I'll wait for an opportunity."

Kenver snatched a portable radio off the desk. "Treave's hardly stupid. He'll check any place that's large enough for someone to hide."

"Doesn't matter if I find him or he finds me," Brando said, his voice grim.

Kenver paused. "He's family, Brando. He's an idiot and a mile-long list of other things I don't have time to mention, but he's still my brother whatever else."

"I'll keep my temper," Brando lied.

Kenver eyed him skeptically, considering, then gave a slow half-nod. "We don't have much choice, I suppose, but I'll hold you to that. All right. Come along."

They jogged out the door and along the courtyard, their steps making satisfying, angry slaps against the cobblestones. The moon flew higher, veiled now and again by tattered clouds, and when they turned into the arched passage that ran beneath the portcullis and out to the village road, the door to the castle entrance opened with a groan.

Janet emerged, carrying Emma's shoes. Spotting Brando and Kenver, she stopped abruptly on the steps. "Are you both going?" She looked from one of them to the other. "All the way to the cove?"

Kenver's expression softened. "We won't do anything heroic—only speak with Treave, that's all. Delay until the Coastguard gets there."

"And if he doesn't want to *speak*? What, then? Will you be letting him go?" She put her hands on her hips and shifted her glare to Brando. "Will you be letting him sail away and take Emma with him? I'm not a fool, Brando MacLaren, and I know you better than you know yourself."

Brando flushed, not willing to lie to her. "What do you want me to say? That I'll stay here and do nothing at all?"

Kenver walked up the steps and kissed Janet's forehead as he gently took the shoes from her. "Trust me. You do, don't you? Trust the both of us. But whatever happens, you and the boys'll be all right. I trust you, too."

She stood on her toes and kissed him so fiercely it made Brando's heart hurt. Kenver kissed the top of her head, held her wrapped in his arms, and then reluctantly turned away. He and Brando were halfway down the hill as they met Tamsyn jogging up the hill from the village.

Her black scarf askew, Tamsyn pressed a hand against her chest. "Don't go. Shipwreck's on the harbor wall," she huffed. "D'you hear me? The cat's down there singing."

MASKS ON MASKS

*"My tongue will tell the anger of my heart,
or else my heart concealing it will break."*

WILLIAM SHAKESPEARE
THE TAMING OF THE SHREW

THE LAST THING EMMA intended to do was get on a boat with Treave. Or marry Treave. She hadn't figured a way out of either of those quite yet, but she was determined to think of something.

Running up the path was out, and so was running into the water. He'd catch her in fifteen steps. She couldn't even try to hit him and buy herself time—there wasn't so much as a piece of driftwood nearby big enough.

Sitting on a rock, she watched him as he paced. Every few turns, he'd pause and try to explain again, a rosy new assessment of how they would get married and he'd borrow against the probate and pay his partners back and everything would be fine. A new explanation about how it wasn't his fault. How he'd had no choice.

"Where's Kenver?" he asked, kicking at the sand in frustration. "He should have been here by now."

"I'm sure he's coming."

"I didn't have a choice, you do see that? I wouldn't survive in prison. I just wish . . . "

"What?" The rock dug into Emma's thigh and she shifted, trying to keep her leg from going to sleep.

"I wish I'd never tried to help Regina, that's what I wish. I knew she'd be trouble, but I took her as a client anyway."

"You think you tried to *help* her?" Emma snorted, then regretted the words as soon as they'd hit the air. Goading Treave made no sense. Regina had written a half-dozen mediocre romance novels and hung around as part of Evangeline's fan club. If Treave had stolen from her, it was because he'd assumed she was stupid, an easy mark, and he'd been wrong.

"I made money for her. For two years," Treave said, crossing his arms on top of his head and looking up at the sky as if there was help there for him. "It was one mistake. If she'd given me more time to pay it back—"

"But it wasn't only her, was it? You couldn't have taken over a million from just her account."

"I could still make the money back. Right now. Tomorrow. All I needed was more money." Treave turned toward her and stood looking at Emma, the knife held down at his side. "You don't want to come with me, do you? You want to be with him."

For the first time since they'd left the cove the night before, there was sadness again in his voice instead of fear or anger. Despite everything, it tore at Emma's heart. Treave had made mistakes before she'd ever met Brando at all, but everything she'd done since then had made things harder for him, pushed him closer to the edge. Watching him now as he stood backed by the moonlit sea, he looked like an overgrown child after a tantrum, one who didn't know how to fix what he had done.

"People can't love to order," she said gently, remembering what Brando had said to her. "The human heart isn't made for it. I don't know why I fell in love with Brando instead of you—chemistry or biology or brain cells going supernova. I fell in love with his thoughts, his heart, and his humility all at the same time, and I didn't even realize it until you put that knife to my throat. But none of that makes me love you any less. I'm just not *in* love with you. The same way I don't think you're really in love with me."

"Of course I am."

"No, you love me enough that you feel guilty about marrying me for money. That's not the same thing, but I'll forgive you for it."

That was almost true, she discovered. She wasn't angry at him. Only sad and disappointed and afraid. Weeks ago, she couldn't have seen past the injustice of it all, and she would have gathered anger inside herself and nursed it, hoarded it, as if anger would keep her warm through long nights of solitude. Now she simply let it go.

Survival, not anger, that was what she needed.

Treave sighed and looked away. "Are you really going to marry me so that I can have the money?"

"I said I would," she said to soothe him.

He was silent another moment and then he nodded. "We should go to Russia anyway. My partners said they wouldn't call the police if I paid all the money back, but they might. They probably will. They're just trying to limit their losses for now."

"Wherever you want to go," Emma said as the castle's big powerboat appeared at the mouth of the cove. A sailboat would have been better. A powerboat didn't have a boom that could swing unexpectedly and give her a chance to escape, and since the engine was faster, it would give her less time to get over the side before they got too far from shore.

BRANDO SLIPPED OVER THE side of the boat while Kenver brought her into the cove at an angle steep enough to hide him from view. The water was unexpectedly cold—it surprised him to be able to differentiate between physical sensations and the cold rage he felt inside. Cold, not hot.

Not hotheaded and half-cocked, not this time.

Kenver cut the engine and let the cruiser drift toward the white mooring buoy that bobbed a hundred feet off the beach as he went forward to the bow. Holding the boat hook out, he snagged the yellow pick-up line and looped the bow line through. Brando ducked toward the stern to keep out of sight as the starboard side of the boat began to drift around.

Stooping beside the cleat to tie off, Kenver called to Treave. "This is what you asked for. She's gassed up and ready, but I'm asking you not to do it. You don't have to do it, Treave. We can put our heads together and find a different solution. If it's St. Levan's bell you were looking for, Perr and I can help you find it. We can open the tunnel to the cove, or get someone down here with ground penetrating radar. If it's there, we'll get it for you."

"You always did think I was stupid, didn't you?" Treave grabbed Emma's arm and pulled her back in front of him. "Given a choice between me and your precious family history, don't you think I know what you'd choose? You'd sooner die than let the island go. Sooner see *me* die. You pretend now, but you and Perr never wanted me around anyway. No one did."

Kenver finished tying both ends of the bow line to the cleat and straightened to his feet. "We were children. We all did stupid things, including you. But we're brothers. Every passing year, having my own boys, I see how much that counts. In the end, family is all we have. Living family, not history. If I'm fighting to save the island, it's because there are living people on it I care about, and they're all family by now."

"Jack and Cam will be happier with the idea of a fugitive uncle than one rotting away in prison, believe me." Treave grunted and pushed Emma to the water's edge. "Get off the boat and swim to the far end of the cove. Brando, too. I know he's here."

"He's not," Kenver said.

Treave shoved Emma forward and put the knife back to her throat. "Don't you sodding lie to me, Kenver. Not this time. This is your fault—and you're still blaming me. Making other people blame me. Why did you have to try to hold on to this place? If you'd just sell the things off, we'd all have a fortune. But you're bloody St. Levan, aren't you? Sainted Lord of the Mount. Can't do anything wrong." He sucked in a breath. "Just tell Brando to come out and get off the boat, the both of you."

Brando's head buzzed with rage, a swarm of impulses and thoughts and firing nerves that wanted to propel him through the water, to plant his fist in Treave's face, to snatch Emma away and keep her safe. But he had to be smart. Cautious. He had to breathe himself calm and clear like the patient water.

Kenver had already delayed too long in answering. Lying clearly didn't come easily for him, but he raised his head and attempted it again. "Brando's back at the castle, Treave. It's only the two of us here together, and you're right, it's long past time we sorted things between us."

"More lies. Lies on top of lies on top of lies. That's

how you sort things, is it? I'll tell you what, you radio back to the castle and tell them to send Brando over here in another boat. Emma and I can wait."

Brando saw the stunned, defeated set of Kenver's shoulders, the stillness that said he was trying to think of an out. There wasn't one.

Brando threw a leg onto the swim platform at the back of the boat and pulled himself up. Dripping water from his hair and boxer briefs, he padded to the bow. The air was warmer than the water but fear for Emma made him feel as cold as he imagined the knife felt at Emma's throat.

"What do you want with me, Treave?" he asked, though it wasn't a question so much as an acknowledgment of defeat.

"I want you and Kenver to both swim to the far side of the cove and stay there until we're gone."

Brando glanced at Kenver and saw the glassy panicked look in Kenver's eyes as he slipped off his loafers and watch and tossed them down into the cabin then peeled off his shirt. "Nothing for it, mate," Kenver said. "You coming?"

He dove into the water still wearing his slacks, and with a sigh, Brando followed suit. Swimming, he concentrated on not losing sight of Emma, on trying to find a solution, but his brain seemed to have soaked up water like a sponge and sputtered to a halt.

EMMA'S STOMACH WAS A tangled knot as she stood at the bow of the boat, her back to Treave and his arms around her while he tied her hands with a piece of mooring line. She hadn't counted on him tying her hands. That would make escaping harder.

He finished and stepped back, taking the knife from between his teeth. "I'm sorry about this, Em. I really am, but I can't have you trying anything."

"I said I would marry you. What more do you want?"

"I saw the way you were looking at him."

Emma's head bent beneath a wave of fury and frustration that threatened to tow her under. "Don't make me do this, then. Turn yourself in. Let Kenver and Perran find the bell. You said yourself repaying the money isn't guaranteed to keep you out of jail."

"*Money* will keep me out of jail. There are places we can go. If not Russia then Ukraine, Andorra, the Maldives. Croatia. Once I have the money, you don't even have to come with me if you don't want to."

"Then see? Why wouldn't I marry you? I want to help you. Just untie me."

He stooped to cut the bow line, his face gaunt and haunted, desperate and despairing as he flicked the knife through the rope. She could see how much he wanted to believe that this would all turn out, how tightly he'd been clinging to the illusion of normalcy these past days while everything he'd done unraveled around him. And she could see how it had all happened, one bad decision at a time that turned into a runaway snowball. Investing his own money a little too recklessly. Winning at first, then losing. Losing bigger. Needing a bigger investment to recoup his losses. Losing everything and borrowing—just a little—in the hope of getting it back. Borrowing from someone else to repay the other, the snowball rolling faster and faster while he stumbled, lost his balance, lost his grip. Fortunes took ages to build, an instant to vanish.

As if he saw her thoughts, as if he hated her pity, he turned away and yanked her with him toward the cabin. She threw a last look toward the far side of the cove, but in the moonlight she couldn't spot Kenver and Brando at that distance. Then Treave pushed her into the cabin and shoved her down into the chair beside the helm as he turned the engine over. He didn't seem sure of the controls, all the knobs and switches, but he set the knife down on the cabinet, pushed the lever forward and turned the wheel, and the boat straightened back out toward the mouth of the cove.

Emma was still sideways in her chair with Treave just three feet away across the aisle. He stared intently at the controls and gauges, studying them one by one. The door out of the cabin was seven or eight feet back and five steps led up to the deck. If she just got up and ran, she would never make it.

Fear was an ache, so familiar that it settled into the nooks and crannies of her chest with a perfect fit. And abruptly she realized that fear could too often masquerade sometimes as anger, but it was like a stranger at a masked ball pretending to be a friend, a mask within a mask. Anger could galvanize you into action. Fear just left you paralyzed.

Which left Emma no choice at all.

She brought her knees up onto the edge of her chair as though she was simply trying to get more comfortable. Treave glanced over but she didn't react, just sat there with her bound hands on her kneecaps. He pulled over a stack of laminated charts that hung on a hook on the wall and started flipping through them.

Emma twisted to the left, pretending to stretch. Exhaled a breath and closed her eyes. She twisted to the right, balled her hands into fists, braced herself, and kicked out at Treave's shoulder with every particle of anger that could lend her wings. His head slammed against the window.

She fell, but she was already crawling toward the door, scrambling to her feet, pulling it open, stumbling up the stairs.

Treave bellowed behind her. Swore. She heard his footsteps, breath and outrage bursting from him as he reached for her. He caught her ankle as she dove onto the deck. She twisted as she fell, kicked him again. Pain sank sharp teeth into her leg. The knife. He must have snatched up the knife before coming after her.

Blood smelled coppery in the air, blood and fury.

Treave stared at the small pool of it, entranced. Horrified. Emma stared at him, then shook herself and scrambled up. Dove off the side of the boat as he reached for her again.

The water was disorienting in the dark. Salt blurring her eyes, she searched for the shine of lights, then swam away from them, bound hands extended in front of her, kicking like a mermaid beneath the surface. She tried to head toward shore, though after a while she wasn't sure where that was. Things brushed against her, kelp probably—hopefully—then something that felt alive, that she tried not to think about. Only when her lungs burned and threatened to betray her did she start back toward the surface, but it was farther than she'd expected.

Gulping air like a stranded fish, she turned toward the sound of the motor and found Treave had already started to swing the boat around. She dove again, angling herself so that she wasn't going at the shore directly, so that Treave couldn't predict where she would go.

Adrenaline and the current swept her along, but even adrenaline had its limits. Her legs tired and her body grew heavier. It was harder and harder to catch her breath. But finally she was level with the white mooring buoy, and a bit farther, the water grew shallower, shallow enough that she could stand, then fall to her knees and crawl.

The boat was close, Treave steering from the flybridge at the top of the cabin and trying to keep it from drifting in. She could see his silhouette up there, and she wanted to run up the path, run and run in case he was panicked enough to beach the boat and try to catch her. In case he tried to moor it. But her leg ached and she had no breath. She watched him, wary, waiting to see what he would do.

A second figure appeared on the boat, crouching as he ran bare-chested along the deck, his movements graceful and familiar and frightening. Treave still had the knife. What if he heard Brando before Brando was close enough, before Brando was ready.

"Treave," she shouted, getting his attention. "You have the boat. Just leave."

"I didn't mean to hurt you," he screamed back. "I never meant that. Come with me."

A third figure ducked toward the cabin, and Brando swung himself up onto the roof of the cabin and launched himself at Treave in a flying tackle of shouts and chaos. They both went down, and Emma couldn't see, only hope and pace, feeling helpless. Then came a splash. Two splashes.

She held her breath, searching for a head to appear in the water. Two heads. Treave swam toward the shore and Brando followed him, caught him. Treave stood up in the shallows. Moonlight gleamed on the steel of the knife; Brando grabbed Treave's arm and wrenched. The knife fell.

The rest was mercifully short. Treave threw a punch and went down with a spray of water when Brando hit him back. He stayed down, half-sitting, looking up at Brando. Shoulders clenched to his ears, hands fisted, Brando bounced on his feet waiting for him to get up, waiting to hit him. Wanting—needing—to hit him. Ready to hurt himself.

"Don't!" Emma ran into the surf, water splashing to her knees. "It's not worth it, Brando."

"No," he said, turning his head toward her. "Are you all right?"

She looked beyond him to where another boat was entering the cove, and then she looked at Treave still cringing in the water and at Brando standing there in the moonlight with his face in furrows of worry. And she was standing there because she hadn't taken it. She'd fought back, and she'd escaped, and she'd found the courage and the anger to do that.

She let the anger go. "I'm fine," she said. "Really, truly fine."

TWICE RUNG

"Women want love to be a novel."

DAPHNE DU MAURIER

T HE WIND WHIPPED OVER the headland, singing through the ruins of the priory bell tower and sending the gossamer fabric of Christina's bridal veil billowing. She and her father, with Janet and Dena Libby behind them, approached from the castle. Perran waited for her, his face so full of anticipation it was clear he didn't care one bit about the cast on Christina's arm or the still-healing scar on her temple, if he so much as noticed them at all. Behind him, the sea was calm, with gulls surfing the wind, and over his head the wedding arch made by an old shipbuilder in Mowzel had been twined through with heather, sea rock lavender, and roses so that it looked beautiful and wild.

"It's all perfect, isn't it?" Emma said, taking it in. "The ceremony is so much more right for them here than some stuffy service in a church would have been."

"Aye, and I'm glad they didn't postpone it." Brando caught Emma's hand and brought it to rest against his thigh, smiling at her in that way of his. A smile that was gentle on the surface, with a dangerous little spark of mischief that could bloom into fire at the slightest provocation. A smile that promised and teased and made her want to pull him up and drag him behind the bell tower and . . .

Not that she would.

"A penny for them," Brando leaned close to whisper. "I wonder if your thoughts are the same as mine?"

She shifted to look back at him, giving herself some distance. The silver buttons of his short jacket gleamed, and the dark material stretched taut over wide, strong shoulders. He made her ache to trace her fingers over his cheekbones, to curve her palm over the back of his neck and watch his eyes close in response.

But she didn't tell him that.

"You look handsome in a formal kilt," she said.

"You're thinking of kilts, then, are you?" he asked, his eyes laughing. "The kilt's the same every day, lass, more or less. Always here."

"Then it must be the tie." Emma could picture herself untying it the way one unwrapped a package on Christmas morning. "Or maybe it's the shirt. I do love a man in a nice white shirt."

"Do you?" He leaned closer still, his breath warm against her cheek and his skin smelling of wind and sunlight, his expression grown suddenly serious. "Any man or one in particular?"

Emma opened her mouth and no sound came out. Fortunately, a moment later Christina and the bridal party passed the gate at the path down to St. Levan's Cove, and the orchestra struck up the wedding processional, the joyful beginning from Vivaldi's "Spring." The music soared, mixing with the cries of the seagulls and the distant sound of waves breaking against the rocks.

The photographer whom Emma's publisher had sent for the cookbook dropped to one knee, positioning himself for a better angle, and every unmarried girl in the vicinity took a second to sigh over him instead of watching the bride approaching. The regular wedding photographer, the young red-haired woman from Mowzel who stood behind the last row of chairs, had been snapping dozens of photographs at a time all afternoon. Gabriel O'Connor always waited for the perfect shot, the perfect light, the perfect motion. What he'd been doing with the food and the table settings for the cookbook was practically magic— he was practically magic himself. But Emma hadn't been the least bit tempted by him, not even once.

She wasn't sure why she'd avoided the word love since that night at St. Levan's Cove. It wasn't that she hadn't thought it often in the aftermath and since. She would turn and see Brando as they worked together on the book, or cooked together in the kitchen, or helped to plan the wedding, and emotion would kick her in the chest like a jolt of electricity. When he smiled at her from the stove or accidentally-on-purpose brushed her hand at the worktable, coherent thought vanished from her mind. But everything between them had happened so fast, and she knew how quickly fairy tale endings could disappear with the turning of a page.

There would be time enough, she told herself. Time in Scotland. Time for hormones to settle, excitement to fade, and fairy tales to lose their gilded edges and turn back into pumpkins.

Brando was still watching her, though, as Christina reached the start of the long red carpet between the aisles of fabric-covered folding chairs. He was still waiting, hurt and confusion growing behind his eyes.

Swallowing hard, Emma nudged him with her elbow, and he finally turned around to watch the ceremony, but all through the service while Christina and Perran promised each other forever, she couldn't help thinking about fear and courage. And after the vows, when the guests had moved to the carriage house for dinner and the food had been photographed and consumed, she spotted Shipwreck washing his face behind a potted topiary, and she wondered again about the different masks of fear.

If she hadn't conquered her fear and jumped off the boat, if she hadn't taken that risk, would she have been here to see Christina get married? Would Treave have been sitting in prison waiting for extradition? Treave hadn't meant to use the knife when he cut her leg, Emma was convinced of that, but he *had* used it. If she'd stayed on the boat and the Coastguard had caught them, what would he have done?

Her heart broke all over again for the tragedy and stupidity of it all. For Treave, and for Kenver and Perran who had promised to support him and stand by him but who still looked brittle and broken beneath their smiles whenever they thought no one would notice. Throughout the toasts, they both avoided the word brother, and they'd both winced slightly every time they'd mentioned family.

Emma wondered if Treave was thinking about them now, whether he was imagining Perran getting married and not being there to see it.

"Time to cut the cake, love." Brando got up and pulled out Emma's chair. "I'll come help you bring it out."

Emma checked her watch, and he was right. Everything was timed down to the minute, and the slightest glitch would ruin the final moment of the night.

She signaled the temporary servers, and then she and Brando went back to the kitchen. For extra drama, she added a final dusting of sugar crystals to the candied roses, and with the help of the newly hired chef, they wheeled the heavy cake down the tunnel to the carriage house while Gabriel O'Connor positioned himself and snapped a half-dozen careful photographs.

Kenver tapped his glass with a fork, and everyone rose to watch the cutting. But Christina whispered something into Perran's ear and ran over to throw her good arm around Emma and kiss her cheek.

"I just had to come thank you again," she whispered. "The cake is perfect. Everything is perfect." Her smiled dimmed as she glanced at Perran. "Well, nearly everything. I think this is the first time in his life Perr's genuinely regretted not having Treave around."

"Me, too," Emma said, and for all she was coming to

realize that heartache was the spice that allowed you to taste the joy in life, she still wished it hadn't had to happen like this.

Then again, she wondered, as the cake was cut and eaten, whether it could have happened any other way. Whether there was any one decision that she or Treave, or anyone, could have made since they'd arrived on the island that would have led to a different outcome. Had there been something she could have said or done that would have made a difference? Or had it all been like Treave's embezzling, a series of small choices that all added up to the inevitable?

The orchestra stopped playing, and the dance band struck up outside in the courtyard. Perran pulled Christina out of her chair and led her out, and Brando offered his hand to Emma.

"Ready?" he asked.

"Let's hope it comes off." She slipped her arm around his waist as they walked out beneath the strands of white paper lanterns and fairy lights that had been strung across the courtyard.

Kenver took the microphone, and everyone turned to look toward the bell tower, waiting for the sunset to fall just right. Christina's hand was tight in Perran's, her face suddenly gone tense.

"Are you sure about this?" she asked, studying Kenver anxiously. "We could still make the first ringing a whole separate occasion. Bring in the press—charge a fortune."

"This is beyond price, and with all the bitterness we've had lately, it's time for as much luck and joy as we can cram into the moment. I want you and Perran to have it." Stepping forward, he kissed Christina's cheek beneath her scarred temple, and then he held out his hand for Janet to come and join him.

Brando, too, shifted Emma in front of him, wrapping his arms around her. Everyone else gathered close: Tamsyn holding the twins, Dena Libby with her parents, and Nessa Rowe with her own mother and David Evans' father, Winnie and Bren and all the staff, the rest of the lifeboat crew, John Nance in a wheelchair with Gwen standing beside him in a walking cast mildly scowling, friends from the village and as far away as London, and Christina's family and friends as well.

The sun descended another inch. The light caught the intricate gold and silver patterns inlaid onto the bronze surface of St. Levan's bell, making it glow where it hung on the freshly cut beams and restored stonework in the belfry. Kenver leaned into the microphone.

"Ladies and gentlemen," he said, gesturing Christina and Perr to step forward. "I give you the first dance of Mr. and Mrs. Perran Nancarrow, may they have a long and happy life together."

The courtyard rang with the high and haunting peal of St. Levan's bell.

No one moved. Emma wasn't sure that she took a breath.

For all the hard, human work that had gone into finding the missing tunnel with the hired radar, retrieving the bell, and hanging it these past nine days since the night at the cove, the sound that rang in the hush of the courtyard was unearthly, full of awe and magic. If joy had a single note, this was it, sweet and clear and carrying on the wind. Even Shipwreck, on hearing it, sat down facing the tower and puffed out his chest to sing along.

With Brando's arms around her, the cat singing, and the song of the bell fading in Tristan's tower above the courtyard lit softly by the strands of glowing lanterns, Emma couldn't deny that fairy tales sometimes did come true. Maybe not because you wished on a stone or a star, but because you simply believed in the outcome so hard that you made it happen. Wishes could too easily turn to dust, but belief created its own reality. Fear, after all, wore many masks, and caution was one of them.

She had promised herself she was going to be brave, hadn't she? She had wanted to dance on the clifftops with her hair free. Well, now it was time to let her heart dance, too. To throw caution and fear away.

Turning in Brando's arms, she put her hands up on his shoulders. "Do you remember what you asked me earlier, before the ceremony?"

"The question you didn't answer?" he asked, his expression growing wary.

The band struck up "A Thousand Years" for Christina and Perran's wedding dance, and she had to raise her voice to be heard above it. "There's only one man," she shouted. "You're the only one I love."

He pulled her closer and kissed her soundly. "Didn't I know that already? But it's about time you admitted it. My poor ego's been bruised something awful."

"Oh, we wouldn't want that, would we?" she said.

"I love you, too, Emma Larsen." His eyes grew tender, and he brushed his thumbs against the corners of her lips. "I love you, and it seems to me I always have."

Her heart beating like thunder, Emma scraped her courage together. "In that case, I was thinking maybe I should make an honest man of you. A respectable man. What do you think?"

His hands stilled and he studied her. "Are you asking me to marry you?"

"A year from now, or any time after that." She nodded. "But, yes, I'm asking."

"I'll marry you any time and anywhere you like, *mo chridhe*," he said. "You were my fate from the first moment I ever saw you." He pulled her closer and kissed her until she couldn't breathe, and then he picked her up and twirled her while the falling sun turned his hair to fire.

His expression filled with joy, slowly, the way the sun rises and lends color to the world. That in itself somehow made Emma love him more. Everything he did seemed to make her love him more. He was her fairy tale, her happy ending. She couldn't doubt that any longer.

A cheer went up behind them, mixed with laughter, and a moment later St. Levan's bell rang in the bell tower for the second time that night.

AUTHOR'S NOTE AND
HEARTFELT THANK YOU!

Thank you so much for reading this story! I truly hope you enjoyed it, and if you did, I hope you will take the time to write a brief review. Even a sentence or two can make an enormous difference in the success of a book and in my ability to keep writing new books.

This book is, obviously, a work of fiction. As with my other books, I connected bits of genuine history and legend with some of my own flights of fancy. The story of Tristan and Isolde is told in many different ways, and many different places claim a connection to the legend. My own St. Levan's Mount is based loosely on St. Michael's Mount in Mount's Bay, Cornwall, a very real and magical location owned by the Lords St Levan. Like St. Levan's Mount, St. Michael's Mount has a wishing stone and a saint who warns of shipwrecks, but astute readers will notice that I have placed my island castle on the other side of Mount's Bay from the real location, on the Mousehole side instead of on the Marazion side. And because it's all fictionalized, I've renamed Mousehole to Mowzel, which is how it is commonly pronounced.

Apart from wanting to make it clear that the story and

setting are fiction, there's a reason for these geographic liberties. Mousehole was the community most impacted by the sinking of the *Solomon Browne* lifeboat from Penlee Station in 1981. Reading about that disaster—and eventually researching the tragedy of it—is what got me thinking about small communities and family traditions of service. Combined with the wisps of story connected with shipwrecks and miracles involving St. Michael's Mount, that's what provided the fuel for my island with a tradition of lifesaving that goes back thousands of years.

The real heroes, when it comes to lifesaving in Britain, are obviously the volunteers of the Royal National Lifeboat Institution (RNLI). What they do is truly astounding and inspirational.

SPECIAL OFFER!

If you've enjoyed *Bell of Eternity* or *Lake of Destiny*, the next new destination in the Celtic Legends collection, *Echo of Glory*, will take us to Ireland, and *Heart of Legend* will take us to Wales. Look for them beginning in Spring of 2018 in hardcover, trade paperback, and ebook. Please also look for *The Magic of Christmas*, which will be revisit the Balwhither glen in the Scottish Highlands, coming December 2017. Order them early to get exclusive introductory pricing!

To stay on top of all the news, special offers, giveaways, and more romantic Celtic recipes, sign up for my newsletter via my website (http://www.MartinaBoone.com) and stay connected.

Adult Fiction Available Now

The Celtic Legends Collection
from Mayfair PublishingSimon & Schuster/Simon Pulse

YOUNG ADULT FICTION
AVAILABLE NOW

YOUNG ADULT SOUTHERN GOTHIC ROMANCE
from Simon & Schuster/Simon Pulse

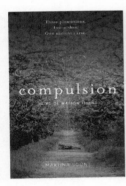 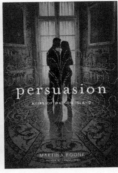 

More Information:
http://www.MartinaBoone.com
Twitter: @MartinaABoone

ACKNOWLEDGMENTS

As always, enormous thanks to my family and wonderful husband for their encouragement and patience. And again, as always, this book simply would not exist without Susan Sipal and Erin Cashman. Their warmth, support, and insight not only made it possible for me to believe in this story, their talent and generosity made the final version a thousand times better.

Thank you as well to my lovely readers and friends, and especially to my Advance Reader Team—all those who have been so excited about *Lake of Destiny*. That enthusiasm means the world!

Finally, deep gratitude to Jennifer Harris and Amanda VanDeWege for their editorial wizardry, Kalen O'Donnell for a gorgeous cover, Rachel and Joel Greene for another great interior, and everyone involved at Mayfair who made all this possible.

ABOUT MARTINA BOONE

Martina Boone is the award-winning author of the romantic southern gothic Heirs of Watson Island series for young adults, including *Compulsion*, *Persuasion*, and *Illusion* from Simon & Schuster, Simon Pulse, and heartwarming contemporary romances for adult readers beginning with *Lake of Destiny*. She's also the founder of AdventuresInYAPublishing.com, a three-time Writer's Digest 101 Best Websites for Writers site and is on the board of the Literary Council of Northern Virginia.

She lives with her husband, children, Shetland Sheepdog, and a lopsided cat, and she enjoys writing romance set in the kinds of magical places she loves to visit. When she isn't writing, she's addicted to travel, horses, skiing, chocolate flavored tea, and anything with Nutella on it.

http://www.martinaboone.com/

Made in the USA
Monee, IL
04 December 2019